DATE
WITH A
DEAD DOCTOR

To Sasha and Alice
with love and
Kisses!

Kane Brill

and her
close
friend

DATE
WITH A
DEAD DOCTOR

TONI BRILL

ST. MARTIN'S PRESS · NEW YORK

Library of Congress Cataloging-in-Publication Data

Brill, Toni.
    Date with a dead doctor / Toni Brill.
        p.   cm.
    ISBN 0-312-05409-2
    I. Title.
PS3552.R478D38   1991
813'.54—dc20   90-15540
                                                                        CIP

First Edition: April 1991
10 9 8 7 6 5 4 3 2 1

To Bubby

DATE
WITH A
DEAD DOCTOR

1

"MIDGE? Baby doll? Listen, it's Mommy, is this a bad time? Are you busy? Can you talk?"

The absolute smartest thing to have done right then would have been to disguise my voice, growl "Wrong number!" unplug the phone, and go back to my dinner in front of the TV, which I say not only because the titles of my beloved Mary Tyler Moore rerun were just then coming onto the screen, and my take-out moo-shu's were already congealing in that little white box with the wire handle that you see only when you buy Chinese food or live goldfish, and my tumbler glass full of nice cold white zinfandel, which I had been looking forward to since about three that afternoon, was already growing warm on the radiator cover I use as my table when I eat in my big comfortable armchair. Those are the little reasons. The *big* reason was that there are only two things that make my mother pant like that on the phone: some dress she has seen at Loehmann's that she thinks would look marvelous on me so I should run right up to the Bronx and buy it.

Or nice men who what would it hurt me to meet them and at least give them a *try*?

In other words, my mother had fixed me up.

AGAIN.

Well, actually that sort of misrepresents matters, because it is only four years ago February that I walked out of marriage and into this three-room apartment on Ocean Parkway in Brooklyn that Aunt Dora had willed to me, the bequest dropping down on me like a hammer from heaven. An entryway too small for anything but a telephone table, a living room to the right, into which I could fit couch, chair, desk, coffee table, and television only by pretty much doing without any floor space, bedroom and bathroom to the left, and straight ahead a kitchen that if Aunt Dora invited you to Thanksgiving, you had to have capon, because there wasn't room for guests and a roast turkey. A space that was, for the first time in my life, wholly and entirely mine.

Which my mother, Pearl, seemed to understand. For about six months. Until her friend Estelle's daughter, who is two years younger than me but is married to a Hasid and actually lives in Israel, had her *fourth* child, and some kind of biological Big Ben went off in my mother, since which she has been driving toward grandchildren with all the subtlety of one of those salmon who flop up over waterfalls and dams in a frenzy to reproduce or become lox trying.

At first, even though I am her only child and agree with Pearl that "children only come before marriage in the dictionary, sweetie pie," meaning I would obviously have to meet a man if Pearl was going to get her grandchild, I did my best to be firm about her new mania for matchmaking, but, even without that to feel guilty about, Pearl can be murder, and I had just walked out on a wonderful Jewish veterinarian, which is almost like divorcing a doctor.

"Fixed up!" I yelled. "I'm not broken! Why should I need fixing up!?"

After a couple of months of trying guilt, Pearl switched tactics. "Of course you're right, dear, the single life can be rewarding too. And it will give us lots more time to be together."

Which, since I am trying to make it as a writer and thus work at home, was *lots* of time. I would sit and stare at my blank page while Pearl unobtrusively dusted my apartment, humming. Or unobtrusively rummaged through my kitchen, unobtrusively checking to see what I was out of. Which she then bought and put away. Unobtrusively. Which was the same way she went through my closets to discard "what they're not wearing now." Plus which Pearl doesn't drive, and she's lodged complaints against so many car services and taxi companies that I swear she's on some kind of blacklist, so sometimes to get a driver you have to phone clear over to Jersey, or way up in the Bronx. As for the subway, "You know what it would DO to your father to know his widow was riding the train? He didn't leave me comfortable? He didn't take good enough care of me?" Meaning I not only had to endure Pearl's torture by vacuum cleaner and dust-rag, but I usually also had to schlepp over to Two Fifth Avenue to pick her up so she could administer it. Bringing the vacuum, no less, since she preferred her Electrolux to my Dustbuster. You know what it feels like to carry a vacuum out of a fancy building like that?

Still, it wasn't *just* the guilt, or the possibility that I would be unobtrusived into a nervous breakdown, that made me answer, "No, mother, it's fine, really, talk about what?" instead of doing what I *should* have done, which was pretend I was a Chinese laundry or something.

I've learned a secret, you see, about *most* of these "great catches" whom Cupid Cohen hooks because she is the only dental receptionist in Manhattan who asks you which tooth hurts and whether you're married, and that is that they prove to be as unenthusiastic about the romance we have been assigned as I am, and that if matters ever even get as far as them calling me, we can just agree that all of next month looks kind of inconvenient, and why don't we do lunch in the fall sometime, when things settle down?

Which is why at the time it didn't seem *so* stupid that instead of listening to my mother's sales pitch for this latest guy, I watched the television, which my phone cord is just long enough to permit, if I kind of stand on one foot and peek around the corner into the living room, taking care not to laugh and making sure to mutter from time to time, "No, he sounds very nice. A urologist you said? Imagine that. . . ."

That's how I missed a few important points. Such as that this promising single urologist was going to come over TONIGHT.

Which I learned about forty-five minutes later, when my visitors call box squawked.

"Midge Cohen? This is Dr. Leon Skripnik. I think your mother called. . . . A little while ago? To ask if it was okay, maybe I could drop in?"

Dr.? I just caught myself from asking out loud, is this a date or a house call? And as for pointing out that my Ph.D. also entitles *me* to a Dr., that *never* works with M.D.s, or psychologists either. They just give you that superior little smile they all practice in medical school to intimidate you out of asking how come they were two hours and fifteen minutes late for the appointment, spent less than ten minutes with you, and then charged you thirty-five dollars. So that's why instead of letting Leon Skripnik know what was what when I should have, the only protest I made as I buzzed the door release for him was, "My name is Margaret, damn it. *Margaret.*"

Midge, which I hate, is the price I will probably have to pay forever for having decided that if Jackie wasn't going to J.F.K.'s inauguration in a plaid dress with a Peter Pan collar and shiny black Mary Janes, then neither was I. After all, the inauguration was an *occasion,* which I knew because my father bought us our first color television to watch it on, even though the broadcast was black-and-white. However, when I teetered into the living room on Pearl's high heels, her mink stole draped over my shoulders, my mother collapsed in laughter. "A midget! She looks like a little midget!"

It stuck. Almost thirty years have passed, I'm the tallest woman our Cohens have ever produced (five foot four, but the tallest nonetheless), I've published two novels—and I'm still called Midge.

Oh, I agree that Margaret isn't a whole lot better, but by now most people have forgotten about Princess Margaret Rose, who was actively hunting for a husband when I was swelling Pearl's belly. Lord Snowden and I turned up about the same time, so I got to be Margaret, because, as Pearl explained it to me many times without me even once understanding the logic of it, "Your daddy is a photographer too!" Still, a Margaret at least you shake hands with; a Midge you pat on the head.

Except, I realized just after I buzzed this terrific doctor into my building, right then I didn't *look* like much of a Margaret. Only a Midge could be wearing a lime-colored RALPH'S PRETTY GOOD GROCERY T-shirt that already had moo-shu spots on it, which at least went nicely with the paint spots on my jeans, which I always seem to get when I visit my painter friend Sasha. Shouldn't a Margaret wear a blouse, and maybe a nice tailored skirt, I wondered, and then I wondered whether maybe I shouldn't worry about my apartment instead.

After I moved in, I boxed up Dora's collection of porcelain shepherdesses and balloon sellers, took out her plug-in fireplace, and had some guy whose address I got off the Laundromat bulletin board build me bookcases along three walls of the room, which I didn't think to have painted until *after* the bookshelves were in. The couch had been bought at an Abraham and Straus Labor Day sale when Truman was president, but my intentions of replacing it had lasted only until I priced something of even *half* that quality, also at an A&S sale, whereupon I decided that I liked the sag that my long-dead Uncle Bernie's tush had left in the middle. I had also kept the big comfy chair that came with the couch but replaced Dora's TV, which she had had only for the noise the last few years, because she was almost blind. I had gotten a new Sony, a little one, to prove I am an intellectual who doesn't watch much, but with an excellent picture and a remote, so I can change the channel without getting up. With all my books and photos set out, this is the room I have always dreamed of living in, the outer manifestation of the real inner *me*.

Except that in the dream someone other than Pearl also comes in regularly to dust and straighten up, which in real life no one, including me, had done since the last time I laid down the law to my mother. The *Times* since maybe Tuesday lay around, and my desk, between the two windows so that as I work I can look out onto the three mulberry trees on the Parkway outside, was littered with wadded up paper, casualties of the terrific struggle I was having with my characters.

A peek in the hall mirror made me realize that if this doctor was going to get the wrong idea about anything, it had better be about the room, and not me. My mother says I'm *zoftig* anyway, which is Yiddish for you should lose maybe ten, fifteen pounds, and without my bra on, the lime T-shirt made me look like an entry in a watermelon-bagging contest.

Of course, it would have helped to know *why* this doctor had come, and what he had in mind for tonight. I tried on a cotton blouse with a Fair Isle sweater, figuring that was okay with jeans, but then that was too hot, so I yanked down this khakhi military thing, like a shirt but with pockets on the hips, that I bought at a Banana Republic and hated as soon as I tried it on without all the plastic palm trees and stuffed monkeys around. It *still* looked stupid, so I was just ripping it off when the doorbell rang. I yanked it the rest of the way off and threw on my Ithaca College sweatshirt, which I then realized had a great big mauve splotch across the belly. Peeling it off as I ran, I screamed "Just a MINUTE!" at the door, wadded the sweatshirt up behind the couch, scooped up the dirty moo-shu plates and glass, ran to the kitchen, and scooted back to the bedroom, where I put the khakhi thing back on, only to discover that I had popped the top button off, so that want to or not I was going to spend the evening looking like Liz Taylor showing off her diamond necklace, except that I had no necklace.

Why am I doing this? I fumed as I finally unbolted and yanked open my door, smoothing my hair, which I had forgotten to comb, with my left hand. It's not as though I *want* to meet anyone. . . .

Especially not someone who looks the way Pee-Wee Herman would if he shopped at Barney's.

"Leon?" I managed to beam as if with pleasure, instead of laugh out loud at this latest of my mother's "finds," who was proof of the minor flaw in my present policy of nonresistance to the evil of blind dates, which is that only the very best of Pearl's have-I-got-a-man-for-*you* men never called. Based on first appearances, this Leon Skripnik was pretty representative of the others who were willing to pursue the possibility of chance romance arising from their need for oral surgery.

"You're Midge? Listen, it's terrific that you—I mean, it's a good thing . . ." Skripnik wasn't as tall as I'd first thought he was, maybe just over six feet, but he was so gangly that I involuntarily glanced at the top of my door-frame, wondering whether he'd clear it. A bald patch surrounded by frizzy clumps that looked more like stuffing leaking from his head than hair, a long neck with a prominent Adam's apple that must be hard to shave—it had a little island of stubble on it—a nose that might as well have had FIXED tattooed up its spine, and bony hands so big they must look like balloons in the Macy's Thanksgiving Day parade, once he was gloved up for work.

"Margaret," I repeated wearily, *"Margaret,"* stepping back to let him in.

Skripnik stumbled over the little curl of lineoleum at the door sill, glanced at my face, spent a little longer on my thorax, then looked around my apartment, which apparently he didn't like sufficiently even to come far enough into it to let me shut the door.

"Your mother wasn't lying?" he demanded suspiciously. "You really do know Russian?"

Lord, what has Pearl said to this man? I wondered as I pulled him away from the door so I could shut it and then kind of steered him toward the couch, which was not so easy, since the doctor kept glaring at me and so stumbled over most of my furniture.

"I don't know what my mother's been telling you," I said with that inane brightness that always takes control of you at the start of blind dates, making you feel like a babbling ass, "but yeah, I know Russian. And you're a urologist, right? Listen, would you like some wine, or I think maybe I've got a beer?"

"No, I mean do you *really* know Russian? That's not just a line or a come-on?" Skripnik was right against the couch but still resisted sitting.

"A *come-on*?" I couldn't help gaping at him, and it took all my self-control not to add, for *what*?

Skripnik smiled unpleasantly now, as though I had just admitted I was after his money, not his mind. "You're not from Russia, are you? You're American, so how can you know Russian? Just knowing the alphabet or how to read menus, that won't help. I need an *expert*."

Why is Pearl never here with me at these moments, to share the fruits of her labors? Trying to be patient and remembering the Jimmy Stewart movie on Channel 9 that I had decided not to watch but which was now suddenly seeming a lot more interesting, I said, "Russian restaurants never *have* menus, and anyway, I don't know what you want, but Ithaca College thought I was good enough at Russian that they paid me to teach it for six years."

That at least made Skripnik blink, nod, and sit down. Dora's bottomless couch and his own greenish madras coat and bright green slacks contrived to make the doctor look a lot like Jiminy Crickett, knees and elbows folded into all sorts of angles.

"Well, all I meant was, it's a very important letter." He sounded reluctantly conciliatory.

"Letter? What letter?"

I swear that Skripnik looked around my living room before he pulled from his jacket pocket a fat business-size envelope of grayish brown kraft paper, which when he held it out at me proved to be plastered over with Israeli stamps. "*This* letter, that I just got, and has to be translated right away."

"Translated?" I echoed stupidly as I sat down, astonished—at him some, at my mother some, but most of all at *me*. I mean here was a guy I had said I would see only as a favor to my mother, who turned out to be the type you'd normally go out with only if one of you could wear a brown paper bag on your head, and even so I was offended that all he wanted was a translator, not a date? "I don't really *do* translations."

"This isn't really a translation," he said confidentially, lowering his voice. For the first time he was looking a bit uncertain. "It's just a letter that I can't read. Your mother said that since you aren't working, maybe you could take the time . . ."

I've heard this "not working" business before. This is an occupational hazard for writers, whose work looks to other people like just sitting pounding at a typewriter, no different than being a secretary, except that you do it at home, don't quit at five o'clock, and never get a vacation.

In fairness, I have never actually explained to Pearl that I hate that she thinks I am "not working," because every time I have to say, "I'm a writer," I still half expect Herman Melville, Fyodor Dostoyevsky, and Stephen King to jump out from behind my bookshelf and chant "No, you're not! No, you're not!"

If this were someone else, I would call this hesitancy neurotic, because while it is true that nobody will give me the Nobel Prize in literature for novels about Mysterious Doings at Girl Scout Camp Poncatoncas, for girls ages eight through twelve, it is also true that I *have* published two of them, with a third under option. Since I wrote those books and did not find them under cabbage leaves, I must be a writer, right?

While I was thinking all this, Skripnik cleared his throat and blinked again, in that ticky way nervous wearers of contact lenses have. "Oh, I'm not trying to offend you, Midge—I mean, Margaret. I wasn't offering to *pay* you or anything. I just hoped . . . I need this right away, and your mother said you could do it quickly." As if to convince me, Skripnik pulled what seemed like reams of onion skin out of the envelope, the pages all covered back and front with a spidery, dark blue script that showed through to the other side. "I just got this, from Israel, I think from a relative I didn't know I had. A relative from *Russia*," he added, as though that might entice me.

Russia. I have *drawers* full of letters like this one, from the days when "underground Russia" seemed the most fantastically romantic place in the world. I had gone there in 1979, ready to be bowled over, and I was. I fell in love with poets and with painters and with philosophers, whom my wedding ring could keep out of my bed but not out of my heart. I drank tea all night and wine all day, I walked from one end of Moscow to the other, and then I walked back, listening, arguing, expostulating. And when I left, eight marvelous months later, I corresponded with them all, getting long demented passionate letters back, which I cherished.

Until my correspondents started to emigrate. Then I began to get long demented passionate telephone calls, and even two long demented passionate visits, the second of which ended when my mild, bland, long-suffering ex-husband Paul finally pointed out, "You know, you don't have to be nice to them just because Russia wasn't."

Put another way, Aunt Dora's unexpected but blessed legacy of apartment furnishings, and $120,000 not only let me jump out of a stupid marriage but also out of a tangled web of Russians.

To which I was not inclined now to add this Dr. Skripnik's relatives.

I guess I must have looked as though I were still considering his offer, because Skripnik now leaned forward, took my right hand in his left one, stroked it with his right, and said so low in his chest it was almost gargling, "Please? As a favor to me?"

"Some wine! I'd really like some wine!" I leapt out of the chair, almost sprinting to the kitchen, calculating on the run how many *pounds* of chutzpah it took to presume upon our five-minute acquaintance for this "favor," while the tingle in my hand made me wonder what other favors my guest might get around to asking before this magic evening was over.

I spent a long time putting together a tray of cheese and crackers to bring out with the two glasses of zinfandel, but I don't think that I need actually have worried about cooling Skripnik off, because he seemed to be a lot more infatuated with himself and his Russian relative than he could ever have been with me. As I sliced and slathered his voice kept me company with tangled, breathless tales of Russia and relatives lost and found.

You've all heard the story, in one variant or another. The old country and the big family there, cossacks all the time making pogroms, so everybody leaves for America, except for one brother, who stays behind, and then the revolution comes, contact is lost, the family in America knows nothing, until at last the Jews are let out of Russia.

To Skripnik it was all a tale never before told, which he related with much waving of hands, strewing cracker crumbs and spilling wine liberally about my living room. "The Russian Skripniks are all big people, very important and learned! Doctors of philosophy, real *European* ones—those are hard to get, not like in America—and top government people. One of my cousins was even a financial adviser to *Stalin,* very high up in the Kremlin. . . ."

I sat as far across my tiny living room as I could and sipped my wine, entertaining myself by wondering whether people always seem to speak about distant relatives with special pride because the relatives make the speaker more important, or because having such relatives now proves that the speaker is as great as I should have known all along he was.

Why was Skripnik obsessed with his family?

Well, to condense what he told me quite a bit, he was over forty, an only child, and his mother had just passed away. His father had been dead for some time, and the more the modest doctor brooded upon life, the less he understood how *he* had proven such a plump ripe fruit on the Family Tree of Mankind, when the shoots nearest him were the few drab and sickly cousins and uncles he knew about, wholly undistinguished shoe store owners and accountants making less money than Skripnik did. Knowing the family legends about Those Left Behind, and reasoning that *they* might have produced someone approximate to him in caliber, the modest Dr. Leon cast his nets wider, placing ads in Jewish newspapers, here and in Israel. You've seen the sort of thing I mean: Seeking relatives Avram and Ruchel Buchbinder, born Chernigovka, sailed NY on *Ostsee* 8 Aug. 1906; reply this newspaper, box such-and-such.

I sipped and wondered, at my mother for thinking this was a catch, at myself for letting him spend all Saturday evening scattering crackers around my apartment, and at him, for being so volubly impressed with what seemed a thoroughly ordinary bunch of Russian relatives. Leon had received one answer to his ad, about two months previously, from the children of the one brother who stayed, and even though they were émigrés now and having a rough time of it, they had been tremendously important people back in Russia who had suffered terribly, which is why they gave it all up for freedom. I tried to remember what émigré I had ever heard admit that he was nothing in the old country. They're all doctors and lawyers and important artists whom America forces to work as beauticians and cabdrivers. Who get mad when you ask, if things were so terrific, why did they leave?

And now here was a second letter, presumably from *another* cousin, Skripnik concluded breathlessly, pushing the envelope toward me across the coffee table.

The woman I am hoping will agree to become my agent—which depends upon how the book I had spent that day working on goes—she would have known what to do. A highly successful big-city businesswoman with a voice that can open tin cans, she would not only have gotten him out of the apartment but would probably have done so by crumpling him into a ball and rolling him to the elevator.

My mother's solution would probably have been to fluff up his pillows, pour him more wine, offer more crackers, and gently steer the conversation around to his net worth, and whether he had children from a first wife to worry about.

Me? I said okay, I would translate his stupid letter. Why did I do this? Well, for one thing, if I hadn't, he might *never* have gone home, and then too, knowing Russian is kind of like double-jointed elbows or being able to cross your eyes and wiggle your ears, a skill you possess that is basically useless in everyday life but is sufficiently rare so that if anyone asks you to show it off, you generally feel you ought to oblige.

Leon immediately brightened. He picked up the letter and took it over to my desk, where he stood, waiting.

"Right now?" I asked after an ear-popping yawn. "You want me to translate it *right now*?"

Leon's pleased triumph was replaced by a grim, almost haunted look. "This is important, Margaret. Tremendously, tremendously important."

"You don't even know what's in the letter!" I pointed out. "How can you know whether it's important? Besides, does this apartment *look* like Translations-While-U-Wait? I can't work with someone breathing down my neck!"

"Okay, how long will it take you? I could, uh, go out for a cup of coffee or something . . ." He looked out the window at Ocean Parkway below.

"At this time on a Saturday night the nearest open coffee shop is all the way out at Coney Island." I was finally getting irritable. "Anyway, I don't know how long it will take to translate. I haven't even *looked* at the thing."

"I *could* pick it up first thing in the morning," he conceded reluctantly, "but you'd have to promise to be real careful. I'd die if anything happened to this letter."

"Like I'm going to stay up the rest of the night to translate this for you?" I finally was mad enough to do what I should have done in the first place, which was shout. "It's almost midnight right NOW and the letter is *twenty-two pages* long! Not to *mention* you could go blind trying to read it!"

"But it *has* to be translated tonight! It could be *very* serious."

"Monday evening," I decided rashly, seizing his arm and pulling him toward the door. "Call me Monday, and I'll tell you when to come pick it up."

I had to promise to treat the letter like it was part of my own body, but since the choice was Monday evening or not at all, I finally got Dr. Leon out of my apartment and into the elevator.

"I'll call you tomorrow, to see how it's going," he said while we waited for the box to clank up the four flights to us; maybe I'm making it up now, but I remember this as intense, almost desperate.

"I'll be waiting." I smiled as the elevator door slid slowly closed between us and then wondered all the way back to my apartment, why had I said that?

Well, at least it made the postmortem with Pearl a bit easier.

"Honestly, Mother, he promised to call again. . . . No, Mother, I didn't say anything. . . . No, look, what do you want me to do, *throw* myself at him? He said he would call, so how can you say I'm always *cold* to these . . . MOTHER, I swear I'm not hiding anything from you! He was a very, well, interesting sort of person. . . . Of COURSE I'll call you the minute he calls me."

But I wasn't surprised that even though I had his letter, he failed to keep his promise to call, which is what happens with all but the most desperate of the blind dates that Pearl thrusts upon me, because—she is actually correct—I don't go out of my way to encourage them. Whatever momentary enthusiasm had made that letter so crucial to him had obviously evaporated by morning. I didn't worry about it but instead set about finishing the translation and daydreaming about what to demand in payment. A ticket to *Les Miserables*? Lunch at Lutèce?

Bagels, cream cheese, and the serious people's parts of the *Times*—book review, front page, entertainment, and travel section, plus crossword for the bathroom—were the only break I permitted myself, in order to have the letter well in hand by Sunday evening and so be able to go back to my book—my *work*—on Monday. I confess though that what *really* kept me chained to my desk that whole Sunday was my growing pleasure at the thought of telling Dr. Skripnik all about his distinguished, accomplished Russian cousin.

Because although a few passages remained as undecipherable as if in Etruscan, the letter did a wonderful job of introducing Shmuel Skripnik, sixty-seven years of age, "son of your father's only uncle," once of Russia, now of Tel Aviv, who was nearly blind with cataracts.

Which an operation would probably cure.

Which he half asked, half demanded dear Cousin Dr. Leon should pay for.

Which they could discuss right after Shmuel had the pleasure of planting a big cousinly kiss on each of Dr. Leon's cheeks.

Which he would do at 3:48 P.M. EDT next Thursday at JFK, when Shmuel would arrive on El Al from Lod, the ticket for which had been bought with his last shekel, which Shmuel had gladly paid, in the full confidence that dear Cousin Leon would be happy to provide food, transportation, and roof.

2

MONDAY I took my Sunday sleep-in, letting my Girl Scout heroines Tammy and Tanesia have the morning off. Until eleven thirty, when there was a hammering at the door, which I finally opened to find my mother.

In black.

"My *God*, Midge," she said sailing in, "don't you *ever* answer your phone?" She was trailing my painter friend Sasha, who, embarrassed, was shrugging apologies at me behind Pearl's back, indicating that he couldn't help but let her into the building because Pearl knew he was the super. I shot him a glare of both anger and understanding and did my sleepy best to focus on Pearl.

Pearl is five foot two, rinses her gray hair but won't admit it, and wavers in her taste in clothes between thinking she is ten years older than she really is, and twenty years younger. Today, to judge by the black hat, black and white dress, and black patent leather bag, she had chosen ten years older. I hadn't even shut the door and she was already straightening my coffee table, talking fifteen to the dozen. "Come on, Midge, the car's waiting—where do they *find* such rude drivers? This one told me to 'shake it,' can you imagine? We have to be there in lots of time. It doesn't start until one, but there's sure to be a crowd, and who knows what the traffic is going to be like. You go take a shower and freshen up. But don't get *too* made up, like you did when we went to Altman's that time, and the man asked whether we were sisters. Just some lipstick and blush. No eye shadow, it wouldn't really be proper, and I'll go get that black dress, the Anne Klein, remember, that you didn't want to look at at Loehmann's? But I said if you just moved the top button it would look stunning—"

"Mother!" I finally managed, "what on earth are you *talking* about? And anyway, the man was just being polite."

She put down the pile of newspapers she had been straightening, pages aligned, section B inside section A, arranged by date, and immediately began dusting my desk as she looked at me, surprised.

"You with your hair dyed blond and all made up? Certainly not. Why did you ever *do* that?"

I tugged self-consciously at my hair, which was almost completely back to its normal chestnut, and wondered how to explain that temptation to experiment: once you've kicked over one box in your life, why not kick them all over? I had taken stock in Aunt Dora's bathroom mirror one morning, decided that the round face with maybe one chin more than it ought to have wouldn't look so round if I could pick up the yellow in my light brown eyes a little, which I might be able to do by, well, *brightening* my basically dark brown hair. I mean, if I could decide that marriage was wrong for me, and Russian was wrong for me, then why couldn't I decide that chestnut-brown, naturally curly hair was *also* wrong for me? Why *couldn't* I look like Mary Travers, with gorgeous straight blond hair?

Because it turned out that the highlighter stuff made my hair so stiff and yellow that I looked like the Scarecrow in *The Wizard of Oz*, that's why.

So I didn't argue with Pearl anymore about what I should wear. "That's not what I'm talking about. What do we have to be on time *for*?"

"The funeral, of course. You haven't seen the *Times*? There was even a story."

My mother is hard enough to follow when you're wide awake and prepared for her. Going from a dead sleep to Pearl is impossible. We don't have any relatives who would merit an obituary in the *Times*, probably not even if it was a courtesy one, like if maybe someone was a victim in a hijacking or, what was more likely, given the way some of them drove, if they had caused some spectacular calamity, like a thousand-car pile-up on the FDR.

But maybe the dead person was a celebrity? Sometimes when someone like Fred Astaire dies, my mother goes up to the funeral parlor to watch the old stars coming to pay respects. But she never makes me go along. *Asks*, maybe, but she doesn't come by in a car to pick me up and all. And certainly not dressed in black.

I gave up. "What funeral?"

"Leon's." I must still have been saucer-eyed and slack-jawed, for she slapped my arm lightly and added, "Dr. Skripnik. Now, go on, get dressed!"

She pushed me into the bathroom and threw a towel at me. Dead? He can't be dead, I just saw him! I kept thinking as I hopped shivering from foot to foot on the checkered bathroom tiles while the dribbly shower dragged hot water up from the boiler in the basement. (I had given up complaining to Sasha about the shower, because whenever I did, he would tell me that in Leningrad, nobody's shower works, and there's nothing to eat. Here at least there's food, so I should be be grateful.) But my disbelief grew steadily into something else.

Envy.

Skripnik rated an obituary in the *Times*?

I soaped myself slowly and thoroughly, trying to scrub the emerald green out of my complexion. An obituary in the *Times*, for crying out loud? With a story, even?

And now my mother even wanted that I should go to his funeral? Why? So I could listen to even more detail about why this schmuck Skripnik, who was not only a total stranger to me but also one of the most ordinary and annoying people I have ever met, why *he* rated an obituary in the *New York* god-damned *Times*? Over my dead body was I going to that funeral!

Sasha's boiler decided I'd had enough warm water, and offered instead a squirt fresh from under the ice up in Pepacton Reservoir. Which cooled me down enough to remember that, in the first place, whatever the justice of Skripnik getting a *Times* obit instead of me, in one regard at least his claim was superior, since he was dead.

And in the second place, I not only still had Skripnik's letter, but I was the only one who had *read* it, and therefore the only one who knew about Cousin Shmuel.

Who would arrive at JFK on Thursday, feel his way

through customs and out into the arrival hall, where he would grope his way along that opaque glass wall that keeps relatives out of the customs area, touching strangers' faces with his bony rabbinic fingers, until someone took him somewhere and robbed and killed him.

So now that I was in a hurry to leave, to find someone to pass the letter to before the funeral, Pearl decided I needed breakfast. Three-minute eggs, which for thirty years I've been telling her make me gag.

"So don't eat them. You'll probably spill yolk on your dress anyway. But if there's a lot of people and we have to stand, you'll wish you'd had something to give you a little strength!"

"Mother, I'm not going to the funeral. I didn't even know the man!"

"Such a young man, too! A doctor, and something like this happens. It's a tragedy, a real tragedy." Pearl shook her head, lips tight.

Which made me suddenly wonder: Could it be what he died of that got Skripnik on the obit page? Some obscure ailment that there was some basis for? Should I be worrying about what he drank out of in my apartment that night?

"This was like some . . . *disease* he suddenly got?"

Normally, I try not to ask many questions, because my mother is not good at answers. Even a simple inquiry about how she's feeling can sometimes involve how the Balducci's boy had put the eggs in the bottom of the bag, and that A&S was advertising hypo-allergenic pillows two for thirty-five dollars, but when she called up to have some sent they were out and weren't giving rain checks. With something like Skripnik's untimely demise, it was to be expected that Pearl's account would last us the rest of breakfast, out the door to the car, up Ocean Parkway, and all the way to the Manhattan end of the Brooklyn Bridge before I finally got most of the story clear enough to make me shudder. Which I did because I was probably about the last person Skripnik ever spoke to.

The story was page four of section B, not the obituaries. When Skripnik's housekeeper had unlocked the house to clean, she had discovered the doctor's body stretched out on the floor of his kitchen, something heavy having recently descended upon his head.

"Murdered?" I asked with that very urban little shudder, mostly horror at what a hell the city can be, seasoned with something almost like pride that at least it's never dull.

"You know the *Times*," Pearl nodded, "so proper about those kinds of things that you can never find out any of the things you really want to know. Believe me, as soon as I saw it there I ran right out and got the other papers too, even that Long Island one . . . well, you can never tell, can you? He might have had some family out on the Island or something, some connection that they'd write it up . . . Here, driver, turn here, it's up at—"

"*Mother,* this is Broadway!"

"Well, I know that." Pearl leaned forward, trying to tap the driver on his skinny shoulder. "And we've got to get up to the West Side, so . . ."

"It's one-way, Mother! *This* way, not *that* way!"

Fortunately the Jamaican driver paid no attention, continuing to slalom the scruffy Oldsmobile up Sixth, dodging other cars and bopping his head to some music only he could hear.

"Drugs," Pearl pronounced. "I'm sure it has something to do with drugs."

"MOTHER!" One of New York's unwritten rules is never to accuse your driver of being a junkie while the car is still moving.

"Not him, silly, Dr. Skripnik."

"Dr. Skripnik had something to do with drugs?"

"Of course he did, he was a doctor! Everybody knows doctors keep drugs around, in case they have to make house calls or something."

"Urologists don't make house calls, mother."

"Crack addicts, I'm very certain," my mother went on, paying no attention to my interruptions. "To beat another human being like that? The *Post*, they tell you what the *Times* won't. The head they say was all blood, and there were signs of a struggle. What else but drugs would make a person do something like that to a useful, upstanding citizen who does a great deal of good for mankind, and leave him *dead*? Not even an animal does such a thing!"

By the time we were finally deposited in front of Tennenbaum and Levy, Counselors to the Bereaved, my mother had me nearly convinced that we had come to mourn Dr. Albert Schweitzer Skripnik, and not merely my chance to land a urologist. Tennenbaum and Levy looked like a miniature of those wedding palaces out on Sheepshead Bay, the kind of place that can feed four hundred Italians in one room and three hundred Jews in another, cannolis on one dessert cart, babka on the other, an open bar, roast beef cart, and twenty-eight people with video cam-corders in both, a big curved driveway out front lined with symmetrical little fir shrubs set among blinding white marble chips, where hordes of sparrows pick at the rice that gets thrown at brides and grooms, who depart with about the regularity—and individuality —as the Trump Shuttle. Since funerals don't usually draw the crowds that weddings do, Tennebaum and Levy was about one third the scale, a short curved driveway up to a canopy, velvet and brass ropes directing us through the heavy carved doors of the flagstone-fronted building, where we were met by a lugubrious attendant in a morning coat, whom I half expected to ask, "Bride's side or groom's?"

In other words, it was the pretentious sort of funeral parlor that I wouldn't get caught dead in, which helped restore some of the sarcastic sense of scorn that I usually need to get me through funerals. Sarcasm helps at weddings too, but generally there you can address yourself to the open bar if the sarcasm won't come. After all, I reminded myself while Mother tried to get fifty cents change of a dollar from the driver to make the tip come out precisely, *I* wasn't here to mourn; I was here to deliver a letter.

So I marched into Tennebaum and Levy behind my mother and the dolorous attendant, determined to find some Skripnik to pass my letter to and be gone. I didn't know precisely who I was looking for, but the best bet would have to be the Russians, the cousins that Leon had been boasting about. The way he talked of his American family, I wasn't even sure they would be there, and the Russians at least would probably already know this Shmuel. And Russians would certainly stand out in the crowd the funeral of an unexpectedly dead Manhattan urologist would no doubt draw.

That's the thing about the émigrés; you can always spot them, because no matter how long they've been here, there's always some little made-in-Moscow detail that gives them away—the olive and lilac checked sports jacket from GUM, the white vinyl elevator shoes, the skirt that's far too long or far too short, hennaed hair or kohled eyes or steel teeth.

We were led with professional murmurs and perfect taste across the plush wool carpets and through the carved wooden halls of the funeral home. Music was playing very low, so that you not so much heard it as absorbed it, becoming weepy before you even reached the room with the box.

The funeral home was divided into several rooms, which unlike those in wedding palaces were identified simply by letters, instead of being named things like the Chapel of Love. Ours was E, at the end of a longish corridor off the main hallway, so that I was not wholly unprepared when we entered to find, instead of a big room crowded with Skripniks, a chapel about twice the size of my living room. Even so, there was lots of room for the eight or nine people already sitting there to keep a couple of chairs between them and their neighbors. Everyone had that straight-backed, decorous look of mourning, which dissolved instantly when they all turned to goggle at the newcomers, which at least let us goggle right back.

The woman in black who might have been Pearl except she was about forty pounds heavier, weeping noisily near the coffin, could have been Leon's mother, the way she was carrying on, but based on what he had told me Saturday night, I guessed her to be a cousin-in-law on his mother's side, whose husband had died uninsured, and who Leon thought was after his money. The two women about my age who were patting the cousin-in-law's hands and giving her handkerchiefs would have been the daughters, one as plump as a chocolate chip Danish, the other anorexic. The man who looked like a heavier, much shorter version of Leon was probably a cousin too, although he looked so bored that he might almost have been in the wrong room. I tried to guess from his feet whether this might be the cousin-accountant or the cousin-shoe-store-owner whom

Skripnik had savaged on Saturday night, but then gave up —wing tips are wing tips. The very non-Jewish-looking, severe blonde in the stiff clothing and tight bun might have been a receptionist, or perhaps a nurse. So far the only mystery was the lone black woman who sat in the back, just inside the door, who was too old to be a lover, not dressed like a nurse or receptionist, and too sad looking to be just ducking in to get warm.

"*Her* family wouldn't come, of course," Pearl whispered, far too loudly, as we took our seats. "It was a *very* nasty divorce, and just last year."

You know, since it was Pearl who sent Skripnik to me, I had never even wondered about a wife, but I might have known there would be one somewhere in the background, even if Dr. Leon hadn't struck me as the most desirable of men. Since all this AIDS business, Pearl feels a little more comfortable with divorced men; as she says, "Well, *these* days you just have to wonder about a man who reaches *your* age and is still single." What did occur to me though, was that I probably ought to pass the Israeli's letter on to Skripnik's ex-wife, since she would know who was next of kin now.

Which could be all right or could be a disaster, depending upon what kind of an ex-wife this was, a problem I worried at for a moment. Then there was a hush, and a man and woman came in through a side door, followed by a boy so awkward and gangling that he might have been half giraffe, had his face not made it plain he was Leon's son. The poor blushing creature had even inherited the huge Adam's apple, now bobbing up and down like one of those glass elevators that fancy hotels have in their atrium lobbies. The pair in front of him looked enough alike to be brother and sister. The brother wasn't Clark Gable, and his pursed-lipped expression of distaste didn't help much either, but it wasn't until the woman turned around to give us all a bewildered glance before sitting that it became obvious that young Skripnik had in fact gotten the best deal he could have, given the contributing genes.

Mrs. Ex-Skripnik may have had the only middle-class buck teeth to escape braces since World War II, and certainly the only nose of its proportions not to be lopped. What really set the poor lady off, though, was a pair of spectacles so thick-lensed that when she peered directly at you her eyes seemed to leap backward, shrinking like startled gerbils.

The organ and violin music came up, bringing tears even to my eyes, and we made ourselves comfortable, ready to hear Leon's virtues extolled by the sleek young rabbi who stepped up onto the little stage next to the closed coffin. I half listened to the rabbi, who had a thick beard, full cheeks, and bright black eyes that made him look like a beaver, and who clearly had never met Leon, while I rehearsed polite ways to say I'm sorry your husband is dead, here's a letter from his cousin, pick him up at JFK on Thursday, good-bye. Skripnik's widow at least seemed satisfied, whenever I took a peek at her. She kept looking back over one shoulder or the other at us, nodding emphatically, as though the rabbi were taking her side in some argument we had all been having with her.

Frankly, Mrs. Ex-Skripnik made me nervous. There is something intimidating about a person who is *that* plain. Her hair was expensively cut, but the style suited her face so poorly that it looked almost like a practical joke, two shoulder-length wings that fell around her glasses and made her nose look like Pinocchio hiding in shrubs. The same thing with her clothes, which were expensive and well made but entirely the wrong shape for her figure and the wrong color for her skin. You might have taken this for some kind of mourning thing, that you shouldn't look pretty when your husband is dead, except that Mrs. Skripnik obviously wasn't mourning.

At least, a yellow skirt and a tropical print silk shirt with magenta palm trees seemed to make it pretty obvious. Her bright azure beret also reinforced the suggestion that if she wasn't quite dancing on Leon's grave, she maybe wouldn't mind stamping her foot on it a time or two.

When the service finally ended, we all shuffled into a line to tell Mrs. Ex how sorry we were about Leon. The avaricious cousin was first, weeping and beating on her chest, the two daughters grabbing her arms and eyeing chairs to sit her in should she faint. Mrs. Skripnik, looking mouselike, murmured something, and the plump cousin, indignant, stomped out, the daughters following dejectedly. Even though he hadn't sat with them, the male proved to have some responsibility for them, because he hurriedly shook hands, and scurried out, evidently in pursuit of the three women. I wondered then whether I shouldn't maybe have handed the letter to one of them, since this Mrs. Ex-Skripnik did not project like a woman anxious to be clearing up the dead man's odds and ends. I began to panic a little, fingering Shmuel's letter and trying to think up a quick but certain method of getting her to take it.

Which I never did, because I never got to try.

The nurse-receptionist–looking blonde shook hands briskly, her squared shoulders quivering and tears making mascara festoons on her cheeks, and marched out of the chapel, purse tucked under her right arm like Field Marshal Montgomery's swagger stick.

Which left me next. Mrs. Ex-Skripnik peered at me

expectantly. When I finally shuffled over, she clutched my arm and stage-whispered, "So *you're* her. I had wondered whether you'd dare come."

The boy and the man standing just behind her looked at me intently, and the black woman behind me snorted and looked away. Even my mother cocked an eyebrow. Realizing what Mrs. Ex meant, I blushed so furiously my earlobes throbbed. I didn't even know which was more embarrassing, that I should be cast as the Homewrecking Tootsie in this Skripnik family drama, or that *anyone*— the woman behind me, the plotchy-faced son, even my own *mother*—would for a moment think that I would . . . with *Skripnik*?

I thought of his narrow shoulders, his gangly legs, his silly little bow tie, his . . . his . . .

His BRASS!

I looked down, to see that I had just tied my scarf into a knot that I would never get undone, and then looked up, trying to be calm.

"There's some mistake, I think," I began, opening my purse to get the letter.

Mrs. Ex kept the upper hand, though, for she clearly had thought about this confrontation and decided that breezy superiority would carry the day. Head back, shoulders square, she smiled at me, to suggest that I was maybe some sort of mud that naughty Leon had been playing in.

"My dear, the burial is on Long Island, *quite* far out. Naturally, the *family* will accompany poor Leon, and I'm sure you won't want to bother."

"But . . . but . . ." Knowing I was sputtering, I said, "I have to tell—"

"Well, I really don't think you do, dear, but if you feel it makes your burden lighter, I suppose . . ." She shrugged, with a graciousness that I almost slugged her for.

"You don't—Mrs. Skripnik, believe me, Leon and I—I mean, Dr. Skripnik. He left—"

Now Mrs. Skripnik clutched my arm hard, looked me closely in the face, and whispered loudly enough for everyone to hear, even the sad-faced attendant, who was plainly trying not to snigger, "*This* isn't the place to tell me about what he left at your place, is it?" Since I was still stunned, she had the time to rummage in her handbag and dig out a card, which she put in my hand. "This has my address on it, the place my son and I have been forced to live since . . ." She shrugged. "Well, I expect you know since when. We won't be back from the grave until, oh, five or six. So why don't we say you'll come to see me at seven?"

By now I finally had Shmuel's letter out of my purse, but it was too late; Mrs. Ex walked out of the chapel, head up, back straight, as I waved my letter in feeble farewell.

The philandering hussy, played by a speechlessly angry, livid-faced Margaret Cohen, crumpled the card into a ball and threw it to the floor, turning to glare at her mother.

"Pick that up, dear. I expect you'll be wanting it," Pearl said mildly, and followed Mrs. Skripnik out the door.

"Seven years I mopped her floors, and I never could get that woman to listen to me." The black woman, shrugged philosophically, stepped around me, and left.

Behind me two attendants stepped through the velvet drapes to push the casket out on its little trolley. I took a deep breath and left the chapel, still so angry I was seeing spots.

"Family?" a man asked me, just outside the door.

I turned on him, ready to let whoever this was have both barrels of what I had never gotten the opportunity to say to Mrs. Skripnik, but Pearl glided smoothly up.

"No, officer, we're friends of the family, and . . ."

"I DIDN'T EVEN KNOW THE MAN!" I shouted at both Pearl and whoever this flatfoot was, standing under a downspot that threw thick shadow below his brow and nose and made him look like something you'd throw candy at on Halloween. Then I spun around and stomped off, until I remembered I was in the black Ballys that I had bought on sale two years ago with my first Tammy and Tanesia check, and that I couldn't even dream of replacing now. Impatiently I turned back around, just in time to hear Pearl saying, "Not seriously, of course, but she had seen . . ."

"*MOTHER!*" I shouted, then waved that she should come on. I mean, let Pearl open her mouth, and the next thing you know the police would be putting us down as suspects!

3

"MOTHER, why in God's name would the *police* be at Skripnik's funeral?" I hissed as we slid into the booth. The waiter smiled beatifically.

"Oh, I *love* this place." Pearl settled herself on the broad banquette instead of answering, and patted the seat with both hands, bouncing a little before she accepted a menu from the waiter. Then, just as she did every time we ate there, she said, "Do you know that they share the kitchen with The Four Seasons? It's the same food here, but cheaper!"

Like most writers, I'm smarter on the page than I am in real life. When they want information, I make Tammy and Tanesia, my two Girl Scout heroines, clever and resourceful. (In *The Secret of Indian Rocks,* my first Camp Poncatoncas mystery, Billy Bates from the Boy Scout camp on the other side of the lake refuses to tell them where he had been going on the night that the ghostly light was seen burning on top of Indian Rocks. My girls tie him up and threaten to tickle him until he barfs.) To get information out of my mother, though, all I can ever think of is lunch at the Brasserie. Whether it really does share the kitchen with The Four Seasons, I don't know, because I have never set foot in The Four Seasons and probably never will, but I decided to humor Pearl and not say anything. Unless Steven Spielberg decides to film Tammy and Tanesia, one hundred dollars a plate is likely to remain deeper than my pocket reaches. I can tell you, though, that while its food may be cheaper, the Brasserie certainly isn't cheap.

But then what place in midtown Manhattan is? Down in that part of town even the panhandlers beg you for dollars, not quarters, because of the overhead they've got to cover. God knows the Brasserie's deep thick booths and big shiny brass plates on the wall and well-polished brass railings can't come cheap. In fact, though, probably the most expensive thing in the restaurant is the space, because the tables and booths are actually far enough apart that you can eat lunch without your elbow in someone else's salad, or someone's tie in your soup. It is not every restaurant in midtown that can make that boast.

And anyway, when you pay $9.95 for a hamburger and fries, you feel like you've *done* something.

"Of course I know that, Mother. I *also* know that I've now got to hang around in the city the rest of the day, waiting for some woman I've never seen before in my life to come back from burying her husband. And it's all your fault! So I really think you'd better—"

"I told you, didn't I?" Pearl looked up from the menu triumphantly.

"Told me what?"

"I *knew* there was something strange about his death. I bet it had something to do with a will, or maybe—"

"Mother," I interrupted, "in the first place, you said you were sure the death would have something to do with drugs—"

She interrupted right back. "And maybe it does! But it'll be something in the family, you can bet on that! Because why else would they have a detective right there, interviewing people as they came out of the service?"

It was only because she buried her nose in the menu that I never got to my "and in the second place," which was to ask why the hell if she thought the police would be looking for suspects was she doing everything she could to get me included among them? Pearl is too vain to wear her reading glasses outside her apartment, though she always claims she just forgot them. The sight of her trying so hard to fake a youthfulness that even I didn't have much left of filled me with pity. As always.

"Since when do burglars come to the funeral? Come on, mother, I have to go see that woman and I don't even know—"

"That's not my fault." Pearl looked up from the menu. "I never saw her before either, you know."

"That's not the *point*, Mother," I slapped my menu down hard enough to make two of the pinstriped munchers at the counter look up from their onion soup. I did my best to hush my voice. "The point is, just Saturday afternoon I was working happily away in my own apartment, not even aware that there was somebody named Dr. Leon Skripnik in the *world,* and just because *you* gave him my number, I'm not only in *mourning* for him"—I pointed down at my dress, which, I had to hand it to Pearl, *was* stunning—"but I've got to go see his widow, who is convinced I was Skripnik's *mistress.*"

At which point, of course, the waiter materialized at my elbow. I blushed furiously and studied the menu blindly while Mother discussed every entrée on the menu, and then, as she always did, chose onion soup, a hamburger, and cottage cheese, with Black Forest cake and coffee to follow.

I gave up trying to read the menu and just handed it back. "For two."

"Even the cake?" Pearl sounded surprised. "I don't remember that that dress was so tight the last time you wore it." She looked at the waiter, as if expecting confirmation. The waiter diplomatically examined his order pad.

I shrugged, nodded. I wanted to fight about choosing my own men, not about dessert. "No cake for me." The waiter nodded, snapped up the menus, and whizzed away, while Pearl, looking triumphant, carefully rearranged her silver. I had the distinct impression I had already lost round one.

Polishing her water glass, as if it was all by the by, she asked, "Well, were you?"

"What?"

"His mistress."

"MOTHER!" I had a brief vision of myself in bed with Skripnik, who was folding and unfolding like a flesh-colored carpenter's ruler. "How could I be his mistress, when I never *saw* him before that night? Or after either? And anyway, you *saw* the man, how could you *ever* . . ."

Pearl, looking satisfied, sniffed delicately, and said with an air of finality, "So don't."

"Don't *what?*"

"Don't go see her. Go back to Brooklyn. Or if you're lonely over there, come home with me; it's been a long time since you came to visit me. You aren't still angry that I moved to the city when your father died, are you?"

Sure, what am I making myself nuts for? Why *don't* I forget about this world full of Skripniks and just go *home?*

Except it was impossible to think about that, because my mother was off, justifying her decision to sell the house I grew up in, on a cul-de-sac in Midwood, because the house had seemed so enormous with Max gone, and so full of memories, and besides, with four maybe five synagogues in the neighborhood and the Orthodox who have to walk to services on the Sabbath moving in like crazy, spending fistfuls of money just to get hold of the *lots,* because the first thing they would do is knock the house down and build one bigger, to hold all their children and the kitchens with the two of everything, dishwasher for meat, dishwasher for dairy, so that maybe for someone who grew up in that house it should stay like a shrine or something, but believe me, Max would have understood.

"Mother, I was never upset that you sold the house."

"Was that why you moved to upstate? Because you didn't like the house?"

Seeing that the conversation was getting even more tangled, I picked up the butter knife and pointed it at Pearl.

"Mother, you sent Skripnik to me, and now I've got Skripniks up to my ears. Don't you think you owe me an explanation?"

"Thirty-two is so old? One man dumps you and suddenly you're an old maid who should stay indoors all day writing books for children she can't have herself? What kind of men do you meet sitting at that desk all day? The super? Or electricians maybe? Exterminators?"

I looked up sharply at that crack about "the super," because in fact Sasha and I . . . Well, that's another story. But then I smiled, because I realized that Pearl was conceding my point. Not only did she know that it was I who had left Paul, not the other way around, but she had also encouraged me to do it. As for that swipe at my books, well, I know for a fact that all the doormen in her building got copies of *Indian Rocks* for Christmas the year it came out. True, each copy had a twenty for a bookmark, but still.

And as for that business about thirty-two, that's the age we both seem to have agreed I will stay, because otherwise Pearl would have to be more than fifty-five.

"Not why you send men, why you sent *him*."

Now it was my mother who looked uncomfortable. "Okay," she said after a moment, "I'm sorry. I was trying to be nice. It just didn't work out, that's all. Maybe next time will be better, right?"

The thought of a next time made me dig my spoon into the crust of my onion soup so hard that the melted-cheese-and-toast thing on top capsized, sending a bloorb of greasy soup splattering across the pale pink table cloth toward Pearl's butter plate. I looked around guiltily, and set the bread basket on top of it.

I have to tell you that when my father was alive Pearl was not as domineering as she is now, though no one would ever have thought she was one of "those" mothers, the kind who let their high school daughters drink beer, run around with boys who smoke cigarettes, or leave the house without a sweater. As I was growing up, Pearl and I had had a proper New Frontier kind of mother-daughter relationship, a little bit Donna Reed, a little bit Dr. Spock, a little bit Tevya the Milkman. We did the usual mother-daughter things, like when I joined the Girl Scouts and she drove me around to make her mah-jongg friends buy cookies, or when I wanted to do science projects and she paid the Puerto Rican gardener to bring me a jar full of bugs. Once she even got the seamstress to make us identical mother-daughter Passover dresses, with matching hats, which she put veils and feathers on herself.

Nevertheless, we somehow managed to make it through my teenage years and remain pretty good friends, especially in comparison to what some of the nice Jewish girls I grew up with were managing to get themselves involved with back there in the early sixties. Probably because Pearl actually can be sensible, when the occasion demands. Like when I insisted I was going to Cornell, just like Vanessa Liebowitz on the next block, and Pearl spent two days talking nonstop about how good Brooklyn College is and trolling Barnard and Hunter past me as the other possibilities, and then, after a telephone call to make certain Cornell had a big Hillel chapter, she agreed that if I insisted my college *had* to be out of town, Cornell was just fine. Vanessa's mom, on the other hand, faked a heart attack, made Brooklyn College her deathbed wish, and then got better, so Vanessa went to Brooklyn, where she took up theater and ran off with a road show of *Hair*, and the last anybody heard from her was the publicity still she sent from El Paso or someplace, which showed her wearing a crown of flowers, a dazed smile, and not much else, a peace symbol painted—tattooed?—on her very bare bosom. Mrs. Leibowitz had another heart attack, this time for real.

In fact, by the time I landed Paul Blank, it turned out that Cornell had been Pearl's idea all along. When I finally had my veterinarian-and-husband-to-be under that wedding canopy, three weeks after graduation, Pearl was beaming wider and hotter than the June sun that winked through the patrician oaks of the Blanks' country club.

Paul's father had a fantastically lucrative job doing something complex on Wall Street, and Max was determined to feel no shame in front of "that Montclair crowd." Nor should he have, even if I did almost die of embarrassment when he set up with his camera just behind the roast-beef carver so as to get each guest's picture, exhorting, "Eat! Drink! Enjoy! This is the only wedding I ever get to pay for!" Paul and I left for our honeymoon (a week in Europe, with stops in London, Paris, and Tel Aviv, all paid for by the Blanks) so stuffed from hot-and-cold hors d'oeuvres, prime rib, potato puffs, and glazed miniature carrots, followed by a Viennese dessert table, that it was three days before we could manage the belly-to-belly necessary to (in Paul's romantic words) "do it legal."

"It was the proudest day of your father's life, seeing you married! Thank God he didn't live to see—"

This was Pearl's gloomy-day refrain, always punctuated by a discrete biting of her upper lip, and a moist-eyed look into the middle distance, as though she were still distraught over my divorce.

A good act, really, because at the time Pearl was very understanding and supportive, an absolute angel in fact, which is doubly amazing given that there wasn't really a *reason* for the divorce. Paul didn't beat me, didn't drink, didn't run around. Our almost decade of cohabitation had been calm, even placid, with plenty of money for furniture and movies and trying the overpriced restaurants that Cornell Hotel School graduates are always opening around Ithaca. In fact, Paul didn't do *anything*, except talk constantly about cows.

Even that was no surprise, because it was the cows that had attracted me to him in the first place. Cornell was a weird place back then; the Black Student Union was carrying shotguns and demanding "cultural autonomy," hippies were into drugs, rock and roll, and revolution, and there *we* all were, over at the ZBT fraternity house, dancing to bands that could play "Louie, Louie" fast *and* slow.

Oh, maybe I did try one or two of the other "life-style options" that Cornell was offering then, but marijuana made me choke and made my hair stink for days, the one time when I let myself be talked into skinny-dipping down in one of the gorges it rained and I caught the flu, and whenever I visited my friend Rachel at the commune she lived in—a run-down house near the railroad tracks called Free Love America—it seemed like however little cooking and cleaning and grocery-buying actually got done, she was the one who had to do it.

So I roomed with Sara Zolotar, who was in the Labor Relations school and planning a pregnancy scare to land her ZBT. With no steady of my own, I went to ZBT parties to amuse myself by being sarcastic to the other wallflowers. Until one day when this guy overheard me being snide about how rich all the brothers claimed they were going to get in the stock market, and shot back a question about why the girls were any better, studying our elementary education homework in the law school library in the hopes of landing young lawyers. I informed him haughtily that *I* wasn't in ed, I was in Russian, and that furthermore, if I was going to teach, it would be as a *professor*, with a *doctorate*.

We leaned on the beer-stained top of the fraternity's piano for about four hours, sparring about our futures— me mostly making it up as I went along, Paul incredibly definite and firm about veterinary school—until finally he invited me to drive over to the agriculture school barns, to look at a new cow. I was pretty sure this was just an excuse to go necking, but Paul really did take me into a barn. Unexpectedly, I found this all so impossibly romantic—the air redolent with hay and cow, myriad motes dancing through Paul's flashlight beam, the light making the cows' eyes a sudden brilliant blue, the dark around us filled with the deep gentle breathing of large creatures asleep—that I still remember the breed of cow we had come to see, and Paul's awe as he discussed her. An Irish Dexter, small enough almost to keep in a yard, but a great milker, with high butter-fat content.

By next spring I was wearing his ZBT pin, and by senior year when we went to the Hillel services together for Rosh Hashanah, I had a brand-new diamond ring to fidget with and admire during the interminable shofar-blowing and college boys stumbling through Torah passages in Hebrew they had mostly forgotten. Paul was accepted to the Cornell veterinary program, I got into the graduate program in Russian, and we got married.

Did we love each other? Were we happy? I don't know. Mostly what I remember is that we didn't get in each other's way. He had organic chemistry and anatomy and long practicums way out in the country, while I had the library, irregular verbs, tons and tons of reading, and, for recreation, wrestling with the eccentricities of the drafty old farm house we had used our wedding gifts to put a down payment on.

And so we lived, for almost ten years, until one icy morning when I was running through the halls at Ithaca College, late as usual because, also as usual, my VW had spun out climbing the hill up to campus. As I puffed and pushed my way through the knots of students leaving their classes, one black kid bellowed at another, "What we here for, man? Ain't nothing here but white folks and *cows*!"

That simple and highly accurate description of life in upstate nagged me through all my classes, through supper with Paul, and well into the night.

Around four the next morning I piled as many of my clothes and books as would fit into my cranky but well-loved VW 412 wagon, left a note for Paul on the kitchen table, and headed for New York.

Don't sell Dora's apartment, I telephoned Pearl from a McDonald's in Binghamton. I'm going to move in after all!

That was the sequence of events, but it makes my divorce sound a lot flakier than it really was. The fact is, even though it never seemed it when I tried to explain to Paul, my mother, and sometimes even to myself, it was the marriage that was flaky, not the divorce.

"Isn't it *funny* that a city kid like me gets so hooked on mastitis?" Paul use to chortle on his especially good days, when one of his papers got accepted or a symposium had gone well. Actually, "bizarre" would have been a better description, and after about five years, which is how long it took to figure out that the fancy French poodles and Persian cats that I suppose I had unconsciously assumed Paul would one day move to Manhattan to treat don't get mastitis, "infuriating" became fairly apt too, because the rewards of what you can do upstate—rake leaves, plant zucchini, and go for endless bicycle rides—had long since been dwarfed by the irritation of what you *can't*—watch French movies, eat new ethnic foods *before* the *Times* writes about them, and, most important of all, go window-shopping on Fifth Avenue so you can plan what you'd be buying six months later at Loehmann's.

What I'm saying is, I was unhappy, and I would have

known it if I'd had the brains to listen to myself. And then one day the lawyer called, to inform me that Great Aunt Dora had left me everything—the apartment, the furnishings, and all her savings, which after all estate expenses and taxes were about $120,000.

Suddenly I felt like one of those sheepish contestants on *Let's Make a Deal* who has chosen some joke prize like a year's supply of cat food or two tons of lettuce or life with Paul Blank and his black-and-white cows. Just to make clear to the audience—and you—what a schmuck you have been, the announcer then shows you the *other* prize, the *real* one, the one you *should* have chosen: a trip around the world on the QE II, with Marcello Mastroianni. Or, in my case, life in the big city, an apartment I could afford, and enough money to support me while I figured out at least what I wanted to do with the rest of my life.

Which is why that particular morning, when the furnace hadn't come on and the kitchen pipes had frozen again, and I had made us coffee out of Sanka powder and microwaved snow and argued with Paul about who would stay home to wait for the furnace guy, that what the kid had shouted at school made so much sense that less than twenty-four hours later, I was watching the sun rise over the George Washington Bridge and the bare trees of the Palisades Parkway.

Pearl took my exit quite calmly, not trying to talk me out of leaving Paul or anything. She listened to the whole, tangled, breathless explanation before asking, "Well, maybe so, but what are you going to *do*?"

"WRITE!" I roared.

To which my mother, bless her, said only, "Well, if you think you can . . ."

Oh, the idea wasn't out of the *blue* or anything. Don't

most of us have that feeling at one time or another? You're reading some best-seller that has made the writer a quad-razillionaire and the whole *shtick* of the novel is that Hitler turns out to be Winston Churchill's prep school roommate, or it's the umpty-third exposé of the perils of being a rich, beautiful woman with big boobs, or it has everything you never wanted to know about twenty-year-old boys who can't figure out whether they're gay or investment bankers, and you read to the end but the whole time you want to throw the book across the room? FEH! you think to yourself, I could do better than that! And maybe you go a little bit further even, and watch some late geese honking south through a hazy November evening, the air smelling of leaves and slightly rotting apples, your cardigan warm around you and the house lights glowing orange behind you, and you think about how one day, maybe, you'll write all this down.

Even so, that still leaves you well back from the window ledge that I suddenly had perched myself on, ready to fling myself out of marriage and job and at least twenty years of being the Midge I had always thought I was.

Because outside of wanting to be a writer, my writing experience was kind of limited. A doctoral thesis, a review of *Contemporary Feminist Thought in the USSR* published in an obscure Slavic journal, and an article called "Isomorphism in Fet and Annensky" that a Canadian journal was either still considering or had lost.

On the other hand, though, Dora's three rooms with a view of the Ocean Parkway mulberries, just a few blocks' walk to stops for both the D and the F subway lines, and generally even with parking in front of the building, gave me a better safety net than most writers get, and I had read enough mysteries to have a pretty good idea of what I wanted to write, even though it turned out to be a lot harder than I thought. You want to know how hard it is just to get some bozo you've invented through a door and across a room? You describe too much, you describe too little, and *then* you remember that in the last chapter his eyes were green and now you just made them blue.

However, that certain *zetz* you get when you throw yourself out of the window and know you have to learn to fly before you hit the pavement, that gave me the energy to put in twelve-and fifteen-hour days at my typewriter, where I started and ripped up three mysteries for adults before I finally hit on my two girls and their Girl Scout camp in the woods. Thinking about my own camp experiences and my junior high girlfriends and the way we talked about teachers, boys, and our hair, I banged out *Indian Rocks* in two frantic months and then, systematic daughter of Pearl that I am, began contacting children's publishers. In alphabetical order, of course. By great good luck Apple Publishing had mapped out a new niche in the young adult market: parents who feel guilty about packing their kids off to camp and so want to convince them it will be fun. "Your book is terrific, but you know what? Two white girls . . . what if you called this Teresa Tanesia instead, and made her black?"

Apple was going to publish my book? If they had wanted, I'd have turned all my characters into dolphins and put the book underwater!

Indian Rocks did not set the world of eight-to-twelve-year-old girls afire, but advance sales were strong enough that Apple not only bought *High Water at Lake Poncatoncas*, but also took ads in *Library Journal*, *Parents*, and *Scouting* for the first book, touting "Tammy and Tanesia, the only multiracial mystery series for Girl Scouts of all ages." Which was enough to get me an agent, who then got me $500 against first refusal on a third book, which I had to show them by June. Which is next month.

So, now I'm a writer.

Not Cinderella, though, and not Irving Howe either. The *New York Review of Books* hasn't reviewed me, and the *Times* hasn't either (which is why it made me so mad when I saw that they had covered Skripnik's death). Maybe more important, Tammy and Tanesia have not only not made me rich, they can't even support themselves yet. One hundred twenty thousand dollars sounded like a lot of money, but it only works out to about nine grand a year in interest, and I'm damned if I'll touch the capital. Which is why about every third month I have to cash one of the checks that Paul faithfully sends me. Unasked, I might add. Each time I have to slink to the bank instead of grandly returning the envelope unopened, I'm depressed for three days, but that's a lot better than the alternative, which would mean taking money from Pearl. So, fudging a little, it's not even three years, and I really can say that I am on my own, doing what I want to do, answering to no one.

Except maybe for this business of grandchildren.

My mother swore that it was not just to find men for me that she went back to work. I didn't believe her though, because long before Skripnik had started his treatment for gingivitis, Pearl had worked out a smooth routine.

"You look at the ring finger, of course," she now confided over her cottage cheese and hamburger, "but these days, what does *that* tell you? Two days in a tanning parlor and you're as single as you want to be! But when this Dr. Skripnik came in, well, I think, *doctor,* but what kind? There's psychologists, there's GPs, you even get some professors who like to be called doctor. But I looked him up in the phone book, and . . . he's a urologist! *And* with the office in the West Seventies! Plus he's looking! How do I know? Because, caps *and* grinding! Those are very expensive operations. And painful! Four visits at least, maybe six if you're a smoker, which he wasn't ever by the way, and all of it is just for looks! So the girls should like your smile! Okay, your movie stars, dental surgery like that makes sense, but a man like Skripnik, to me it can mean only one thing." Mother smiled, proud of her own cleverness. "He wants to get married."

More like he's looking for chickies, I thought sourly, staring at the rumps of the businessmen over at the counter. They make such a fuss about our hormones and menopause, like it's perfectly *normal* that a man will grind all his teeth off, take up jogging, dye his hair brown, and run off with a secretary half his age, just because he's forty.

Mother was still talking. ". . . not really gingivitis, but some sort of complication from the first job, and he'd never had orthodontic work, so it really was a tangle. The doctors had him back several times, and what with one thing and another, well, you know how waiting rooms are, so we talked quite a bit."

Pearl paused to cut some of her burger, lips pursed as she pondered whether to divulge a secret. Then she lowered her voice to a half-pitying, half-accusing tone, "I must say that he didn't seem overly interested in meeting you, the first few times the subject happened to come up."

Which in translation meant she had bent the good doctor's ear about the many splendors of her daughter. I got seriously involved in cutting my own hamburger for a moment, suddenly squirmy with embarrassment, and even a little sorry for the doctor. What *had* she told him?

Pearl happily chewed her hamburger. "I expect it was

the divorce, of course, which I gather was still pretty raw. Once burned, as they say, and he certainly had a lot to say about that woman!" Pearl smiled, nodding her head in the general direction of the funeral parlor, many blocks to the north. "But she can't have been as cold as—I mean, there is a son, and men don't understand how we feel about those things. So it was probably mutual, just one of those things that happen to couples. *Restlessness.*" I got a pointed, rather severe look here, which I ignored. "I am quite certain though that Dr. Skripnik did not get divorced *for* someone, if you know what I mean. In fact, after we got to know each other a little better, it seemed to me that maybe he was at loose ends, even downhearted a little. You know how men are, they think all they want is a fast little red car and a house full of toys, and then when they come home to a microwave dinner in a cold dark kitchen, they know in their hearts that life isn't meant to be lived like that, it's *empty*, they want some *warmth*."

Granted our acquaintance hadn't been long, but I had trouble imagining that Skripnik would find any world empty, as long as he had himself there for company. I had no trouble, though, imagining my mother *saying* this to him as poor gawky Skripnik sat in the leather-chairs-and-phony-hunting-prints waiting room, flipping through back issues of *Money* and *Fortune,* fantasizing about the fabulous girls he was going to get between his sheets as soon as his gums quit bleeding.

Pearl may be persistent, but she's not obstinate; once it was clear I wasn't going to sell as a homemaker, she started pushing me as an intellectual.

When, lucky me, my candidacy improved.

"It was the Russian that really seemed to catch his fancy." Pearl laid her knife and fork neatly on her plate, brushing nonexistent crumbs from her skirt. She pointed to her chin, meaning my face was dirty. "His people were Russian, and he was getting terribly interested in them, so I told him about how we were from Russia too—"

"Oh, *Mother*," I interrupted peevishly, scraping whatever it was off my chin, "*everybody*'s people were Russian!"

"I know, sweetheart, but Dr. Skripnik had just found some relatives, a cousin I think, who had just moved here. An émigré."

"Did he say who?" I sat bolt upright, because some Skripnik relatives right then would have greatly simplified my afternoon. I had counted on finding a roomful of people at the funeral, among them *somebody* who would take the letter—and its blind author—off my hands, but instead had found only that handful of tearful petitioners, and the colorfully clad Mrs. Ex, whose behavior this afternoon left me suspecting that what made her my best hope for taking care of Leon's arriving cousin was that she was my *only* hope. If I could turn up another Skripnik, especially another Russian, then I would not have to hang around Manhattan until seven; I could pass off the letter, wish them a happy reunion with blind Shmuel, and be back in my apartment with enough day left to make it worth trying to work.

Pearl was enjoying the Black Forest cake so much I had to repeat the question.

"I don't recall the name. It wasn't Skripnik, because there was a niece or a daughter. Something else Russian. This is good!"

I tried not to look at the forkful of gooey chocolate crumbs she was holding up. "But how come they didn't come to the funeral, if they're such close relatives?" I asked.

Mother put the last forkful in slowly, chewed lusciously

and dabbed her lips with her napkin. She sighed. "That's such good cake. I admire your willpower, not having any. I don't know, probably they don't read the *Times,* or maybe even they don't know English. How would they find out about the funeral?"

"Wouldn't someone else in the family have telephoned or something?"

"No, I don't think so, because no one else knew about them, I don't think. Dr. Skripnik was all excited about them, but kind of secretive, like he didn't want anybody to know, but he couldn't help boasting. I got the impression that he was, well, *saving* them. For himself."

Which didn't contradict the picture I had formed of the late doctor. "He boasted, you say. About what?"

"Oh, he said they were big people in the old country, all of his family."

"Yeah, I know, he told me too, lawyers and doctors and Indian chiefs. I mean *here.* Did he say anything about what these people are here? What they do, where they work, where they live, *anything?*"

Pearl cocked her head at me, curiosity aroused. "Baby doll, I thought that . . . you said you and the doctor . . ."

"The doctor and I," I said with icy fury, "met *once,* when he showed up on my stoop with some stupid letter—"

"He *said* it was important," Mother interrupted, a pink flush edging along her collar. "I thought it was odd, because he'd just been in on Friday and hadn't said much, but then when he called on Saturday he seemed *so* anxious to get a hold of you."

"To *translate,* Mother, to *translate.* He couldn't read the letter and he wanted a translator!"

Mother's flush now became a full-fledged blush. "Well, I didn't think you'd mind," she admitted timidly. "It wasn't such a big thing, and at least . . . Well, I thought maybe if he *met* you . . ."

I must have looked awfully furious, for Pearl nearly wailed, "I'm sorry, darling, if I did wrong, I know I'm a buttinsky. I just wanted something *nice* for you. Really!"

The afternoon sun was bouncing off the window opposite our booth, lighting Pearl's face, showing the wrinkles at the neck, the crow's feet, the skin beneath the powder . . . and all my fury unexpectedly drained into some kind of warm gushy hole in my heart. Tears prickled my eyes and my throat clogged.

She *is* a buttinsky, and one day, if he's Jewish, single, and needs dental work, she is going to give my phone number to Jack the Ripper, but she's all I have, and I'm all she has, and maybe she's even right, that it's time there were more of us.

I have never actually asked why I am sibless, and in fact the general reluctance with which Pearl has always addressed all sexual questions made me suspect for most of my adolescence that I was probably adopted, since I couldn't imagine Pearl doing *that,* but the infrequent, enigmatic comments that she did let drop left me with a hazy impression that it had something to do with the war, and the difference in age between my parents. My father had been fourteen years older than her, and their marriage had been delayed not only by the war itself but also by the occupation. His skill as a photographer and his knowledge of Yiddish had gotten him involved in the openings of the death camps and in testifying in the war crimes trials that followed. About this part of my father's life though I know nothing, for he refused to discuss what he had seen and done. Pearl, I'm certain, does know, and sometimes hints that whatever it was, it was sufficiently shattering to explain why it was so long before I came along. So since I'm the only one, I'm going to have to carry the ball, reproduction-wise, if Max and Pearl are going to continue on into a third generation.

I reached across the table and squeezed her hand. "I know, Mother. I know. Come on, I've got time still, let's go look at shoes."

Pearl brightened immediately and slid out of the booth. After the necessary stops, she was waiting for me at the door, diplomatically looking away while I counted the meager change I got back from my two twenties and a ten. Not enough for the tip. I sighed and opened my purse again.

"Thank you, dear, it was lovely," Pearl said as we pushed out into the street, which seemed horribly chaotic and crowded after the tranquility of the Brasserie. "And I *am* sorry that this has turned out so—"

"Don't worry about it, Mom." I pointed at the cab we should try for, which was just disgorging passengers across the street. "Besides, things could all work out yet, you know."

Pearl grabbed my arm and looked up at me, trying to tell if I was teasing. "What do you mean, baby doll?"

"That cop at the funeral, remember? Maybe he'll have questions, find out who I am. I'll get a good look at him and maybe he'll be handsome—and single. Come *on,* that guy in the three-piece suit is after our cab!"

4

IMELDA Marcos buys shoes by the thousand; Pearl just tries them on. Clerks in two dozen boutiques had been left exhausted and empty-handed, glaring daggers at our backs, before I finally convinced Pearl that no, I wasn't mad at her for all the trouble she had caused me, and no, I really couldn't come up to her place, even for just a minute, because I really did have to go on to Mrs. Ex-Skripnik's, since all Pearl could remember about the other Skripniks, the ones Leon had been so proud of, was that she was a singer, they were both from Odessa, and maybe the man was named Sasha. For finding Russian émigrés, that information was as helpful as telling me they had two legs, so, like it or not, Skripnik's ex-wife was going to inherit the blind cousin. Still, once the cab finally left Pearl at 2 Fifth Avenue and I was alone, staring at the back of the cabbie's neck, I felt relieved; this unpleasant day was at last almost over. The funeral, the sixty-dollar luncheon, and the three hours of tormenting shoe clerks were already behind me, leaving me just a bad ten minutes with Mrs. Ex, after which I could return to Brooklyn, my typewriter, and more problems at Poncatoncas.

Which I still believed right up until about two minutes after Mrs. Ex herself opened the door. Wearing a peacock blue full-length skirt of heavy brocade with a green fringe running up the front slit and a shirt of raspberry silk that, I was abashed to realize, I had once admired in the window of Altman's. Even away from the store window, it was *raspberry*!

At the funeral parlor I had already gotten the idea that this woman wasn't sitting *shiva* for her dead ex, but this colorful combination took my breath away.

"Mrs. Skripnik?"

The hand she extended across the threshold was as bony as Leon's, and no warmer, but her manners had improved a little since the funeral parlor. "I am Phyllis Smolensky."

Cowed and confused, because the card she gave me had said otherwise, I sputtered, "Uh, look, we spoke at the funeral, remember? I'm sorry to be disturbing you at a time like this . . . Phyllis, but—"

"Ex-wives don't mourn," Phyllis cut in tartly, as if I had asked. She spread her hands outwards and down to indicate her clothing.

I had spent a whole afternoon with my mother, which is why I almost said, Too bad, because black *has* to suit you better than peacock, but instead I shifted from foot to foot and mumbled, "Uh, no, of course they wouldn't —uh, you wouldn't."

I was getting more certain that whatever business we were going to do, it was going to be done right there at the door, because getting stuck in the doorway seemed to run in the Skripnik family. Not that there was much about the room I could see over her shoulder to beckon me in, except maybe the fact you could sit down there.

Peter Cooper Village, the address on her card, is quite nice, and the area is very clean and safe, considering that really it's the Lower East Side, but the apartment still looked awfully pokey. If they hadn't been curtained, the living room windows would have looked right out on the FDR Drive, where maybe a million cars poured by every minute, and the living room had so much furniture in it that the shutters only made the room seem more airless. By the looks of things, though, the room was only half as crowded as it might have been, since all the pieces were broken sets. One end table with a cut crystal lamp, one easy chair upholstered in chintz of blue flowers the size of pizzas, three leather and chrome sling-back dining chairs, which didn't go at *all* with the maple dining table.

Meaning, I guess, that the Skripniks had divided every-thing right down the middle. Except of course the address on the Upper West Side, one block from the Park, which Leon had kept for himself.

"*You* may feel some regret," Phyllis said, sailing jauntily on, even if her voice cracked to a squeak, "but as far as I'm concerned, Leon had burned his boats, or bridges, or whatever it is that people burn when they leave their wives, their *sons*—"

"I *tried* to tell you this afternoon," I interrupted, sidling around her to at least come in out of the entryway before I gave her the letter, "Leon—your husband and I—"

"I don't think I should have to hear the actual details of your . . . relationship," which the way she said it made me feel like I was covered in running sores or something. "Leon was a grown-up, and he made his decision. If he wanted his freedom, fine. But I *was* his wife for fifteen years!" she stepped in front of me to stop me getting any closer to her chintz-covered chairs than I already had. "If he left clothes or something in your apartment, you can keep them, or give them to a charity." Looking fierce, in a badly nearsighted way, she added, "Or sell them."

"WHY WOULD HE LEAVE HIS CLOTHES AT MY HOUSE? HE WAS ONLY THERE ONCE!" I shouted.

Phyllis gave me a superior smile. "Well, if that's the case, I can't imagine he would have left you very much in his will, if *that's* what you're worrying about, but you'll know when the will is read. If there *is* a little something for you, his lawyers will contact you, I suppose." Then she crossed her arms and did her best to look worldly and wicked. "In your line, though, isn't it more customary to get paid after each time?"

I inhaled to erupt, but surprised myself by sagging instead. You know, there's only so many times you can explain nicely that you're not a whore, and the fact that the woman I was trying to explain it to was wearing a tablecloth for a skirt didn't make the situation any better. So instead of shrieking again, I let that breath out as a sigh, took Shmuel's letter from my purse, and said as flat calm as I could, "I only saw your husband once in my life, which was last Saturday night, when he asked me to translate this letter."

The wicked look disappeared, but otherwise Phyllis

Skripnik née Smolensky didn't move. She peered uncertainly at the envelope, light brown kraft paper, scrawled over with a leaky ballpoint in three alphabets, plastered with Israeli stamps. Then at me again.

"Translated?"

"It's in Russian."

"Leon doesn't know Russian."

"That's why he wanted me to translate it."

"*You* know Russian?"

Phyllis was peering at me with a puzzled intensity that gave me some idea of what a bug feels like under a magnifying glass with some saucer-eyed entomolgist trying to reclassify it.

"You and Leon, you weren't . . . didn't . . . weren't lovers?" Phyllis stumbled through the realization that she had been mistaken in assigning me to the genus *Home-Wrecking Woman of Sin,* her voice dying to a harsh whisper on the last word, as if it hurt her even to pronounce it.

It seemed kind of rude, even if she was a divorced widow, to tell the bereaved Mrs. Skripnik that the idea of her husband so much as *touching* me was enough to give me a rash, so I stifled my startled snort of a laugh into a cough. Which, as it happens, started me choking, so I did not immediately realize that Phyllis was now gripping the doorway with both hands, tears streaming down her face.

Streaming. Like someone had emptied a bucket on her head.

I was dumbfounded, too startled to move, and with no idea what to do if I had. If you grow up with Pearl, you see the occasional fit of hysterics, many of which you may even have to throw yourself if you are going to get permission to do things like go out on dates, attend sleepovers at girlfriends' houses, or wear white shoes after sundown, but I had never seen anything *remotely* like the despair of Phyllis Smolensky. In fact, we might be standing there still, I with mouth agape and she drenching her raspberry silk in tears, saliva, and makeup, had Phyllis not begun to hiccup.

And hiccup. And hiccup. Convulsive spasms that sounded like her diaphragm was ripping loose from her rib cage, even as the sobs made her shoulders heave and quiver, until her face began to turn purplish, and I wondered whether she was choking.

That at least got me moving. I dropped the letter and my purse and put my arm around Phyllis. She collapsed against me like a sand castle when the tide comes in.

Less than a half hour later, when finally I had her sitting up in bed, her hiccups gone, a cup of chamomile tea steaming on the flouncy pink-skirted night table, we had become lifelong friends.

Or so Phyllis had decided.

"*I* didn't want the divorce, that's why I put up such a fight! Leon was no angel, he had his faults like any man—and in *his* line, well, the temptations must be everywhere. I did my best to, uh, meet his needs, but, well, it became an *obsession*. And not normal, if you know what I mean. He'd treat a patient for something, ask how it had happened, and then he'd come home, all steamed up. But . . . I *tried*, I really did, but we always ended up fighting. I mean, the boy was *right there*! What if he came in and *saw* me dressed in one of those . . . And then one day, we were in the Bahamas at this convention, and there was another couple, he was in his *sixties,* and she was about *nineteen,* but *hard*? Eyes that seemed to know *everything*. And Leon wanted us to . . ." Phyllis began to shudder with tears again, and I *certainly* knew more about the Skripniks' sex life than I wanted to, so I tut-tutted and told Phyllis to hush, she needed to rest. Leon had apparently gotten custody of the connubial mattress—which, God knows, judging by what Phyllis was telling me, he was the more likely to need—because I had to sit perched on the crepe de chine counterpane of a narrow and unpleasantly soft single bed, which kept trying to throw me onto Phyllis or dump me on the floor. My back was getting distinctly stiff, but the little bedroom had no place else to sit, so I couldn't think what else to do. Leaving her alone, tempting as it was in the abstract, certainly seemed out of the question; would you like it on *your* conscience that you let a perfect stranger *hiccup* to death?

Fortunately, the tea and sympathy seemed to have Phyllis on the mend. She sniffed heartily through a nose the color and texture of a scrubwoman's knees, and rearranged the bedclothes around her legs. "Anyway, that was when I gave up trying. To please him, I mean. Do this or it's divorce, Leon always was threatening, so one day I just decided, let him *have* his divorce! Let him see what it's like to make your own dinners and wash your own socks and pick up your own shoes at the cobbler's and . . . the shirts . . . and eat alone." Tossing her head back, and fixing me with a stare that would have been defiant if she hadn't been so nearsighted, Phyllis continued fiercely. "I mean, I knew we *had* married young, too young, I suppose I would have to say, and, well, we had been the first. For each other. In . . . bed. So I thought, I guess, with Leon just getting into his forties . . . I mean, I always supposed that one day, when he got it out of his system . . ."

Then, with a blind wet despairing shudder, all of her defenses collapsed, and Phyllis turned her head to the wall, wailing, "But now he's DEAD!"

I patted her heaving back. "More tea, I think."

I didn't hurry with the boiling and teabag dunking in her tiny, very neat kitchen, because following this emotional yo-yo up and down her string was wearing me out. When I finally pushed back into the creamy pink room, fresh tea steaming in a checked yellow mug, I found Phyllis embracing an eight-by-ten in a silver frame, apparently snatched from the wide sill of the window by the bed, where the other framed photos that had stood in precise ranks now lay scattered. Since the ones I could see were all of the Skripnik trio, I assumed what she was clutching was a particularly loved variant on these posings of gangly Junior, hostile and somewhat aloof Leon, and earnest, bat-blind Phyllis, her glasses invariably removed for greater photogenicity.

"Always they wear glasses and then take them off for the photographs!" my father used to shout in exasperation. "And THEN they complain it don't look like them!"

"Uh, Phyllis, I brought you more tea."

She jerked upright, holding the frame at arm's length, which let me see I was wrong. Leon, about nineteen, in a Brooklyn Dodgers sweatshirt.

"He's DEAD, Midge, and there's no hope, ever. We'll *never* get back together! My life is as good as OVER!"

I don't *think* the bedside clock was actually defective, but the glowing green digits blipped over as if they were mired in molasses. Each time I sneaked a peek during Phyllis's rambling account of what she could have been and should have been and would have been, had not handsome Leon ridden up on his white charger, offering her home, hearth, and huppah, invariably it was only about two minutes since the last time I looked. Trying to sound sympathetic enough that she would eventually cheer up and take her husband's letter, but not so sympathetic that she would remember newer and better complaints to wander on about, I patted and tutted and handed her tissues, grateful that she couldn't see my face and my incredulity that she ever was premed.

"And I was *good* at it too! I *always* had to help Leon with his homework in organic. *I* should have been the doctor, not HIM!" She thumped her chest with a hollow, bony authority, and I wondered how it was that my mother always got me into these things but was never around to *go through* them with me. After about an hour I started nudging Phyllis in the direction of the letter I had brought, but she proved awfully impervious to nudging.

"*Russians,*" she sniffed disdainfully, somewhere around eleven o'clock. "Leon was *obsessed* with Russians, almost as bad as he was about . . . the other thing. Sometime before the divorce he got it into his head that he must have really important family, because someone of his accomplishments couldn't just pop out of nowhere, the way his schlubby cousins and uncles made it seem he had. Actually, I believe it was his nurse started him off originally, because she's one of those genealogy buffs. After a while Leon went plain *nuts* about the family-tree business, like he was some sort of WASP going back to the *Mayflower,* or the Skripniks were all Einsteins and Rothschilds that the tsar had to force to emigrate to America, to keep the revolution from happening for a while. I kept telling him he's *crazy,* what kind of a family tree can our people have? His people lived in a shtetl just like mine did, and they came to America because they couldn't stand the mud and the poverty and getting beat up. Sell everything you own, you come to America in rags, and some half drunk, illiterate clerk on Ellis Island writes your name down however his Irish ears can make sense of your shtetl Yiddish! Not to mention that by the time Leon finally got interested in whatever family he might still have over there, there's been the Nazis, the Reds, and God knows what else, plus all of the old people in this country who knew the real family name are either dead or senile, and even if you can get anything out of them, all they can remember is how wonderful everything was in the old country, so it doesn't even make sense that they came in the first place!"

Which seemed as good an opening to mention Shmuel as I was going to get.

"That's why I came, or why your—Leon came to me. That letter is from Israel, from a cousin, who's coming to America."

"He found relatives?" Phyllis looked at me over the tea she was sipping. "He never told me. Embarrassed, probably. I always warned him, what happens if you do find them? They'll want money, and how are you going to say no?"

"He's coming to see Leon," I said, rather than confirm that she was correct.

"But Leon's dead," Phyllis pointed out reasonably.

"I know that, but this man doesn't. He expects to be picked up."

Phyllis stared at me, as though I had begun a joke but had forgotten the punchline.

"At the airport," I tried again. "Someone's got to meet him at the airport."

Phyllis put her cup down, unconcerned. "Tell him not to come."

"How can I tell him not to come? I don't have his phone number, and no letter's going to get there in three days, and besides, he's not my relative, he's *your* relative."

"*Mine?*" Phyllis was genuinely shocked. "He's *Leon's* relative. He's not *my* relative!"

"Well, how about one of the other relatives then?"

"*Leon's* relatives? He's insulted them all so badly I think they only came to the funeral to make sure he was dead!"

"Look, Leon definitely told me that he had these Russian relatives who live in Brooklyn somewhere. He never mentioned them at all? To your son maybe?"

Phyllis shook her head vigorously. "The boy refused to see his father after . . . well, after. He's a good boy, very sensitive and loving. He wouldn't . . . forgive his father, for what he had done to me."

That degree of devotion, especially in a teenage boy whose father was single, and rich, seemed unlikely, but I wasn't going to pursue the point.

"Could I maybe ask him? Just to be sure?"

Phyllis got frosty and distant, pulling the counterpane tight around her legs. "I sent him to my mother's, in New Jersey. She thought he shouldn't see the actual burial. He has nightmares."

I slapped the letter against my leg, feeling like the Ancient Mariner, with the dead albatross around my neck. "Look, *somebody's* got to do something. There must be some way we can contact his other relatives. Your husband must have had an address book, at least."

Phyllis looked thoughtful, shrugged. "I suppose so. But I don't know where it would be."

"In his house? In his office?"

"I guess so. But the police have sealed up everything. They're investigating."

It was my turn to wail. "But this blind guy is arriving on *Thursday*! What am I suppose to do?"

Phyllis tucked her hands around her knees and studied

me with nearsighted confusion before asking, not nastily, but like she really wanted this information, "Why do *you* care?"

"Because he's blind and he's expecting Leon and he'll get off the plane and—and something *terrible* will happen."

"Golly, if you really think so . . . but shouldn't somebody do something about it? Like pick him up or something?" Phyllis finally said, clearly mystified but obviously feeling that she had to say *something*.

5

I WAS floating about in that warm soup that comes between sound asleep and totally awake when I remembered
what Phyllis had suggested: tell blind Shmuel not to come.
Last night that had seemed so impossible that I shrugged
it off, but this morning it made so much sense that I could
only figure three hours of shoe-shopping with Pearl had
rendered me temporarily crazy. Excited, I swung my legs
out of bed and started looking for my clothes.

"Where are *you* going?" Sasha mumbled, throwing his
arm around my waist.

"To phone Israel." I kissed him on the ear, which

smelled of turpentine, and slipped out from under the arm, grabbing the black Anne Klein from the floor. "I'll just call this cousin, tell him what happened, and he won't come."

How it was that my Anne Klein came to be in one corner of the super's apartment while I was in another, and not for the first time either, is something I've never really explained to myself, and certainly never to anyone else. "Your *janitor*?" I can just hear Pearl sputtering, which makes me think of sputtering back things like how Sasha is smart and funny and I like talking Russian with him and he's a janitor only because he needs the time to paint, until finally I remember what I'm *really* supposed to say: "It's MY life, Mother!"

To which I'm very sure she would say, "Well, is he single at least?"

As it happens, he is, or at least I *think* he is, but it would sort of miss the point even to tell Pearl that, since one of the reasons why my clothes and I sometimes come to share opposite corners of that canvas-filled basement apartment reeking of paint, pine gum, and boiled food is that Sasha is the most self-possessed man I've ever met. Not selfish. Not self-centered. Self-possessed. Content with himself and with what he's doing, whether it's painting huge canvases, which he fills with intricate, slightly surreal scenes of epic battles in some ancient, fairy-tale Russia, or fixing leaking faucets and helping the old ladies in the building unstick their windows. Humming Vysotsky through his thick black beard as he does so. We met when I couldn't get the pilot in Dora's stove relit; he came in all bushy and fierce, his tools clanking in an open tool chest, which he thumped down on my floor. He squatted to look the pilot light over, then began humming the song about the wolf hunt. Surprised, I laughed, then began to sing the words, trying to make my voice as gravelly and whiskied-out as that of the original singer.

It tells you something about Sasha that he fixed the pilot light *before* he asked me how I knew Vysotsky. But then we talked about which songs we liked best, and I found a tape I had made from someone else's tape when I was in Moscow, and then we went to his apartment to find *his* tapes, and of course I couldn't help but notice his paintings, because they kind of gathered around us as we drank wine in broken coffee cups.

Eventually I came to know that Sasha is gentle, and funny, and very kind to me, and that that is a wonderful combination in someone whose mind it would never cross to marry me, nor mine him. No doubt saying that makes me sound like the sort of girl I had spent all yesterday loudly proclaiming I am not, which is why I haven't ever said it to anyone, but that isn't really the way I mean it. All I mean is that what Brenda Starr never let us know about the life of the career woman in the big city is that *sometimes* you want very much to be held.

Like after yesterday, when instead of getting rid of Shmuel Skripnik, I had gained Phyllis Skripnik. And then had realized, already out on First Avenue at nearly midnight, that all my money had gone to lunch and cabbies, and that Pearl had confused me so much in the morning that I left with the handbag that goes with my dress, not the one that my bank card is in. Leaving me with about two dollars, just enough for a subway token and so little change that if you get held up the robber is likely to be insulted and maybe kill you. Not a calming thought when you have to ride the D train back to Brooklyn alone, and then walk four blocks in a black dress that you moved the buttons on to make you look stunning.

Days like that, I sometimes go to Sasha's. Sasha is the only émigré I have ever run across who doesn't seem to have noticed he's left Russia; in Moscow he lived among the steam pipes, here he lives among the steam pipes. There a super, here a super. There nobody bought his paintings, here nobody buys his paintings, probably because he almost never shows them to anyone, and certainly never a dealer. And here as there, he rarely cuts his thick black beard and never combs his tangled hair, which by now has some gray in it, but has always had fuchsia too, and magenta, and cobalt, and any other color that he happens to brush against without noticing. That is Sasha: he never seems to have money, but neither does he seem to need any, the fridge always holds just enough food for whatever meal I want to make for us, the wine bottle always has a few glasses more, and his clothes, though never changed, also never seem more than comfortably dirty and old.

In fact, I would say that Sasha notices nothing, except that he also notices everything. Sasha can tell you the precise color of a bird's shoulder as it flicks by, and sees the stainless steel gargoyles on top of the Chrysler building, and knows precisely when I want to be held. He entertains me when I'm with him, and doesn't worry me when I'm not. Since I don't think I have him, I never fret about losing him and never feel my style is cramped, but at the same time I don't have to face the terrifying loneliness of freedom. It's like going abroad for a while, or back into my youth. The canvases among the steam pipes and the potatoes boiled in a tea kettle that never gets washed and the walls covered with photos cut out of magazines, and the huge smile Sasha gives me when he sees that it's me; well, sometimes I just need that, okay?

Which is why when I came out of his appallingly dirty

bathroom he was sitting on the fold-down couch, jeans on, shirt unbuttoned, and one black nylon sock dangling from his toes. He scratched his jet black chest hair and yawned, which didn't make his Russian any easier to understand.

"You have this man's telephone?"

"No, but I know his name, and his address is on the envelope."

"And you know Hebrew?"

"Is that a nasty crack? What do I need Hebrew for? The man is from Russia, and maybe I don't talk perfect, but *you* understand me just fine!"

Sasha smiled sleepily. "Relax, my little sun. Why so excited? You talk just fine! What I meant, the address on the letter, it's in Hebrew."

Which of course Sasha had noticed, and I had not.

Hoping no one was coming down to complain about a stopped-up sink, I crept out of Sasha's place and back to mine, puzzling at that problem as I changed into clothes a little more appropriate for Ocean Parkway. In fact, I was already around the corner on Ditmas Avenue before I realized what a goose I was being.

After all, Ocean Parkway is only in the middle of one of the biggest Jewish neighborhoods in New York!

To look at, of course, it looks like most of the rest of Brooklyn, mostly two- and three-story brick buildings slowly giving way to taller and taller apartment blocks, the four-story walk-ups that once anchored the corners of the blocks now run-down and dilapidated next to the mushrooming condo buildings. There was a time even when the city was putting welfare families into those corner buildings, and Dora's neighborhood started to get the abandoned cars and the trash in the front yards that tell you an area is sliding fast. Dora was even talking of moving, and then suddenly, almost overnight, the whole neighborhood changed again. One cause was the Russians, whom the agencies began to settle there in large numbers. Those people sit outside on the benches and stroll the streets, most of them such busybodies they won't let you leave the house in mismatched socks, let alone with someone else's TV if you happen to be a burglar.

So then the Orthodox Jews started to move in. There already were several large shuls along that stretch of the Parkway and on the shady avenues which cut across it; now they moved their large families in, made little synagogues in their basements, tore down the old houses, and built grand new ones. They too walked the streets, and their children played on the sidewalks, the boys with the boys, the girls with the girls, hissing at you if you drove on Saturday, muttering at you if you wore shorts, which sometimes made running down to the corner store feel like a trip to the Holy Land, a discomfiting thing when all you really need is a quart of milk or a box of tampons. In fact, some days it seems like the only people on the whole block who aren't Orthodox are me and the delivery boy from Hunan of Midwood.

Today, though, I was looking at the good side of this, which is that the local branch of the Brooklyn Public Library could be counted on to have a Tel Aviv phone book.

In many ways, I consider this branch library to be one of the best parts of my windfall from Aunt Dora, because it is just around the corner, in a storefront on the avenue. It used to be a shoe store and still sort of looks like it, with the books jammed onto every surface flat enough and wide enough to hold them, and aisles so narrow that when you bend down to look at a title on the bottom shelf, your rear end chooses two or three titles on the other side. About half of the people who frequent it are deaf as posts, so it's not an ideal place to work, everyone bellowing the latest news at one another, but it's a friendly place, and my tush has knocked some good books off the shelves for me. Besides, I'm a celebrity there now, the Neighborhood Writer. Mrs. Plotkin, the librarian, kept my first Tammy and Tanesia by the checkout desk for almost six months, and once she even tried to have me read from *High Water at Lake Poncatoncas,* except that the women brought all their toddlers and tots, a wriggling, runny-nosed gaggle of ear-locked, yarmulke-topped Orthodox who had no more patience for my two Girl Scouts than I had for them. I got my revenge, though; I read them *The Three Little Pigs* and *Green Eggs and Ham* until their mothers finally picked them up again.

In fact, Mrs. Plotkin is the closest thing I have to a public, because whenever I go in she sails up to ask loudly when my next book is coming out. I like that a lot, when the answer is "Next month!" Now that "God knows!" is closer to the truth, the question is not so much fun. Mrs. Plotkin also introduces me to people in the checkout line. "Mrs. Schulman, this is our Margaret Cohen, the writer!"

To which the Mrs. Schulmans always say either "Oh?" or "That's nice," since being Margaret Cohen means I am neither Belva Plain nor Sylvia Tennenbaum.

On the other hand, Mrs. Plotkin *also* lets me have the new mysteries as soon as they come in, because "I know you need them for your writing, dear." And occasionally she lets me bend the rules and do things like take the phone book out of the library.

"Phone books are not supposed to circulate." She pointed at the stamped mark on the tattered blue cover, her half glasses set sternly on her nose. "And this one, it's the only one we've got. Somebody donated it."

"But I only want it for maybe a minute! And besides, who's going to want to read it?"

Librarians don't like it if you suggest nobody will want one of their books.

"Oh, you'd be surprised." Mrs. Plotkin pursed her lips and let her half glasses fall on their chain to her chest. "At the holiday times, people wanting to send their cards use it all the time."

"But all I want is to take it up to the corner so the man can help me with a number!" I fanned the book, noticing that most of the pages were torn.

"Well . . . I guess it's okay, since it's you—and the book *is* ten years old." She smiled in bright consolation.

I went back up the avenue with a sinking feeling, wondering when Shmuel Skripnik had moved to Tel Aviv.

The store around the corner from my building once sold candy and soda and cheap toys that came apart right after Aunt Dora bought them for me, but then the son inherited it and sold it to some Pakistanis, who sold newspapers and magazines until the man got more fundamentalist, put up a big sign in Arabic, and started spending most of his time in the back, poring over a Koran. This did not go down well with the Orthodox, who didn't like the inscription, nor with the rest of us, who didn't like the wait. I always waited a bit, then slapped down my coins for the *Times*, but I think a lot of people must have just taken the papers, because about two years ago the Pakistani went out of business and was replaced by a religious goods store, which even though it was brand new immediately got that dusty, always closed, definitely hostile look that those shops usually have, as if they don't really want you buying their sun-faded books and prayer shawls. Still, it was close, and since not counting the age-old Coca-Cola decal that told you where to push on the door there wasn't a sign in the place that wasn't in Hebrew, I figured maybe they could help me.

I peered through the rusty grate at the jumble of menorahs, hand-knitted yarmulkes, prayer shawls, and spice boxes, and timidly pushed open the door, only to bump into a faded and torn foil holiday stringer that spelled CHANUKAH; that much Hebrew at least I can read, but I wondered about the demand for such a decoration halfway around the year from the holiday.

The store was a clutter of books on tables covered in plastic sheets, spinner racks filled with books slightly too large for the pockets, Israeli toys hanging on hooks in pegboard fixtures, and locked display cases jammed with silver menorahs and *pushka* charity boxes, so at first I didn't notice the proprietor, who sat behind the counter, eyeing me glumly.

I smiled timidly. He blinked slowly and straightened his neck. He was a round man with short arms, which were crossed over his chest. He had a long scraggly beard just going pepper-and-salt, and earlocks that curled up around his ears.

"I wonder—" I heard my own voice sounding like a mouse singing in a barrel, so I coughed and started again. "I was wondering, maybe you could help me?"

"What, you read the ads those Lubavitchers in the paper put, and now you are wanting candles to light?" he grunted without moving.

"No, no." I took the letter out of my purse and held it up. "I got a letter—"

"Every Jewish woman should light candles, say the prayers!" He shook himself, spreading his arms. "Who is saying this? Schneerson is saying this! You are at maybe your tennis, you're dancing in clothes too tight, and the guilt, the guilt it *bites* at you a little," he said, hitting himself in the breast with the fingertips of both hands. "So you think, I buy candles, I say the prayer, and then!" He raised his hands to the ceiling in triumph. "I have a Jewish home, hurray!" Then he leaned across his counter, raising dust puffs as he slammed both hands onto the plastic sheet that covered some sort of cloth. "NO! That is a Schneerson home maybe, but a *Jewish* home? Two candles make you a Jew? *Ptu!*" He spat, turning his back to me.

"No, no, I don't want to buy anything, I—"

"You think this is maybe a club? My heat should keep you warm while the bus is coming?" He turned around again, making the little fringes that hung over his black trousers flare out. "The sign outside says change I don't make."

"Just a darned minute, you!" I was startled to find I was mad. "Suppose I did come in to buy something! Suppose I came in to buy candles, *you* wouldn't sell them to me, so where do you get off yelling at me because I came in?"

"Candles I don't sell, you want candles, you go to Waldbaum's," he said grumpily. "You want to make a Jewish home, that I can help with. Books, on what means such a home. Mezuzot, like the Lord, blessed be He, wants we should put on the doors. Scarves for the head, a woman her modesty should preserve." As he spoke he was scooting down the counter, scooping up the items he was talking about.

I followed a half step behind, waving the letter, trying not to drop the phone book. "No, no, I don't want all that stuff! I just need help with some Hebrew, a letter I got!"

He stopped, glared at me. "Help you want? I look like maybe a library to you? In the UN, big money they pay for translation!"

"This isn't translation! It's an *address*, all I need is the address! So you could tell me where in the book ..." I pointed to the upper left-hand corner of the envelope, then held up the phone book, with the eerie sensation that I had done all this before.

"Not translation, she says. She can't read, but it's not translation," the man said in disgust, but at least he took the letter. He squinted in the gloomy light of the antique fluorescent bulb overhead, bringing the letter close to his face; he held it by the corners, as though I might have AIDS. He looked up, putting the letter down on the counter. "General Delivery, Kiryat Wolfson. Tel Aviv."

"General delivery? No street? No number?" I picked up the letter and peered at it, as if he had made a mistake.

"You want I should *write* this letter, or just read it? General delivery. This person, you write him, he goes to the post office and asks for his letters. General delivery. Listen, maybe you need something anyway, huh?" He looked as gloomy as ever, hope a faint distant spark in his mournful eyes, like fireflies in a June cold snap. "You've got a cloth to cover the challah with, when your husband does the *brucha*? Uncovered, it's no good."

"No, no. I need, I'm looking for a phone number." I held up the phone book. "You couldn't look it up? I mean, I can't read Hebrew."

"How about one of these maybe, for the little one, when he's born?" He held up a yarmulke that had Velcro tabs, for holding it on a baby's head.

"Skripnik, the man's name is, maybe you could look —WHAT LITTLE ONE?" I looked down in horror at my middle, remembering instantly the Black Forest cake and my mother. "I'm not pregnant!"

The man shrugged. "Skripniks you don't find in book what goes *aleph* to *chey*. Look, I help you, why you won't help me? You aren't with child now, your husband will give you one; take maybe this rattle? Soft, with the letters on it?"

"THERE'S NO HUSBAND EITHER!" I yelled, realizing instantly that I had made a mistake, because the shopkeeper's face lit up with what I can only call a Pearl look.

"So?" He smiled. "Such a nice girl, and not married? But there is a man?"

"No, there's no—or no, there is, maybe there is a man, but . . . Look, I have a problem, there's this man coming from Israel—"

"Your man is coming from Israel? He is religious?"

"No. Or maybe he is, I don't know, but—"

"You will marry him and you don't know he is religious? This is not good."

"I'M NOT MARRYING HIM!"

"So." The shopkeeper beamed again. "You are single then. There are many good boys who need wives. You give me your telephone, my wife calls and takes you to *shteibel,* okay?"

Pearl is doing this to me for three years, so I know when I'm licked. I looked frantically around the counters, grabbed the first item that looked cheap, and thrust it at the cash register.

"This, this is all I want, here's . . . a ten, all I have is a ten."

The shopkeeper shrugged, took my purchase, punched some buttons on his cash register, and made change. He put what I had bought in a bag and said, "Very nice, that ice tray what makes cube in shapes of Mogen Dovid. Your man comes, you give him cold drinks, he will see the cubes and think of shul and good Jewish weddings."

You know, the damn thing didn't even make very good ice cubes, because the points of the stars melted so fast. I found that out after going grumpily back to my apartment, having returned Mrs. Plotkin's telephone book to its shelf, and trying to settle down to work. Tammy and Tanesia refused to appear, or when they did, they seemed so stupid that I would type a paragraph, rip it up, and go to rummage in the fridge. Since that particular work habit is the very reason why I never keep anything in my ice box, I finally poured my Star of David ice tray full of flat Dr. Brown's cream soda, from a can I found back near the baking soda, and waited until I had a whole tray full of sticky little ice pops.

Which almost certainly explains why I wasn't as firm as I should have been when Phyllis called.

"You want the Russians' address, don't you?" Exasperation made her sound whiny, after I tried to refuse to come meet her in Manhattan.

"Of *course* I want the address." Especially now that my plan to telephone blind Shmuel before he left Tel Aviv had proven a bust, I didn't add, But does it have to be right now? I mean, it's almost rush hour.

"But the police said it *had* to be today, and I was trying your phone all morning, but there was no answer, and then I had to go out, so . . . Why don't you have one of those machines, like everybody else?"

Ocean Parkway used to really be a parkway, a genteel carriageway for Brooklynites who had made their pile to motor out to Coney Island on the weekends, a broad *allée* between towering maples and mulberries, which screened out the apartments behind. About fifteen years ago they ripped out the cobblestones, cut down most of the trees, and turned it into a drag strip, putting traffic lights at every corner to give the maniacs something to ignore and fool the old ladies into thinking it was safe to cross the six lanes of heat-sticky asphalt. Two in the morning Ocean Parkway has traffic, and at twenty to three on Tuesday afternoon, it sounds like storm-surf building, except that storm surf doesn't also honk. I never will understand why rush hour traffic is heavy coming out of the city *and* going in; it makes you wonder whether Brooklyn and Manhattan aren't just changing places twice a day. What I do understand is that between three and six there is *nothing* that can get me to schlepp from Brooklyn to Manhattan. Forget the subway; it would be *jammed* already, everyone sweating all over me, and then some fat steel drummer would come on, deafen you with a few bars of "Montego Bay," and demand a contribution. If you ask him for what, he says, "To help poor people."

The car, though, that meant the Brooklyn-Queens Expressway, which been under repair since about 1911 and every night from three until seven turns into an overheated parking lot, where people come to practice honking and making rude hand gestures at each other.

On the other hand, if I was going to drive in to Manhattan, which I knew I was, every moment I wasted meant I was that much closer to three o'clock.

Which didn't make it worth explaining to Phyllis Smolensky that I do have an answering machine. After all, am I not a big girl in the big city? How can I be a writer if I don't have a machine to tell all my zillions of callers that I'm too busy writing to talk to them?

Especially since most of those callers were Pearl. Asking me to call. Asking why I hadn't called. Telling me not to call. Demanding that the machine let me come to the phone, because she knew I was in. Finally, one freezing February night in my second year in the city, when I still was doing things like buying half subscriptions to concert series at Avery Fisher Hall, I had finally clawed my way back from Lincoln Center, so bone-weary that I almost went to sleep in the elevator, to discover this message on my machine: "Baby doll, it's okay, the doctors said not to worry. Love you, Mommy."

YOU could sleep after that? Especially when Pearl's phone rang busy from one A.M. to five A.M., when I finally drove over to 2 Fifth Avenue, to discover that Pearl had taken her telephone off the hook, and what the doctors had said not to worry about was the insurance forms that Pearl had misplaced earlier in the day, a story to which I had apparently paid no attention during an earlier call that afternoon.

So, right after I got back home, my answering machine broke down, after I dropped it a couple dozen times.

"You're sure the address is in his office?" I finally asked Phyllis, knowing I was giving in, without even bothering to ask why I had to come all the way from Brooklyn to the Upper West Side to get an address that any normal person could easily have given me over the phone.

It might have been only yesterday we met, but I already knew Phyllis well enough to be certain that she and normal didn't have a lot to do with each other.

Not that I was in a good position to be critical. I mean, how normal could I be, worrying about some blind man I'd never met that I'd gotten stuck with because of some doctor that my mother tried to fix me up with, even though neither he nor I wanted to be fixed up? And why can't I ever just tell Pearl to go to hell and quit trying to fix me up, especially when it gets me into a mess like this, which I only seem to get farther into, instead of out of?

I didn't have an answer, but I had lots of time to torture myself with the question while I bumper-to-bumpered into Manhattan; I was early and traffic was light, so it only took me about three days to crawl through the Battery Tunnel and up the West Side to the West Seventies, where I had promised to meet Phyllis.

"Thank God you're here!" She ran out into the street when she saw me, so I nearly hit her, because I was concentrating on finding the address and looking for parking and ignoring the line of cars behind me and the double-parked delivery truck ahead. "He's been waiting here for hours, I think he's mad at me, but I was waiting for you. He keeps asking questions, like he suspects *me* or something."

"Who does?"

"The policeman. Where are you going?"

"I've got to do something with my car, the people behind are honking."

"Can't you park it?"

Phyllis wouldn't let go of the window, and the people behind were getting madder, and I felt about half roasted from my drive, so I gave up and parked by a hydrant. If the cop didn't like it, let *him* come and move it.

As we walked back to the brownstone, Phyllis clung to me, trembling.

Back in Brooklyn I had asked, "What's so bad about an inventory? The police just want somebody there when they go through his things, that's all. Have your mother come."

"My mother? She *hated* Leon, after . . . what he did."

"Yeah, but he's not going to be there, right? So why do I have to come over?"

"BECAUSE. Because, I just can't do things like that, that's all. It gives me the creeps. It was *our* house, and then . . . We *lived* there, but . . . I haven't been back in that house since, well, *since*, and I don't want to see what he's added. I mean, to *our* things, really. And with the police there. I'll probably cry and get hysterical and maybe drop things, and then the police will suspect *me*. So you'll have to come with me."

Skripnik's brownstone was beautiful, radiating that cheerful air that only money can give a home. Bow-windows up and down, carved stone fruits garlanded above door and windows, steps curling up to a shiny black oak door like the last few steps into heaven, vaulting over the more modest servants entrance below, which now had a discreet brass sign: OFFICE OF L. SKRIPNIK, M.D. The building's stone was a sunny, welcoming color, and behind an ornate, well-painted wrought iron fence the little garden was vivid with daffodils poking through a shiny green ground vine, seeming all the more cheerful for the gloominess of the high rises on all sides. Except for this oasis of a half dozen brownstones, the rest of the block had sprouted in high-rise Manhattification, which is the process by which real estate developers put more people into a neighborhood than can physically come outdoors at one time.

"You guys lived over the store, huh?" I tried to drown my envy in sarcasm, but Phyllis was oblivious.

We went up the stairs to where a man waited, sitting on the low balustrade.

"Come on lieutenant, my friend is here now!"

The man stood. "Russo, NYPD," he not quite growled, nodding at me.

Cohen, World of Letters, I was about to growl back, when my knees developed a strange rubberiness, and all the moisture left my mouth. It was the man who had caught me coming out of the funeral. Even angry as I had been, I had thought the cop was cute.

Now, with him not twenty feet away, the sunlight full on him, I realized I had been wrong.

Russo, NYPD, was *gorgeous.*

Not pretty handsome, like somebody who knows he's handsome. *Handsome* handsome, like Clark Gable, or Marlon Brando before he started looking like Shelley Winters. Russo was tall, maybe six one, six two, and muscular, with the lazy grace of an athlete. His eyes were in the green family but had an undertone of warm brown that made his tan glow like a five-hundred-dollar Florentine handbag. Altogether the sort of man that puts foolish thoughts in a girl's head.

Even if he did have the peevish air of someone who has spent too long with Phyllis Smolensky.

"Midge—uh, Margaret Cohen. Margaret," I mumbled, putting out my hand, then stumbling on the top step so that we didn't actually shake hands but kind of bumped knuckles. "Phyllis asked me . . . I'm sorry, the traffic. She wanted me—"

Russo nodded impatiently, and we both turned to face the shiny black door and its brightly polished brass knocker, while Phyllis rummaged in her shoulder bag, which was big enough to deliver mail with. We stared at the lintel like we were in an elevator, waiting. And waiting.

Phyllis pulled key ring after key ring from her bag, bringing each up close to her nose for nearsighted examination, then, muttering, tossed each back, only to bring them up again. After trying a couple of keys that didn't even go into the keyhole, she turned around, looking sheepish and frightened, as though we might hit her.

"I guess I don't—I mean, I was sure that it was here. I mean I just . . .". She wrinkled her nose and bared her huge upper teeth in what was probably meant to be a nervous grin.

The cop looked at Phyllis, then at me, which sent a shiver of treachery through my soul, because it was suddenly incredibly important that Russo know I wasn't a dingbat like Phyllis and that I didn't even know Phyllis and that she wasn't my friend and—

Which made me mad at myself. Who *cared* what this stupid flatfoot thought? I sat down on the balustrade and put my chin in my hand, feeling about sixteen years old and pouty.

"Jeez, Miz Skripnik, I told you I had to get in the place," Russo said, trying hard not to be aggravated. "And you was sure you had the key."

I looked up, astonished at this first long speech I had heard Russo make, trying not to grin. I've never *heard* a thicker Noo Yawk accent, of the sort Pearl long ago taught me to laugh at—or more exactly, to make a point of *not* laughing at, because we were too refined. To tell the truth, it was the accent that sent the last smidgeon of heart up into my throat; those *looks,* and then he talks like some orphan in a movie where Frank Sinatra plays the priest.

"Well, I *thought* I did, I mean no one else would have it, but I suppose I haven't lived here for a long time, you know, and I don't know. I mean, you said it was for an inventory, so I thought you just needed my *permission* or something." Phyllis flushed, looking more and more flustered.

Russo was rubbing the back of his head. "Well, yeah, we have to have your permission, but what I gotta get is the inventory, so's we can tell if something is missing, like

I told you. See, maybe robbery was a motive, the way your husband was found."

"Ex-husband," Phyllis said sharply.

"Burglary," I muttered.

Russo looked at me, tiny grin beneath quizzical eyes, uncertain whether to bring me into the conversation or tell me to shut up. I couldn't help noticing that the brown undertone in his green eyes was really more golden, almost glittery—and that I was blushing, badly.

"How's that?" he cocked his head.

"We were divorced, I told you that. I'm not his wife, I'm his ex-wife," Phyllis said through her nose, rummaging in her bag again, unaware that Russo was talking to me.

I fidgeted, smoothed my jeans against my tush, straightened my shirt, and mumbled, "Ah, sorry, that was kind of automatic. I mean, robbery is like out on the street or something, and burglary, well, he was found in the kitchen, right? So . . . I'm a—I, uh, do books."

"Are you a lawyer, ma'am?" Russo inquired sternly.

"Me? Oh, God no. I mean, my mother *wanted* me to, but, well, I was never . . . no, no."

"You have some other relationship to the deceased?" Russo's question was thoroughly professional, since after all what the hell *was* I doing there? But since I would rather have had the earth swallow me up than have this Russo person suspect me of the most likely "other relationship" with the loathsome Doctor S., I begin to babble like a half-wit.

"Oh, Lord no, I mean I never even *knew* him, see, it was my *mother,* and then he—"

"She was probably the last person to see Leon alive!" Phyllis said, looking up to peer at me with mingled awe and pride.

Russo stared at me. I stared at Phyllis.

And Phyllis looked at her watch.

"Officer, I have an appointment later this evening," she said haughtily, as though it was us and not her who was holding things up.

Which at least broke up the game of don't blink that the cop and I seemed to have gotten stuck in. Russo gaped at Phyllis, gave me one more searching look—at which I opened my mouth, closed it again and waved my hand —then reached into his pocket.

"*You* don't have a key, do you?"

I shook my head, continuing to study the fanlight above the door, hoping the blush I felt along my ears didn't show.

Russo sighed, shoved his notebook back in the outside pocket of his sports jacket, then dug some keys from his pants pocket. "We're not supposed to do this, but—is there an alarm?"

"Officer, I haven't lived here—been *permitted* to live here for many years," Phyllis said tartly. "Why should I have any idea what security arrangements my ex-husband had?"

"Wait a minute. YOU have keys?" I couldn't help asking the lieutenant. "What, you have passkeys for Manhattan or something?"

"No, they're . . ." Russo looked up and down the street. Apparently satisfied that none of the tottering old ladies, black nurses pushing old white people in wheelchairs, or purposefully striding men in business suits were paying us any attention, he put a key in the top lock, "Evidence," he said. The cluster of keys was on a ring with a brass replica of a Bloomingdale's charge card. He put the second key in. "You recognize these, Miz Skripnik?" he asked Phyllis.

An ear-splitting shriek turned every head on the street our way.

"HELL! There *is* an alarm!" Russo leapt through the door and knelt behind it, fumbling desperately; finally he just yanked some wires free.

The alarm stopped, silence descended. I was feeling goose-bumpy and conspiratorial, to say nothing of impressed with Russo, who grinned as he stood up and said, "Pretty classy. Those ingress alarms aren't cheap."

"Smolensky. My name is Smolensky," Phyllis said coldly, and stepped past Russo and into the hall.

I followed her. "Ingress?" I asked, in that stupid sarcastic way I have when I'm nervous, "You wouldn't mean entrance?"

Russo looked at me, puzzled, then muttered, "One way, so you don't have to reset them every time you go out." He looked after Phyllis, who was already in the living room. "What was that you said?"

"I said my name is Smolensky, Lieutenant," Phyllis said with her back to us.

"Okay, Miz Smolensky." Russo rubbed the back of his head. "The keys. I asked whether you recognize the key chain."

Phyllis spun around, fixing Russo with a glare. "Should I?"

"Maybe. They were found on that table there." He pointed to an occasional table of some dark wood that was just to the right of the door. There was a china bowl there with some mail in it, held down by a baseball. Russo held the keys up so that the brass charge card dangled in front of us, an engraved P.S. catching the sunlight. "And they've got your initials."

Phyllis turned from her examination of the entryway, her face vague and distracted. "Well, I lived here. I mean

I don't remember what I took and what I left. And any-way, I've gone back to my maiden name." She went back to looking around the hallway.

Russo studied her for a moment, probably wondering about her sanity, after that last remark. He stuffed the keys into his pocket again. "Well, least we're in," he said, and shrugged at me, grinning slightly.

A grin which, I confess, left me a little wobbly in the knees, so it took a moment to catch up with the other two when they moved on into the living room. I don't know what I had expected of Skripnik's house, but certainly not what we saw, which was the other half of Phyllis's apart-ment, only spread out instead of squished in.

A reclining chair covered in the same flowery blue chintz as the chair Phyllis had collapsed sobbing into, though young doctor Skripnik had been bon vivant enough to take the clear plastic cover off. The other three chrome and leather dining chairs, plus the glass and brass table they were meant to go with. The other end table and lamp.

With the right furniture—oh, say, a couple of leather Chesterfields facing each other over a huge smoke gray Aubusson, a Chinese Chippendale dining set upholstered in watered silk, the odd piece of Waterford to add sparkle—the room would have been stunning, because under Phyllis's dreck the apartment was *heaven*. A par-quet floor of two dark woods inset into a honey-colored one—not oak; ash maybe? or linden?—an interior wall with a plaster frieze of dancers carrying garlands under the ceiling, which joined a wall stripped down to the brick, which set the marble fireplace off like a jewel. The room must once have been partitioned, but now it was a glo-rious open space running the full length of the brownstone—forty feet? fifty feet?—from the bow window in front to a huge French door in back, where there must have been a garden, since we could see a small tree glowing green in the late sun.

Which was nicely framed by the newly swinging Skripnik's addition to the decor, two floor lamps in the shape of enormous baseball bats, with Mets caps for shades. *Big* Mets caps.

Phyllis went slowly through the room, looking around like someone on a tour of the White House; Russo followed a few paces behind, notebook and pen in one hand, the other behind his back; I came last, wondering how anybody could choose his decor from the souvenir concession at Shea Stadium. Baseball was everywhere: a baseball-shaped ottoman in front of an armchair shaped like a glove, a Mets beach towel draped over the sofa, a row of signed baseballs on pedestals on the mantel, doubled by the mirror. Mets posters, framed. On every wall. World Series, 1969. World Series, 1973. World Series, 1986. Let's Go Mets banners. Blue and orange curtains, even.

Which Phyllis fingered with bewildered distaste and then went through a swinging door into what proved to be the kitchen.

I was so thrilled that for a moment I even forgot about Russo, who was standing close enough behind me that I could feel his breath on my neck. The scene of the crime! I suppose since I am in the mystery business I shouldn't admit this, but Skripnik's kitchen was the first honest-to-gosh scene of the crime I'd ever been at, and all my nerves were tingling with attention.

The room was big, and it glowed in the afternoon sun. Unlike the rest of the house, it was sleek and uncluttered, with deep blue walls and smooth formica cabinets in lavender. In one corner was a deep stainless steel sink, where a big Pyrex dish was soaking. In the opposite corner was a gas range, surprisingly bare and scrubbed clean.

And that was it. No chalk outline on the floor. No yellow tape with the words Police Line—Do Not Cross. No overlooked button with a dangling piece of thread hiding underneath a dustball behind the counter. No half-smoked cigarettes lurid with lipstick, stubbed out in ash-trays from a cheap motel in Florida.

I looked at Russo, who was looking at Phyllis. Who was washing out the Pyrex dish, scrubbing as if she wanted to break it in half.

And weeping. I came around the counter and gave her a hug, signalling with my eyes that Russo shouldn't worry about this.

Phyllis put the dish on the counter and buried her face in my shoulder.

"We were *happy* here," Phyllis sobbed, her voice muffled by my shirt that she was ruining. "Why did he do it, *why*? Wasn't a family, this house, wasn't that *enough*?"

Russo finally slapped his notepad in his palm. "Okay, that's the kitchen . . . how's about the rest of the house? What's upstairs?"

"The bedrooms, and my husband's . . . his den."

So on we went, up a broad flight of linden stairs trimmed in darker wood, wonderfully elegant but also a little treacherous. The strip of darker wood had come loose on a step near the top, and Phyllis stumbled, righting herself by clutching the graceful, dark wood railing. Up-stairs the space was broken into three rooms plus a bath—probably intended as master bedroom, nursery, and nanny's room, way back when. Now the nanny's room, which had no outside window but did have one onto the hall, high up near the ceiling, was obviously a boy's room, used sporadically, if at all. More baseball, but more prominent was a poster of a Ferrari with a woman's nude hip hovering above it, and next to it a picture of a very tall and very thin blond girl in a very small pink bikini, her thumb hooked through the waist-band of the bottom. At the bed's head was a third poster, of a rock group called Deviant; the band members were made up like demons and played guitars cut into space-age sharply-angled shapes. All of which contrasted strangely with the neatly made bed covered by a Snoopy bedspread.

The master bedroom was in back and looked out onto the garden, which was overrun with ivy, as though the doctor couldn't be bothered. Skripnik seemed to have kept the nuptial night tables and dressers, which only made the bed look even more lurid, a vast circular affair was neatly made up in orange and blue satin sheets. Phyllis approached it with a look of horrified fascination, leaning down to touch it with her palm; the bed heaved up and down suggestively.

"A water bed?" Phyllis asked no one in particular. "For him and his . . . *women*."

Russo snorted, then noticed me looking at him. "Hope he had the joists checked, you know? Bed like that would weigh *tons*."

Phyllis was still staring at the bed, her back to us.

"So how about it, Miz Smolensky?" Russo prompted her gently. "See anything missing?"

Phyllis shook her head slowly. "No, it's all just like it was. I mean," she said, turning to face us, "the stuff I remember is. And the new additions. . . . My son visited, of course—when Leon could be bothered. He mentioned some of the things, the lamps and the curtains. But not the bed . . ." Phyllis shook her head slowly, hair flapping like a spaniel's ears.

"How's about the other room then, the den?"

Somehow I wasn't surprised that Skripnik had stuck his son in the room with no window and taken the front room for his den. I braced myself, preparing for an apotheosis of baseball, and was startled to find an office instead. Metal bookshelves covered two walls, and three file cabinets stood in rank against the third. The desk, far too large for the room, was also metal, but a different shade of green than the bookshelves, and the only light was from a banker's lamp on the desk. Instead of the Mets Hall of Memorabilia I had been expecting, the room looked like the warehouse of a repossessed office furniture dealer, which made the big fat leatherbound address and date book on the desk look all the more glaring. I almost yelped, just barely managing to turn the noise into a cough.

Russo touched the address book, making my mouth go dry. "Your ex-husband worked here?"

Phyllis nodded. "There isn't room downstairs; there's just a waiting room and the examination area. And this way . . ." Phyllis waved her hand vaguely. "He said it was a bigger deduction."

Russo made a mysterious but disapproving noise, looking around. "So anything valuable, this is where he'd have kept it?"

Phyllis had a strange look on her face, as if she'd swallowed something unpleasant. "Oh yes, this was where the *real* treasures were kept."

"Treasures?" Russo brightened. "What? Bonds and stuff? Or like old coins, sculptures, rare books maybe?"

Phyllis snorted and jerked her thumb over her left shoulder at the wall across from the desk.

On the wall hung a big painting in a bronze metal frame, about four foot by five, of a rabbi or some other ultra-Jewish type, long earlocks, black hat and coat, dancing with a Torah scroll, so ecstatic he seemed to be floating, above haystacks and tumbledown shacks and a scrawny spavined nag pulling a cart and, in the far distance, a tiny onion-domed church.

"Nice," Russo stepped closer. "Is it worth a lot of money, or what?"

"Photos of my husband with baseball players are worth money?" Phyllis blinked and turned from the desk. Looking up, she wrinkled her nose to peer, then turned around, puzzled. "No, his baseball pictures. He had them on that wall. He used to go to Florida in the spring and wait outside the training fields. And he never missed a Hall of Fame Game. Once he even gave somebody famous a ride in his car, but I don't remember who." She looked at the painting again, clearly puzzled.

I was so intent on dreaming up plausible, offhand ways to say Hey, who cares about a picture! What's say we take a peek in the doctor's address book, see if he's got any Russian relatives listed! that I didn't look up for a moment. When I did, I could see that the painting wasn't hanging flat against the wall.

"Maybe they're underneath," I said, mostly as a joke; I lifted the edge of the frame and was shocked to see it was true. "These?"

Phyllis took the other corner and lifted. There were several smaller frames, hung neatly beneath the big canvas.

"Yes, but this is *weird*." She turned around, still holding up the edge of the painting, looking bewildered.

Russo stepped forward, grabbed the painting from us, and took it off the wall. "This isn't your ex-husband's? You *sure*?"

"I'm not *sure* sure, but I never saw it before in my life. And it surely doesn't look like something Leon would buy."

"You've been divorced a while," Russo pointed out.

"But he'd *never* cover his baseball pictures. Why would he cover up his baseball pictures?"

"Maybe because that painting is worth a *lot* of money," I said quietly, feeling very shaken. It was only when Phyllis had moved the canvas that I noticed the signature, which was in Russian.

M. Shagal.

You probably know him by the French spelling that he began using later: Chagall.

I was still gaping stupidly when Russo swooped up and took my wrist, to turn my hand palm up. "Where'd that come from?"

"What?" I looked at my fingers, which had something dark brown and flaky on them; whatever it was, it came off when I rubbed my thumb against it.

Russo had already whipped out a handkerchief, which he used to cover his hand as he pushed back the picture frame and, peered behind the painting.

"What is it?" I repeated, alarmed at his sudden interest.

He looked at me for a second, eyes seeming to look right inside me.

"Blood, Miz Cohen. And I don't think it's yours."

6

"BUT he's so *schmaltzy,* all those flying lovers and violin players on the roof!" Sasha threw his bread crust into his soup bowl and turned sideways in his chair, indicating the conversation was over.

I slammed my spoon onto the table, indicating it wasn't.

"I didn't ask whether you *liked* Chagall, I asked you what the painting is *worth*!"

Sasha gently took away the spoon, then put his hand over mine. With the other he pointed at a postcard I had pinned up next to the telephone, so I wouldn't lose my friend Marilyn's new address. It was a section of Monet's *Garden,* from that Giverny show at the Met.

"Perhaps as much as that is worth."

"As much as a *Monet*?"

"Or as much as a postcard of a Monet." Sasha smiled gnomishly into his beard and waggled his eyebrows like Groucho Marx used to, to make sure you didn't miss the joke.

I slowly stirred my soup, trying to accept that; of *course* Skripnik wouldn't have a *real* Chagall in his apartment. Then I stirred the soup the other way; why in the world would anyone put up a *fake* Chagall? Especially if it covered up an autographed picture of yourself with an arm around an uncomfortable-looking Tom Seaver, pitcher for the team you had chosen as your decorating theme?

These questions I asked myself so many times on the way back into Brooklyn that I almost hit the guard rail at the exit to Red Hook.

Skripnik had been found down in the kitchen, my mother said. So it wouldn't be his blood on the picture, which was why Russo hadn't seemed so interested in it. Except that it was only when Russo found it on my hand that he had woken up. But then why was he so concerned about where the picture had come from, if it was the blood that was important? He had mentioned burglary, which would make sense if the painting really was by Chagall—except that what Phyllis was saying made it seem more like the burglars had *brought* the painting, not tried to take it. Maybe *Skripnik* had taken the painting? Only from whom? And when? And why? And if he did, what did it have to do with him being dead?

By the time I had finally wedged the VW far enough into a legal space that I could argue about the back wheels and bumper jutting into someone's driveway, I knew one thing for sure: any answers to this jumble were going to start with whether or not the painting was real, which is why I went down to ask Sasha for supper. Sasha had studied art history. True, it was at the mining institute in Leningrad, where he had to go because his Jewishness kept him out of the university, and instead of getting to *teach* art history, his first job assignment was showing pensioners how to paint Soviet slogans in some godforsaken village two hundred kilometers northeast of Leningrad. It was three days of rehearsing the brushstrokes for THE PEOPLE AND PARTY ARE ONE! that led Sasha into janitoring, which proved to suit him, even in America. He preferred steam pipes to hustling academic or museum jobs, but he never wholly abandoned his first calling either; when he took me to the Brooklyn Museum I learned so much that I came home with a headache.

"Midge, Midge, slow down, I understant *nothing!*" he wailed, reluctantly eyeing the painting he had been at work on when I barged in, calm as a wet hen, and just about as coherent. "Main course *and* soup?"

"And soup," I had agreed. "Even vodka, if you want."

"Okay," he agreed, "but only if talk English."

"God!" I laughed. "Do I really sound that nuts?"

Instead of answering, Sasha screwed his index finger into his temple, crossing his eyes and sticking out his tongue, and made his hand jabber like a demented puppet. "More nuts than poundcake." He put his arm around me, to encourage me up the stairs to my kitchen.

Sasha's gallantry rarely goes so far as to permit me to be the native speaker, which gave me some idea of how wound up I must be. Usually he gets to be the fluent, clever, poetic one, while I have to hack along, wondering about tenses and endings and genders. Unfortunately, though, Sasha's English is . . . well, eclectic. Sash weights, grommets, bleeder valves, drip washers, and other necessities of janitoring he can rattle off fine, and he knows all the Beatles lyrics and most of Pink Floyd by heart, vocabulary which you can understand would have left huge chunks of my tangled story totally incomprehensible, especially since being on native ground also let me be twice as incoherent as I could have been in Russian.

Particularly since Sasha refused to be interested in any part of my story but the blood.

"There was blood all over the back of the picture?" Sasha's eyes went huge and round with pleasure. "It was the blood of this doctor of yours?"

"Not *my* doctor, damn it! And they don't know *whose* blood it is! What I want to know, do you think it's a real Chagall or *not*?"

Even when I'm calm, the thing I make best for dinner is reservations, and I was far from calm that night. The soup was from a can, which Sasha abhors even when it doesn't have all the clots because I forgot to stir while I talked, and then the burgers ended up burnt on one side, almost raw on the other. Sasha pushed away the last lumps of soup and looked at both sides of his burger; he nodded his head and reached for the mustard. Like most émigrés, Sasha is both an insufferable pedant and a terrible snob, which meant he had trouble deciding whether to show off how incredibly much he knows about Chagall or how little he thinks of such piffling daubers, the front of whose canvases are not nearly as interesting as the blood that might be found on the backs.

"Why *shouldn't* it be real?" I shouted now, banging my spoon again, making Sasha wince. "You said yourself it sounds like one of his paintings!"

"Sounds like, sure." He shrugged. "I'd have to see it to be able to say, though. This blood, you think maybe the doctor was murdered?"

I admit, the question had occurred to me too, just as soon as Russo had made me and Phyllis go downstairs without touching anything and sit on the sofa while he made terse phone calls from the kitchen; he talked softly, watching us through the swinging door, which he held open with one foot. Phyllis was white-faced, trembling, while I kept rubbing my hand, feeling like Lady Macbeth, unable to get the blood off.

When he finished talking on the phone, he came and sat on the coffee table opposite us and gave Phyllis a close interrogation about the painting. I kept trying to interrupt, to ask about the blood, but every time I did, Russo looked at me for a second, his lids partly covering those incredible green-gold eyes, and then went back to quizzing Phyllis. I picked up pretty quickly that he was sorry he had said what he had about the blood, because what he really wanted to talk about was where the painting had come from.

About which Phyllis seemed to know nothing, except that she was absolutely certain Skripnik couldn't have bought it, if it really was a Chagall. They were comfortable, sure, she and the doctor had money enough to make ends meet; what Manhattan urologist doesn't? And the brownstone had been a lucky buy, back when the neighborhood was still mostly decaying bowfronts, now pulled down for that canyon of condos that turned the street dark at five P.M.

"Yeah but Miz Smolensky, you've been divorced awhile, like you said, and maybe, I don't know, like a second mortgage or something? Place like this, you could probably get some good dough that way, huh?"

Phyllis shook her head at Russo, her hair woggling emphatically. "No, he couldn't *touch* this place. I still own half the building. He can't even use his half for collateral, not without my signature. Which he didn't get."

I must have looked startled, because Phyllis smiled at me, pleased with herself. "I told him, you want out so badly, okay. But it's going to be difficult." In fact, later on, after Russo finally let us go and I took her back downtown, I began to realize *how* difficult, because not only did Skripnik have to sign over half that brownstone, but she had practically forced him to use his connections to get her an apartment in Peter Cooper Village, where the waiting list is reportedly interminable unless you know someone. "I know I was being uncooperative, but at the time, I didn't really care," Phyllis told me. She giggled. "The judge saw my point, how hard it would be for me to keep up our son's life-style alone."

Russo must finally have been convinced, because he sighed, stood up, and thanked us both in a way that made it clear we should leave.

"But the blood? Whose blood is it?" I demanded, holding up my hand to remind him I had some interest here.

He shrugged, waving vaguely in the direction of the telephone. "That's for the lab boys to figure out." He smiled. "Maybe the guy putting it up cut himself, you know? The corners on those things can be wicked sharp."

After a few thoughtful forkfuls of mustard-slathered charred raw hamburger, Sasha finally said, "It must be his own blood. How could such a painting be real, a Chagall in this man's house that no one has ever seen before or knows where it comes from?"

"What if a patient gave it to him? Some really rich old patient, who's incredibly incredibly grateful for—"

"Midge, this is a doctor of urine! Who gives a painting

for *urine*!" He laughed, reaching for the vodka bottle. I pushed it away.

"Okay, maybe it belongs to his relatives. He just found these relatives from Russia, and they gave him the picture."

"From Russia? What person in Russia has a Chagall?"

"I don't know! Maybe he was *related* to Chagall! Maybe he was Chagall's *cousin*!"

"You said the painting was signed in Russian? Already when he arrived in St. Petersburg in 1906, Chagall was signing his paintings in French."

"So maybe they knew him from before he moved! Why couldn't that be, huh?"

"Before he left Vitebsk he wasn't an artist!" Sasha grabbed the bottle and poured himself a good four fingers. "He was a *baby*! Twenty-one years old!"

"So why did he leave Vitebsk, then?"

"Because he had to study. He had to go to St. Petersburg, because there was no art school in Vitebsk."

"Just like that? He knows he's an artist, so he goes to St. Petersburg? Vitebsk was in the middle of the shtetl, his people were probably religious, right? You're telling me some Orthodox Jew just lets his son go off to the big city, where Jews aren't even allowed to live! To let him be an *artist*? Jews weren't artists then, they were rabbis and peddlers and bloodletters and revolutionaries. But off goes Chagall, twenty-one years old, and you're telling me there was *no reason*? He never drew, he never painted? He just *went*?"

Now Sasha was banging his fist on the table. *"He was a painter! That's reason enough!"*

To which I smiled sweetly and said, "See? You just said he was a painter, *so he must have been a painter in Vitebsk*!"

Sasha said, "Tphhoo! Vitebsk! You ever seen Vitebsk?"

"No, and I bet you haven't either!"

Sasha shrugged, looking angry. "Why do I have to see it to know what it's like? A backwater, the provinces. What kind of a place is that for a painter? Mud and little wooden huts and people walking around in old rabbi clothes, of course he had to go to Petersburg!"

I don't know whether Sasha meant Vitebsk in 1906 or Vitebsk now, but I suspect what he was really describing was a kind of spiritual Vitebsk, the millions of little towns where artists feel themselves dying. Besides, Vitebsk is in Belorussia and was devastated by the Nazis, so even though Chagall's house survived that wouldn't tell me anything—although it is now being made into one of those demented Soviet museums that always scatter copies of Lenin and Marx on the bookshelves and night tables of the formerly famous, I guess to prove that pro-revolutionary Russia was just counting the minutes until November, 1917—because Chagall's Vitebsk, and his world, are as dead and gone as the dinosaurs. What was more interesting was that Sasha's description of Vitebsk also described Skripnik's painting just about perfectly. In fact, when he calmed down a little, Sasha told me that Chagall had been a prolific painter in his early years, but that not very much survived. Most of those very early canvases were presumed lost, victims of the Soviets or the Nazis or simply chaos.

Meaning it *could* be a Chagall. Worth a lot of money, something that people would fight over, and get blood all over. Except that then it would have been stolen, and we would never have known about it, or the blood. So it must be fake. Only why would it be covering up the Tom Seaver pictures and have blood on the back?

I was back where I had begun.

"Come on, damn it!" I slammed down my fork. "Let's go find somebody who *will* know!"

"Who is that?" Sasha looked up, mystified and alarmed.

"The Russian relatives, that's who!"

"But you know nothing of these people!" Sasha objected reasonably, when he figured out who I was talking about. "Not name, not address. Nothing."

"Well, damn it, it's not as though I didn't try!" I shot back. "As soon as he found the blood, though, the cop had us out of the room so fast—and anyway, it would have seemed kind of weird, what with the blood and the picture, and all I'm interested in is Skripnik's address book! Besides, I know *something*. They live in Brighton, his name is Sasha, and she sings. I also know that I have to find them, Chagall or no Chagall, so they can take this damn letter off my hands!"

Sasha smiled sardonically and made a quick and successful grab for the vodka bottle I had momentarily taken my hand off. "So we go to Brighton Beach to look for a guy named Sasha and a girl who sings. What is it in English? Two noodles in a haystack."

"*Needles*. And anyway, we know more than that. The doctor said that they were very important people in Russia, that this woman was, I don't know, like a People's Artist or something."

"And this Sasha was head brain surgeon to the Central Committee! And I am the man who painted Red Square red!" He grinned as he poured another healthy dollop of the syrupy vodka into his coffee cup. "Funny thing, Midge, we were *all* great people back there. That's why we came to America, because it's more *pleasant* to starve on food stamps and live under the train in Brighton Beach!"

"*You* don't live under the train. And anyway, being a

singer, that's doing something. How many lady émigré singers like that can there be?"

Sasha lit a cigarette, which he knows I don't like him to do in my apartment, and looked deeply thoughtful. "Certainly no more than there are painters. Thirty thousand, thirty-five maximum."

"But not all from Odessa, Sasha! The doctor said they were from Odessa, I think!" I was so infatuated with my own idea that I even leaned across the table to punch Sasha in the arm.

He threw back his head and guffawed. "ODESSA! They said they are from Odessa?" He put his elbow on the table and peered intently at me. "You know what it means, a Jew from Odessa? Mark my word, dear Midge, we shall never find these people, and when we do, it will turn out that they never existed!"

Because, of course, Odessa is to Russia as Naples is to Italy, or Marseilles is to France: warm, charming, and capable of stealing the label off your garter belt with you still in it. Which I not only knew but should have thought about, except that all my brain had room for that evening was the maybe Chagall, and the two mysterious Russians that I wished I had listened better about when Leon was explaining. Certainly dear Dr. Departed didn't cross my mind once as Sasha and I chugged our way down Ocean Parkway in my VW, heading for the little Russia that Brighton Beach had become about fifteen years ago.

What *had* he said? I couldn't remember, and it was awfully clear that what I did remember wasn't making a scratch in the memory of the maître d' at the Golden Palace. That's the biggest of the Russian nightclubs, almost at the beach in Brooklyn. The neighborhood is typical Flatbush, blocks of two-story houses so close together you can hear your neighbors changing their minds, huddled around a commercial block of kosher pizzerias, kosher Chinese restaurants, kosher dry cleaners, and, for variety, a Greek diner. The Golden Palace probably used to be one of those; it's got the same stucco exterior, fancy windows frames cut out of plywood, and an arcade with flashing yellow bulbs. Inside, though, it's Soviet heaven, what everybody emigrated to get. Loud pulsing music, so much smoke that Aladdin's genie would feel at home, greasy chicken and beet salad served by the platterful, and everybody dressed absolutely to the tips of their stainless steel teeth. Men in leather jackets, women in floor-length gowns and honest-to-God feather boas. The tables are all pushed together, the vodka is served in vinegar cruets, and bored children crawl around on the sticky floor, tripping the waiters.

It's all a lot of fun, actually, unless you are trying to get information from the maître d'. He was a round, lively man with a quick grin and broad gestures, who rushed at each new party as though they were long-lost relatives, shaking hands with the men and complimenting the ladies as he led them to their tables and then came bounding back, straightening the ruffles on his shirt. In between groups I tried to ask him about a singer from Odessa, but whether from the din or my Russian, all I got was a shrug.

Sasha faced the street, to shout-whisper in my ear, "He has to be bribed."

"*Bribed?* All I want is to ask a question!" I had never bribed anyone and didn't have the faintest idea how it was done. We stood shivering under the flashing lights of the arcade, watching the parties roll up while I wondered what to do. Tuesday night, for crying out loud, and people were coming in by the bucketful. Sasha was looking decidedly glum, which probably meant I had a half hour or so before he got disgusted and asked to go home. And if I didn't take him, he'd go by bus.

"How much?" I finally hissed back.

"Twenty'll do," the maître d' said over my shoulder, rubbing his nose with a cucumber-size thumb.

Which is exactly what was folded up in my wallet. I felt foolish as I dug the wallet out of my purse, then the bill out of the wallet. Wasn't this bribery stuff supposed to be smooth and surreptitious? Bill out and wallet back in my shoulder bag, I didn't know what to do next. Fold the bill up and put it in my palm? Drop it and let him pick it up? Stuff it in his cummerbund?

While I was wondering, the maître d' gave me a courtly tilt of his head, reached over calmly, and plucked the bill from my hand. He took a wad like a gas station attendant's out of his pocket, around which he lovingly wrapped my twenty.

"A singer, alone, right? No band, and of middle years, not old or young. Maybe from Odessa, and possibly with a guy around? We never have single acts here, always bands. But go try the Kaukas. They do singers, and I kind of remember somebody like that. Liudmila, Lidia, something like that. Did gypsy romances, mostly, I think."

A youngish man with a beard and a potbelly strolled up to the door, a girl on either arm, and I lost the maître d'; he ran forward so excitedly I wouldn't have been surprised to see him fall on his knees before whoever this celebrity was.

"Kozlovkin," Sasha said, not quite spitting, as he took my arm and steered me back toward the car.

I planted my Reeboks firmly on the cement. "Sasha, I gave that man TWENTY DOLLARS! And all he can tell me is TRY THE KAUKAS! Don't you *get* something with a bribe?!"

"So ask Kozlovkin then." Sasha pointed at the man in the doorway, whom the maître d' was just solicitously helping to remove his blondes. "A journalist who claims to know everyone. Everything, too."

Still incensed about my wasted twenty, I marched off to do as Sasha suggested, quickly enough that I was almost at the door before he caught me.

"He'll cost fifty at least, little sun," he whispered in my ear. "Come on, let's try the Kaukas first. They won't tell you anything either, but at least it will be cheaper, and there's a chance what *they* say will be true."

When you have to go to the bank machine at night, most neighborhoods look uninviting, but Brighton Beach seemed particularly spooky right then, partly because I wasn't sure how many more bribes I ought to drain out of the Citibank machine. The brass-colored light that passes for night in Brooklyn seemed to swarm with people, all of whom knew a tiny part of the secret I sought, and all of whom would demand bribes. But then, even by day what the émigrés call Brighton Bitch isn't precisely a feast for the eyes. I don't know whose idea it was to stick the émigrés all the way out on the end of the subway line, two blocks from the Atlantic, but I bet it had a lot to do with no one else wanting to live there. For one thing, you're almost as far away from Manhattan there as you would be back in Moscow, and for another the entire street is directly *under* the subway, so everywhere else in Brooklyn it can be the sort of day that makes you feel like a dimple on God's chin, but when you go out there the pigeon muck, wastepaper, and gloom of the elevated makes the world feel like it's two days until the end of the Black Death.

When the street first started to go Russian I got all bubbly and brought Pearl out there for supper, when Paul was away at some mastitis convention. Now that every third teenage girl is wearing some cyrillic slogan that would get her jailed as a Wobbly if anyone could read it, and Bloomingdale's is peddling watches with CCCP on them, I know it's hard to remember not so long ago, when the Iron Curtain looked impenetrable, the only Russians in America were émigrés and defectors, and you saw Russian letters here about as often as you did Etruscan. So I took Pearl through the food stores, saying inane things like "Look! Russian mustard!" and "Kvass! They have actual kvass!" and through the bookstores, chock full of the books by writers who emigrated because they couldn't publish there. I think half my bookshelf space must be filled with those novels, which I finally quit buying because they were so like the academic novels I was addicted to at Ithaca, both seething with the same rage that the author had been squeezed out of life by people stupider and more crass.

Then I wound up my grand tour with supper at some restaurant so authentic it even had a bored pensioner by the door to take your coats and no seat on the ladies' room toilet. Pearl was patient about my enthusiasm until halfway through a pullet tabaka—a Georgian recipe for preparing a young chicken so it looks like a road kill on a sun-baked freeway—when the waiter brought the sour cream he had forgotten for the borscht, his thumb up to the first knuckle in the dish.

"I'm sure it's very interesting for you, dear, but to me it looks like what we worked our tushes off to get out of."

"We" meant Jewish emigrants, which Pearl wasn't. She was born on the Grand Concourse in the Bronx, because her father, who was, did very nicely indeed, thank you, with a line of clip-on neckties he invented and marketed with his two brothers. All those memories of pushcarts in Hell's Kitchen, laundry dangling across Hester Street, bellowing knife grinders, and pale children locked up in cold-water flats because of polio scares I later learned had come out of novels, but Pearl peddled them to me as true, to frighten some industry and responsibility into me, at an age when I preferred to lie on my bed, eat jelly graham crackers, and read *Mad* magazine.

Still, I knew what she meant. The two-block shopping strip under the elevated, the surrounding streets full of narrow asphalt-sided houses built the width of a garbage can apart, the stores-below-apartments-above where the children played in the street and the trains thundered overhead, all of Brighton seemed the sort of place that America had created for the sole purpose of urging émigrés to get on with capitalism so they could buy their way out of those miserable dank surroundings.

The more energetic of the émigrés had, too, opening restaurants and grocery stores and bookshops, until they could buy their escapes to Flatbush and Prospect Park and even to Long Island, so that, by day at least, Brighton is pinched, pale, and stinks of that dry-cleaning, leaky-gas smell from the establishments of those too old and weary to leave.

But it's at night that that kind of neighborhood really gives you the willies. That hard unreal light, the steam writhing from the grates, and the shadowy people muttering words you half understand make Brighton seem the sort of place for which no deed is too desperate, or any act too dark, if only it might help you escape.

Or as Sasha said while I punched my code into the

money machine, shaking his head and pulling his collar up high around his neck, "There always is something dripping out here."

Just then a train car pulled in overhead, making the ground shake and conversation impossible. Jostled free by the racket, a trio of scruffy pigeons dropped out of the gummy black undersupports of the elevated to peck irritably at a paper bag somebody had dropped outside the drugstore. A couple of kids too young to be out alone at that hour dashed for the stairs, running to catch the train, and nearly bowled over an old woman in a shapeless black skirt and a gray sweater; she had a plait down her back as thick as my wrist, and about as stiff.

Wishing I had never suggested we look for Leon's mysterious relatives, I just pointed at the Kaukas, our next stop.

More a restaurant than a nightclub, they had no room for bands. "Singers sure, and maybe with an accordionist, if he's small," the dyed-orange–haired lady with the wen by her nose sniffed, tapping the keys of her cash register thoughtfully. "Most of the singers are women, of course."

Ten dollars got her to recall that maybe there *had* been a Lidia, but she had come from Odessa the restaurant, not Odessa the city. I might have tried another ten, except that the sharp smell of burning onions suddenly billowed from the kitchen, and the sack-shaped lady eased herself from her cashier's stool to waddle into the back.

Sasha took my arm, but I slipped on a pelmeni somebody had dropped and banged my knee into the table by the door, causing the vodka of a little man with a toupee to spill. He stood up and yelled at me about dry cleaning, until Sasha glared at him and steered me out onto the avenue; the fall had started tears which didn't seem to want to stop. Standing between the mounds of trash bags heaped by the parking meters, Sasha put his arm around me.

"Don't cry. It could be worse; we might have eaten there!"

I choked on a laugh, then wailed, "We aren't going to find them, are we?"

He hugged me, patted my shoulder. "Don't worry, there's still the Odessa, and the grocery stores, and the bookshops. We'll find something."

Which of course we didn't, as Sasha had known we wouldn't, and I ought to have. The man at the Odessa didn't even look up from the piles of cash and waiters' checks that he was sorting at a back table. "They come, they go. If they can sing, please, here's my microphone. If they can't, there's my door." Larissa, Liudmila, Lidia, it was all the same to him, Odessa or Omsk.

Information it wasn't, but at least it was free.

At midnight, when the Black Sea Bookstore closed, Sasha finally persuaded me that anything else I might learn about Brighton Beach that night wasn't likely to be so pleasant. "Midge, not *everyone* had to change professions when he came to America." He took me by the arm and steered me back toward my VW, which was against a hydrant of which I could claim ignorance, since it was mounded up with trash bags. "Thieving is a transferable skill, and we have tried all the places where we might find honest people."

Delicate though it was, that hint was enough to make me slide behind the wheel and start back for Cortelyou Road. In fact, to tell the truth, I wasn't even sure anymore what I was looking for. Fatigue, anxiety, and the eerie look of Brooklyn by night, brilliantly lit as if it's were a military perimeter, which makes you think everyone who is still on the streets is probably a criminal, even the old women giving their dogs one last draining before bed, all that had made a muddle of what I had gone to Brighton Beach to search for.

What did I want out of all this Skripnik mystery, anyway? Real or not, the Chagall really had nothing to do with me, right? It's not as if I was in line to get hold of it, no matter how the authenticity issue worked out.

As for blind Shmuel, he was mine only as long as I let myself worry about him. So why, I wondered at each red light, was I so worked up about all this? I caught every red from Avenue X down to Cortelyou Road, in reverse alphabetical order, which made for a lot of wondering, but even so, the closest I could come to an answer was that it was like one of those car wrecks on the Long Island Expressway: you crawl along in a traffic jam for *hours* and finally reach the place where the flares are burning down to ash and the police lights are flashing and people are standing in the broken glass looking grim, and it almost *kills* you not to know what happened, and why, and to whom, and where they were going, and what's going to happen next.

Snoopiness, Pearl calls it. I prefer to think of it as interest in my fellow humans. Stock in trade for us novelists.

Whatever you called it, though, the fact was that I could not put any of this out of my head. A painting worth maybe millions, blood on it that nobody was saying where it came from, a man dead. And the most handsome cop in all of New York investigating. How could I *not* be obsessed?

Cortelyou Road looked much friendlier than Brighton Beach, but even so I was happy for Sasha's company. To my door.

"But Midge, I have given you my entire *evening*," he

said with that grape-eyed look that some men think is foreplay.

"God, Sasha, I'd really love to have you up . . ." I ran my fingernail lightly across the hollow of his throat, a femme-fatale-ism I had seen in a Pia Zadora movie that I chanced on while channel-flicking during an insomnia bout but had never had the guts to try. "But . . . I can't. Not for a few days."

I hate women who do things like that—I mean, jeez, it's only two steps from that to the way my roommate Sarah had landed her ZBT—who later got fired from his brokerage house during the Ivan Boesky thing and last I heard was under indictment, not that Sarah cared, since she was dating someone high up in the Republican National Committee—and when I have to do it, I usually pretend I'm somebody else, but what *can* you do, when some guy really and truly *has* been nice to you, for which kindness he feels he deserves a chorus or two of "Roll Me Over In the Clover"? Someday I'll meet a man who doesn't think sex is some kind of ride at Disneyland, which you get by pulling the right tickets out of your book. Dinner and a movie? No? Okay, then dinner, a movie, and I'll say nice things about your dress. Still not enough? Okay then, dinner, a movie, three compliments, *and* I'll stay for breakfast, but it's my last offer, and you're going to have to spice it up a little, maybe cook the bagels topless or something.

Until I meet that man, though, I'll just keep relying on my period. A wince of regret, a gentle hint, and most men wither like candles too close to the sunny window. Russians especially, but Russian, American, and for all I know, Zulu, *none* of them ever know how long it's supposed to last or when it's supposed to come, so any time you think you really *have* to sleep alone, there it is. No hurt feelings, and you have your time to yourself.

Which I was certain I needed, because even without sex to get tense over, I doubted I would ever get to sleep. Even when I've worked well all day, taken my hour walk up to the Waldbaum's on Avenue K, which is good exercise but also necessary since the roof of my Waldbaum's fell down, and paid all my bills for the month, I still spend a lot of time staring at Aunt Dora's ceiling before the sandman finally agrees, grudgingly, to visit. With the picture, the blood, the police, and the Russians all whirling around like some dumb attempt at a gazpacho you threw in the Cuisinart without even checking to see that you had all the ingredients, I could have had insomnia for days. That's about the only time I miss Paul and our marriage, when I have really bad insomnia. Paul always fell asleep as soon as he got horizontal, and many nights the only way I could finally put myself away was to match my breathing to his. Now that I'm single again, the only thing I have to synchronize to is the *floop-floop* of the cardboard numbers on my old clock radio flipping over, and all that ever does is send me out for herbal tea and television.

Which explains why, Sasha dispatched, disappointed but undefiled, and my clothes exchanged for my beloved flannel nightgown, I didn't give the bed more than a glance before going to the TV and Dora's deep armchair. I nestled down in the semicollapsed chair, put my chin on my knees, and aimed the remote, the magic wand that would get me through the night without thinking of Skripniks.

And immediately fell asleep, or so I figured out when the front door buzzer jolted me awake about six hours later.

You know how stiff you get, sleeping like that? My

legs felt like they had been pickled, and my brain wasn't much better, as I padded barefoot to the squawk box. Seven fifteen, I could see on the kitchen clock.

"Yeah?" I snarled into the intercom.

"Miz Cohen?"

Even half asleep, I wasn't about to fall for that trick; you know how many "Miz Cohens" there *are* in Brooklyn? If you want to get into some building you just jab a button, ask for Ms. Cohen, and you're in.

"Go to hell," I barked, and headed down the hall for the bedroom, hopeful that another couple of hours lying down would make me feel less like a paper clip someone had been twisting.

The buzzer went again, "Shave and a Haircut." I was going to keep walking, but whoever it was left off the last buzz-buzz, which after maybe a minute I couldn't stand. Crazy, I went back and pushed the talk button.

"Listen, whoever the fuck you are, get the hell away from my button or I'm calling the cops!"

"Miz Cohen, it *is* the cops. It's me; Russo, NYPD."

7

OH GOD!

I pushed the enter button immediately, before I remembered I was still in my nightgown. Not to mention unwashed, uncombed, teeth unbrushed, my apartment looked like I was moving, and my sink was full of dishes. By the time Russo knocked, the dishes were in the refrigerator, the old newspapers were in the shower, and I was in my raincoat, because I couldn't find my bathrobe. My hair was combed, my face glowed, and my teeth felt minty ice every panting breath I took. Talk about your aerobic exercises!

When he knocked, I took a deep breath, held it until I

thought my heart might come through my neck, and opened the door.

"Morning, Miz Cohen." He peeked around the door, a big smile on his face. "Listen, you shouldn't just open up like that, it could be anybody."

So I put my shoulder against the door, just about squashing his head. "Okay then, who is it? Show me some ID."

An arm came in, with a wallet. I studied it until I had it memorized, my foot still wedged against the door. Lieutenant Michael A. Russo. Six feet one inch. One hundred seventy-eight pounds. Eyes green. Hair brown. Badge number A327-564. And a photo, of some gaunt, lantern-jawed, hollow-eyed person who looked like Russo after an all-night binge.

"So it's okay? I'm legit?" He peeked around the door again.

"Your hair isn't brown."

He laughed as he took the wallet and put it back in his sports jacket. "Not enough of it left to tell. And I probably don't weigh one seventy-eight no more either." He patted his belly, which looked plenty flat to me. "But it's me just the same."

He was eyeing my apartment, over my shoulder. I stayed where I was. The last time I had a cop in my house was senior year at Cornell, when I was staying with my friend Rachel at the commune, because my roommate Sarah had to get her ZBT guy in a position where he could believe he was the one who had knocked her up. Those cops had been looking for dope, which two of the guys were hastily chucking over the fence into the neighbor's yard, so we had to stand in their way and yell "Pigs! Pigs!" until the guys whistled all clear.

Or at least that's what the other people did. I was in

the living room, praying to God to make the cops believe I was just there to pick up a homework assignment, since I knew neither He nor I could ever calm Pearl down again if I were to get arrested.

But Russo didn't seem porcine. Feline, more like. He smiled, a little lazily, a tabby that has just found a patch of sun. "Listen, I'm, uh, sorry to be bothering you, so early and all, but there's something I wanted to ask you about."

"About Skripnik?"

"Well, yeah, kinda."

You know how it is. Here was this gorgeous policeman, right in my hallway, he wants to talk, and what do I do?

Get bitchy, of course.

"Look, Lieutenant, I thought I made myself clear yesterday. I didn't know the Skripnik family at all, in fact, until four days ago I didn't know any of them existed, so I certainly don't see what I can help you with, especially at this hour of the—"

"One thing maybe'd be a cup of a coffee. You could help me that much, couldn't you?" He smiled more broadly at me, which made my legs feel strangely rubbery again. "Haven't had any yet. See, I'm on my way in to work, I see your address, and figure maybe I'll stop in. But if it's too early . . ."

I stepped back, to let him come further into the apartment, making a sour face, so he wouldn't think I really wanted him to but ready to cut my heart out if he didn't. Which probably explains why I started rummaging around for beans, filter, grinder, to make espresso. Italians like espresso, I explained this to myself.

Russo went past me, careful not to touch in that narrow kitchen, and took a seat at the table, where he brushed some loose sugar from the yellow place mat. He looked around, humming.

"Nice place you got. All yours?"

"Meaning do I live alone? Who's being investigated here, me or Skripnik?" I was still being severe, which is not easy when you are on your hands and knees, trying to dig out the espresso machine from the very back of the cupboard. "How about you answer some questions instead? Like where do you live? In Midwood? Or further out, like Sheepshead Bay?"

Russo pushed his chair back and put an ankle on his knee. A stray beam of sunlight bounced through the trees, lighting up Russo's chin, neck, and shoulders. The stubs of his freshly-shaven whiskers glistened like sand just wet from a wave, so I bent down to rummage again for the top half of the pot, which I eventually found, because I had been holding it in my left hand.

"Naw, but kind of." Russo shrugged, fiddled with the potted violet in the middle of the table. "You don't want to water these so much, it yellows them." He held up a withered leaf.

"Brooklyn?" I snatched the leaf and put it in my raincoat pocket. "Hand me the grinder, would you? It's behind the toaster there."

"More or less." His hand touched mine for a second, making me jump, spilling coffee beans.

"More or less? Where is more or less Brooklyn?" I hastily swept the coffee beans from the sideboard into the grinder, like that's how I made coffee every morning. Then I hit the button on the grinder, so Russo had to say it twice.

"Riverdale."

"*Riverdale?* That part of Brooklyn is called the Bronx."

I banged ground coffee into the tin basket of the espresso percolator and filled the bottom with water. I screwed the pieces together very carefully, trying out reasons why an extremely cute detective from the Bronx who works on the Upper West Side in Manhattan would "drop in on" a once married, maybe not so young, and probably plumper than she should be but still more or less okay-looking sort of writer who lives in Brooklyn. Since that route to work makes as much sense as going from New York to Boston by way of Buffalo, I only came up with two, and one of those, that this was official, seemed unlikely to have started with coffee. The other possible explanation gave me a severe dose of butterflies.

"Yeah, well, my car's pretty fast, and I like to drive. What, your roof leak or something?"

I didn't know what he meant, until he pointed at my raincoat.

I blushed, and cinched my belt buckle tighter. "No, I . . . you just surprised me. Listen, you said you had some questions?" I sat hurriedly, as though that would make my raincoat less visible. Which put him about four feet away, on the other side of my kitchen. Which, with the sun filtering through the leaves outside and hitting my yellow walls, looked very homey. And made Russo's eyes look yellow now, but with a tinge of green . . .

"Yeah, well, just wanted to get a little more info." He made a show of peering at his notebook. "Margaret? Right?"

"Midge," I said immediately, then added, "or Margaret. But I told you that yesterday, when you got my address."

"Midge? What is that, like a nickname?"

"Sort of. An old joke. Short for midget." I toyed with

a button on my raincoat, wondering why I was telling this to this man.

He laughed, head back. "Midget? You aren't so short. What, you were a short kid or something?"

Mercifully the espresso was making the dyspeptic gurgles that indicate coffee was nearly ready, so instead of explaining, I fussed with cups, saucers, and spoons. The coffee smelled delicious as I poured it.

"Got any cream? Or milk?" Russo stood, heading for the refrigerator. Where I had stashed last night's dishes. I stepped forward in panic, bumping into him.

"NO! I mean . . . cream, in espresso? Doesn't . . . Italians drink it black, right?"

Russo looked at me like I was a little nuts, but sat down again. "You want to know the truth, espresso is a little strong for me." He took sugar, four spoons, then sipped. "But this is good. Very good."

I sat too, mad at myself for being so pleased he liked my coffee, mad at myself for still feeling the tingle of our bump, all down my front.

There was a moment's silence. Then Russo said, "Nicknames can be a pain, that's for sure. Especially for Sicilians. You know that?"

"Sicilian? I thought you were . . ."

"All Mafia, right?"

"No, I mean, Italian."

"Italian, Sicilian, it's pretty much the same thing nowadays, for most of us. Not for my grandfather though! He *hates* Italians. *Sicula per siculesi!* Sicily for Sicilians! Anything east of Enna, they're all Romans. Or worse, *Calabresi*. Anyway, Sicilians are very good at cutting each other down. Your mother calls you maybe Salvatore or Ruggiero or Olterio or something, but in school the kids notice you've got one leg too short, and until you die you're Hopalong. Or Squint-Eye, or Carrot-Top. Take me, all day at work it's Lieutenant Russo, or Mike, from the other cops. But soon's I get home, Mama, Grandma, even the people in the stores, everybody calls me Babo."

"At home?" My mouth went too dry to ask, And your wife too? Instead, I blithered, "I mean, Babo, what is that, like papa or something?" I leaned over my coffee, to take the first sip without picking up the cup. I hoped that the top of my head wouldn't give away that I had just about asked him whether he was single.

Or give away my disappointment that he didn't really answer.

"No, it means like 'stupid' in Sicilian, or 'dope.' " He laughed again and sipped his coffee. "Listen, you wouldn't have maybe some toast? I didn't get any breakfast."

Coffee? Toast? This is a *policeman*, who talks about Sicily and nicknames and never *mentions* Chagall, blood, Skripniks? Could it be, I was beginning to wonder, that I really *am* being hustled?

And if it is, what do I think about that?

Would it give you a hint if I told I was scrambling eggs and popping English muffins in the toaster before I remembered that breakfast was one of the first things to come between me and Paul, even before we were married? Paul is into cows, remember? And a big part of the poetry, as he explained once, is that special glow of dawn breaking through the icicles on your eyelashes, when you get up before dawn to go milk the beasts on some fast-frozen January morning. Myself, I have always maintained that if God really wanted people to get up before noon, he wouldn't have made luncheon menus so much more interesting than breakfast ones.

Which is why I was so astounded to find myself there

in my sunny yellow kitchen, humming as the butter sizzled in the pan, watching Russo gingerly drink his espresso, just beginning to let myself believe that, hey, maybe he really *was* interested, I mean it's not *so* crazy . . .

Dark suspicion suddenly clouded the kitchen. This couldn't be one of Pearl's setups, could it?

I sneaked another glance at Russo out of the corner of my eye, and giggled. Pearl? Send me a *cop*? An Italian cop with a Noo Yawk accent and a neck so thick he couldn't keep his top button done up? Pearl sent me accountants, lawyers, urologists. Pearl sent me Skripniks.

Which Russo wasn't. As I got bread and jam and knife and plate, my hands trembled, because I couldn't really believe that this Russo had come all the way down from Riverdale to pretend to interview me, because he was interested. In *me*.

You reach a certain age, you have a job, a mortgage, you're married, or used to be married, maybe there's kids, and those trembly, wonderful pickups just don't seem to happen anymore. Sure, there's sex, and maybe even love, if you're lucky. But you don't have that feeling anymore, the one you get when the best-looking boy in the whole school comes right up to you in the lunchroom and in front of *everybody* asks you to the dance next Friday night, and you go home to spend the entire week practicing writing your first name with his last name.

Yet here was Russo. Gorgeous, tall, handsome, and apparently interested in me. So how did I keep the ball rolling?

"Okay, Lieutenant, there's your eggs and your toast and your coffee." I not quite slammed same down in front of him. "Now don't you think we'd better get on with the questions? I have a lot of things to do today."

Russo looked up, surprised, before he let his face go

blankly professional. He put the silverware down carefully and looked me in the eye. "That's the way you want it, okay, Miz Cohen. But I was kind of hoping you'd get around to telling me yourself."

"Telling you what?"

"You claim you didn't know this Dr. Skripnik, there was nothing between you—"

"Claim? Claim? I don't 'claim' *anything*. I met Skripnik *once,* right here."

"If that's true, then how come you took Dr. Skripnik's address book last night?"

Breakfast went downhill from that point. I sat, hand over my mouth, eyes big as cheese Danish. Since all I had looked at in Skripnik's office was that big leatherbound book, I could hardly say, "What address book?" but maybe I ought to have anyway, since what I *did* say didn't help matters much.

"Me? I didn't take it."

Russo tried not to be obvious about it, but he clearly didn't believe me. He grunted, eyed me, then cut deliberately into his egg.

"You didn't," he said with a mouthful of egg, "then who did?"

I admit, it was not a bad point. After all, why would Phyllis steal her husband's address book?

The book had been on Skripnik's desk last night. So how did Russo know it was missing?

"I have a real good memory," he said matter-of-factly, mopping up with the muffin. "When the guys from the lab finally got there with their truck, we went back upstairs, and I saw right off it wasn't on the desk anymore. And I remembered when you went up to the bathroom."

Which I had done with Phyllis, just before we left. And we had always been together, except for . . .

So it wasn't hard to figure out *how* Phyllis could have managed to pocket that book, but that still didn't mean it made sense.

Russo's polite but firm reluctance to believe me suggested he was of the same opinion, so I got mad, shouting and throwing open drawers, insisting that I have nothing to hide, and that Russo should search my apartment.

"You think I'm lying? Here, God damn it, LOOK! You want to know where that book is, ask Phyllis! *She* was there too, you know!"

"Good idea," he said in a *Dragnet* voice that said plainly he already had asked Phyllis, who had convinced him I was the better one to put the question to. Which made me so mad that it no longer mattered whether he saw the dishes in the refrigerator or the newspapers in the shower or that he found my lost bathrobe under the bed, which is where it turned out to be, fuzzy with dust-balls. I made him search every inch of my apartment, and even forced him out to the parkway and around the corner, to go through the coffee cups, yellowed newspapers, and tangled jumper cables that decorate the inside of my VW.

Would a guilty person behave like that?

On the other hand, would an *innocent* person?

I have no idea. All I know is that the harder I tried to convince him I had not taken the book, the more he seemed to believe the opposite, which made me even more nuts. I was just beginning to think, in the far back parts of my brain, that probably I had overdone things, when Russo turned and went to his low-slung, bright red car, which he had parked in the bus stop at the end of the block. I trailed after him.

"Tell you what," he said, getting in, "you think of anything, give me a call, okay?" He pulled a business card from his breast pocket and held it out his window between two fingers, starting the car with his other hand. Not thinking, I took the card and watched him drive off with a squeal of tires. He ran the stop sign and turned neatly out onto Ocean Parkway, headed for the city.

And, suddenly aware that I was in the middle of the street in my nightgown and raincoat, I went back to my apartment.

My apartment had not been neat before; the search made it look like I'd been looted. Worst of all was the kitchen, where the remnants of toast and egg were a taunting rebuke that I should *ever* have let myself think that Russo's friendliness was anything more than clever police work.

I got dressed, avoiding the mirror, which would explain *why* it had been so foolish to think that someone like Russo would, well, you know, and then set about trying to make enough order in the apartment to allow me to get to work.

About a month ago my editor at Apple suggested that Tammy and Tanesia were old enough maybe to start being interested in boys, and that a little kissing would expand my audience. I had been struggling ever since to incorporate some kind of twelve-year-old love interest, with very little success. Every time I brought a boy into the story, the girls couldn't seem to *think* anymore, so it was always the boys who suggested following the mysterious stranger or who crept up to the windows of the abandoned fishing lodge, where a light had suddenly been seen. Last week I had screwed up all my courage and phoned the editor to say it simply would not work; she had insisted that I bring in what I had and we'd talk.

At three o'clock on Friday. Maybe if you're Judy Blume

the YA editors buy you lunch; we Lake Poncatoncas people come after lunch.

And if I didn't have something more than a wad of crumpled drafts and a page with CHAPTER ELEVEN on it, I wouldn't even get that much of an audience the next time. I tried, I honestly did. As if *anyone* could write, after a morning like that! It wasn't enough that I had had only about six hours of sleep, and that in an armchair, but on top of it I had that damn address book to think about. Every time I attempted to conjure up Tammy and Tanesia, the only thing that would pop into my head was that book. I tapped Xs and Os on my Selectric, getting madder and madder and madder.

That Phyllis had taken the book I had no doubt, so what we were after here was motive. Oddly enough, my first idea was that she must have done so to be nice to me. After all, it was to get the address that she had gotten me to come into the city, and then there was all that fuss with the picture and the blood. So when we went back up to the bathroom, she must have remembered and gone in to get the book and then forgotten to mention it.

The longer I looked at the piece of paper I had rolled into the Selectric two days before, perfectly blank except for the words CHAPTER ELEVEN, the more I began to wonder about the painting. How *had* that painting gotten into Skripnik's apartment? Phyllis had certainly sounded believable when she swore she had never seen it before, and nothing about Skripnik's apartment suggested he'd ever been an art collector.

But what if the painting belonged to some other Skripnik? In particular, what if it belonged to the woman I had looked all over Brighton Beach for, whom Skripnik had mentioned so coyly that night in my apartment? Supposing the painting was hers, what would happen to it now that Skripnik was dead?

For some reason I remember all sorts of perfectly useless things, like my junior high school locker number—4185, fifteenth from the end, starting from the left, combination 2 left, 17 right, 35 left, back to 11—and the flip sides of Beatles singles—"Paperback Writer"? Easy: "Nowhere Man." But I immediately forget things like names, errands I am supposed to run, and what the men I presume are blind dates set up by Pearl are saying to me, which meant that if Skripnik *had* said anything about the painting, it would have gone in one ear and out the other. Still, I did remember one thing from that evening.

Skripnik was sneaky. Evasive. Anxious, insistent that his letter be translated *right now*.

Because it was from another Skripnik relative!

That realization jolted me up from the Selectric to begin pacing the apartment. How could I have missed something so obvious? Why the enormous rush with the translation? Because the painting belonged to the other Skripniks! And now, suddenly, out of the blue, a letter from yet another Skripnik!

Which is only worth worrying about if you somehow have designs on that painting, designs which might get put awry by the arrival of another Skripnik.

Which put a very different complexion on matters.

What's a painting like that worth? Hundreds of thousands? Millions? I had no idea, but I was beginning to suspect that Dr. Skripnik had a pretty good one. Certainly it was enough to make it worth trying to cheat some old-country relatives out of it. Maybe even enough to make it worth getting killed for.

At which point my thinking got very tangled. Skripnik had been found in the kitchen, my mother said, but the painting with the blood on it was found upstairs. A painting is a murder weapon? Somebody beats somebody to death with a Chagall? Then takes it upstairs and hangs it over Tom Seaver? On the other hand, who breaks into a house, makes a bloody mess of a doctor's head with an object unknown, then goes upstairs to daub the back of a valuable painting with blood, and leaves without stealing anything?

This made no sense, but as I pondered, something else began to make no sense. Namely, that since the painting was still in Skripnik's den, unless someone else turned up fast with proof of ownership, that Chagall was going to be part of Skripnik's estate.

Which a nauseating sinking in my stomach told me was probably going to go to Phyllis.

I'll be honest; my first reaction was a jealousy so green that I could have been lady mayor of the Emerald City. The plainest, whiniest, most schleppy woman I had ever met in my life was about to inherit full control of a magnificent brownstone that just happened also to contain a sofa-size Chagall, and all I was going to get out of a lost week was her blind in-law and a near miss with the most handsome man I had ever seen on this side of the silver screen.

But I wasn't *really* mad until I thought about the address book again.

Of *course* it made no sense for her to steal her own ex-husband's address book.

On the other hand, it might make a LOT of sense for *me* to take it. If I was Skripnik's mistress.

Which was precisely what Phyllis had set me up to be, I realized. "Oh, I need your help!" she pleads, getting me to the brownstone when Russo is there and telling him I had been the last to see her ex-husband alive. Then, to make certain he would be suspicious, she steals the address book when I'm in the bathroom.

For a moment I stumbled, trying to think *why* she would do all this, until I realized it made perfect sense, if Phyllis knew the painting was not Skripnik's, realized what it is worth, and was going to make damn certain that she inherited it. I had stupidly made her aware that I knew about the other Skripniks, and she was taking no chances. If she could discredit anything I might say by making me suspect, chances were good she could muddy the waters at least until probate was cleared and she came into full legal possession of the house and everything in it.

Was Phyllis that calculating? I walked back and forth in the apartment, recalling her hiccups, her absurd clothing, her blind-puppy mannerisms. Which didn't at all square with the woman who had tied Skripnik in such knots that she now owned a brownstone on the Upper West Side and had a coveted, rent-stabilized apartment in Peter Cooper Village.

"The judge felt very sorry for me," she had explained last night, with a little smile, that the longer I thought about it, the cleverer it got.

The *witch*, I thought, dumbfounded at the possibility.

The best-looking man I've ever had in my apartment had just stormed out, convinced I was both a liar and, far more horrifying, Leon Skripnik's mistress, I hadn't done any of my own work in five days, and I *still* had damn Shmuel Skripnik hanging over my conscience.

All because of conniving, calculating Phyllis Smolensky Skripnik.

Who was not, I decided right then, going to push ME around.

I covered my typewriter decisively. After a little

thought, I put on my tightest jeans and the snakeskin boots I had blown my entire first royalty check on and never told Pearl about, because they have such high heels, made myself up, and marched the three blocks to the Cortelyou Road subway stop, muttering and waving my arms.

Which at least meant I got a seat almost immediately. No true New Yorker will get out of the way for old people, pregnant women, or anybody disabled, but people we think might be nuts, we can't yield to them fast enough.

8

PETER Cooper Village is practically at the East River,
eight or nine blocks from the train, which meant that by
the time I got there, I was beginning to understand what
I was doing. God *damn* Phyllis and her creepy husband
and her weepy little bedroom and her blind in-law! She
had cost me a week's work, and I had blown it with Russo.
The hell with Russo, who cares about one Sicilian cop,
more or less? The point was that when he walked out, I
had felt he was right. I mean, what did I have to offer to
a man who looked like that?

Which is why I had dressed up as I had. To make it
clear to Phyllis—and to myself—that the answer was

PLENTY! And if Russo didn't see it, then it was his problem, not mine.

So I bounced along, liking that click of my heels and the snug fit of those jeans, not to mention the second looks I knew I was getting from at least some of the men on the avenue. It was one of those days you occasionally get even in New York, when the air is clean and smooth, with just enough chill to make you glow as you stride along, and the city seems alive, vibrant with interesting, occupied people. I was enjoying the walk so much that I even bought a Greek sandwich from a pushcart, which I ate sitting on a window ledge, congratulating myself.

Damn it, I was a grown woman, leading the life I wanted to lead, and no one was going to take that away from me, not my mother, and certainly not Phyllis Smolensky!

In short, I had fire in my belly when I got to Phyllis's building. I would bully the address book out of her, and then just to spite her I would find the other Skripniks, and tell them to reclaim their Chagall. And Russo would be so bowled over by my cleverness and determination that he would invite me into his low-slung red car, and we would roar off into the sunset together.

Or failing that, I could at least go back to my Selectric, my apartment, and chapter eleven.

"Yeah?" said the squawk box.

"Phyllis Smolensky, please."

"Not here."

That was a possibility I hadn't expected, so it took a moment to pull myself together, and realize that *someone* was there. I didn't need Phyllis, I needed her apartment. I rang again.

"Listen, I'm a friend of your mother, and I think, uh, she has something of mine that I need."

Silence. It was the son, of course, about whom I had totally forgotten until that moment. The reason for his silence I discovered when I finally got in, which I did by hanging around the building until an elderly woman headed for the door, her grocery cart squeaking slowly behind her. When she already had her key in the lock, I came up jauntily behind her, jangling my own key chain.

"Oh, hello, here, let me hold the door for you."

"Thank you, dear."

And I was in. Fortunately one of mankind's most deeply ingrained reflexes is to open a door that is knocked upon.

Which Phyllis's son did. Wearing a Twisted Sister T-shirt, his eyes glazed and his hair smelling of marijuana. Some music that sounded like a chain saw hitting a nail was throbbing from a back room.

"Hi." I smiled brilliantly. "I'm a friend of your mom's."

"Oh, shit."

It was hard to tell how stoned this kid really was, because he looked more scared than lobotomized. Having already experienced the Skripnik family's problem with getting stuck in doorways, I pushed on into the living room. The boy pirouetted, mouth agape. At the funeral, when he was dressed up, Leon Jr. had looked to be sixteen, maybe seventeen. Now that I saw him close up I doubted the boy was even fifteen. Most people, as soon as they get through those early teenage years, start to get nostalgic. Golden oldie records, trivia games about the TV shows that used to be on, high school reunions. What we all forget is how incredibly *awful* it is when your body becomes one giant zit-covered hormone.

Leon Jr. was as stretched out as a reflection in a funhouse mirror, with the position of every bone suggested on the surface of his too-tight skin. The male hormones were just beginning to trickle in, giving him a smoky film on his upper lip that made his face look dirty; he was wise not to shave, though, because he could have bled to death cutting off the tops of all the pimples. Add braces and a voice that couldn't stay in the same octave for four syllables in a row, and it's not so hard to understand why the kid was in the back room listening to one of those record albums with a cover no doubt featuring a woman chained to a wall, her boobs about to pop out of her torn tiger skin.

"My mom's not home. . . . You're not the locksmith."

"Right the first time!" I said brightly. "But who needs a locksmith, with you here to open the door?"

"Well, who are you? You can't just come in like that."

Which was true enough, but I was in a nasty mood. "Which do you think would upset your mom more? Me being here or you smoking dope in the back room?"

"Dope? I wasn't smoking dope!"

"Then what's that smell? You burning your collection of Boy Scout knots?"

"How would *you* know what dope smells like?"

Which question made me feel antediluvian. I was tempted for a moment to inform this kid about Woodstock and the *real* hip generation but decided against it, since I had not actually gone to Woodstock, having been away at summer camp at the time. So I simply said, "I used to teach college."

The boy nodded and shut the door, still looking worried. I felt sorry for him, and a little ashamed of myself, so I had to keep reminding myself about the stolen address book his mother had tried to pin on me.

I decided a little sympathy wouldn't be out of order.

"Don't worry, I'm not going to tell on you."

He brightened, even smiled for a second. That made him look like a seven-year-old who had been put through a Xerox enlarger. "Thanks. I was . . . my mom went over to my grandma's, and I figured . . ."

"Needed a pick-me-up, did you?"

"Something wrong with that?" he blazed up, ready to explode.

I just shrugged. "Not my house, is it? It just seems kind of, well, lonely. I mean, sitting inside on a nice day like this, listening to records and smoking dope, alone."

He shrugged. "I'm okay." Macho man. I decided to push a little harder.

"Bad times lately? I mean, I know about your dad."

The boy's eyes looked intelligent for the first time since I'd come in. "That's right, you were at the funeral. . . . You were my father's girlfriend."

I shook my head. "No, I wasn't. I didn't really even know him. Did he—were there a lot of girls?"

He shrugged, that glaze of hostility once more clouding his eyes. "Dunno. His business, not mine."

"Yeah, but didn't he ever take you out or—"

"Sometimes. Museums, that kind of thing. Just him, though."

"You miss him?"

Again the shrug. The kid's hands were shoved so deep into the pockets of his worn Levi's that he looked hump-backed. After a second, he relaxed, a little. "At first, yeah. A lot."

At first? He was dead less than a week. Then I understood what the boy meant, because he went on to say, "But then it was like he never had time. I was little, and I couldn't figure out why I had to go with my mom. I mean, she's okay, but, well, my dad used to do stuff with me, especially take me to Mets games."

"You a baseball fan too, like your father?"

He shook his head. "Naw, not really. In fact, I really

kind of hated it, because my father always wanted me to remember stats and all that, and I'd mess them up. But I liked the hot dogs and stuff. Anyway, it didn't matter, because then like he got busy. After they split up, he was supposed to be sharing custody, but . . ." The shrug was sharper.

"He didn't, huh?"

The boy muttered something, his face sullen.

"I'm sorry?"

"I SAID HE WAS AN ASSHOLE!" he flared, his face bright red, hot with anger. He hit himself on the tops of his thighs with clenched fists, raised his arms again, and then jammed the fists back into his pockets. He started to leave the room but abruptly turned back around, keeping his face turned away, probably to hide the tears I could see trembling on his eyelashes.

I was startled, and suddenly wondered, just how much did his son hate Leon Skripnik?

"Uh, look, can I get you something or something?" he finally mumbled. "My mom won't be back for . . . until later."

Trying to keep cool, I said coffee, because I was pretty sure there wouldn't be any ready, and the boy would thus have to make it. I needed the time to think, and maybe to poke around a little.

I was correct. Leon Jr. withdrew to the kitchen, looking challenged, and left me alone with the living room. I wasn't terribly confident that I would find the address book; if Phyllis had taken it for benign reasons, then it was most probably in her mailbag of a purse, and if she had taken it for any other reason, then it was even less likely to be set out on a shelf, in plain view. Still I had come this far, so I might as well make sure. Spurred on by the clattering and the sound of running water from the kitchen, I did a rapid tour of the shelves, checked next to all the chairs, and even slid open the drawers of an Italianate desk, which seemed to be where Phyllis kept her bills. The bookshelves suggested that Phyllis was the kind of person you'd love if you owned a bookstore but would hate to have to make small talk with: fat studies of modern Zionism, histories of the Middle East, all the novels you get assigned in college literature, and, seeming almost embarrassed in that company, shelved spine to the wall, *The Joy of Sex, Any Woman Can!,* and *Gourmet Sex.*

And, of course, no address book.

"Are you looking for something?"

I spun around guiltily, blushed, and put *The Joy of Sex* back on its top shelf. "Oh, great! Coffee!"

The boy had set a tray with one cup, one saucer, and a china teapot on the dining table, and was now nervously flexing his left bicep, which he was surreptitiously kneading with his right hand. Whatever he had been introducing into his nervous system when I came must have been wearing off, because his gaze was clearer, and less hostile.

I poured, taking great care with what was obviously Phyllis's pot for when the Hadassah ladies come, and took a sip.

"It's okay?" He clutched his arm.

"I like it like this," I beamed, sitting down on the couch, putting the cup on the low table in front of me. The coffee was thick enough to stand a pencil in.

"You do?" He smiled shyly. "I never made it before."

I tried not to shudder at the jolt of caffeine I had just swallowed, somehow squashed my grimace into a smile, and asked weakly, "Just could you get me some milk? And sugar?"

"We don't have any milk, I don't think." He looked

doubtful as he went into the kitchen. After a moment he returned with a yogurt.

"Would this do? I mean, it's almost milk, and if you take the white stuff from the top . . . Or there's some sour cream, if you prefer."

You know? It was an improvement, which will give you some idea of the coffee. I sat sipping café au blueberry yogurt, listening to young Skripnik chat as I tried to figure out what to do next.

For which I at least had plenty of time. Young Skripnik—whose name turned out to be Jason, and not Leon Jr.—proved to be an eager, even thirsty talker, who needed no more than an occasional "Oh, really?" from me to keep rattling on. Talking, he reminded me of his father, flourishes of the long thin fingers, nervous bobbings of the prominent Adam's apple, and a deep, deep interest in himself. With the one difference, a charming one, that Jason shared his self-possession with me eagerly, like he had just discovered the only other person who shared his interest. Papa Skripnik had also talked only of himself, but had done so with the calm assurance that I would be as fascinated with himself as he was; Jason's attitude was more like thrilled surprise, and thanks.

And why not? It couldn't have been easy growing up in the Skripnik household. I was an only child too, but where I remembered my youth as talks with Pearl, skipping down the block to meet my father as he came back from the subway, shrieking as he swung me high, high in the air when I reached him, Jason's story seemed to echo with long silences. Doing models in his room. Playing toy soldiers on the rug. Sitting on the stairs into the back garden, where he wasn't allowed to mess up what the gardeners had laid out.

Had there ever been any love in the marriage? It was

hard to glimpse any through the cracks in Jason's chatter, but that didn't necessarily mean anything; when a marriage dies, it seems never to have made sense in the first place. Especially to a child, who sees only the fights, sees the father stalk off to his den, or the mother angrily stirring soup in the kitchen, slopping liquid onto the burners. The making up, if it comes, the child never sees.

The Skripniks had been divorced for only three years, but Jason's tale made it seem as though the divorce was simply the death certificate of something that had been stillborn and then hidden away for a decade in the Upper West Side brownstone.

And Phyllis, not surprisingly, had put all her excess energy, all her sexuality into the one thing she possessed. Jason.

Who laughed now, but guiltily, like a boy who has gathered courage enough to say aloud, "God doesn't exist!" but who isn't yet convinced he won't be struck by lightning when he does.

"Lessons! I had lessons in *everything*. Viola, because it was bigger than the violin. And piano. And ice skating, and gymnastics, and I couldn't watch television, except for *Mr. Rogers* and Snoopy specials. She used to get me up at *six,* so we could read together—even when I was in *fourth grade*! And *fifth*! And Hebrew lessons too! She made the rabbi let me read the whole Haftorah, not just a couple paragraphs, when I was bar-mitzvahed. The whole—uh, *damn* thing!"

He was sent to an expensive day school. Jewish, but Conservative, so it wasn't really a cheder or a yeshiva, but it wasn't a normal school either. So little Jason learned all about the Sabbath, and then violated it by going to baseball games, like all his fellow students. Whom he was goaded to be better than, and at the same time forced to be just like.

The more Jason talked, the more he seemed like a spring, wound tighter and tighter by his parents. The basic stock of conversation was quickly exhausted, but Jason's chatter was the more fervent for having no content. As Jason rattled on, his eyes watched me desperately, fearful that I was going to leave, or stop listening, or tell him to be quiet.

I would have, too, if I could have gotten him to show the slightest interest in Shmuel or to tell me anything useful about the other relatives. Of the latter, Jason knew nothing. His father had never taken him to visit them, in fact had never mentioned them.

Of the former, he said only, "From Israel? Neat. My mom says she'll send me to camp there, after I finish confirmation classes."

"But this man might be very useful to you there. It always helps to know somebody when you're in a foreign country. Why don't you get your mother to take you out to pick him up? He's your relative; he was coming to visit your father."

"Naw, the camp takes care of all the arrangements, you stay at a kibbutz." Then a sly smile flitted across his face. "The older guys say it's a fantastic summer, because of the girls."

"The Israeli girls?"

"Naw, there's a lot of Swedish girls come, it's right on the ocean." Jason did his best to look like a dispassionate imparter of information, but awed hope shone through his solemn face, making him look like a believer contemplating heaven. "Did you know that Scandanavians don't think bathing suits are healthy?"

I sneaked a peek at my watch and realized that it was now less than twenty-four hours until Shmuel arrived, and I still had not managed to pass him off to anyone, despite having sunk most of the week into the attempt. Tammy and Tanesia were still where I had left them Saturday afternoon, sitting in the abandoned boathouse, debating whether Jerry Hough from the Boy Scout Camp next door should be allowed to kiss either or both of them. What's worse, they had only until tomorrow afternoon to make up their minds, because I had to see my editor. And instead of getting rid of Shmuel, I had gained Phyllis, and now her son. Once again I was sitting in a chair, letting Skripnik words gush over me.

How much is revenge *worth,* I asked myself crossly. I wasn't just wasting my time trying to get even with Phyllis, I was risking my livelihood. My *career.* What, I demanded very sternly, as I shifted uncomfortably on Phyllis's couch, the plastic wrap sticking to my legs, exactly was I getting from all this?

The answer, of course, was nothing.

One borough away, it wasn't so hard to construct an evil genius with Phyllis's face, someone who was trying to frame me so that she could keep the Chagall. Here, in her living room, listening to the desperate freak of nature that was her son, I couldn't make myself believe Phyllis would have the guile to outwit even the pop-top on a can of salted nuts.

So why didn't I just stand up, put the letter on the table, say good-bye to young Jason, and leave?

Because of Pearl.

"Be a mensch," I could hear her say. Be a good person.

Do not confuse this with altruism. My mother has a special deal with God. Every time she does something good, God does something nice for her, which Pearl will demonstrate for you by tracing every bit of good luck back to something nice she did before but didn't want to talk about, such a good person she is. She finds a cab at five o'clock on Fifth Avenue, in the rain? That's because she gave two dollars to the old bag lady in Washington Square, the one with the bag from Ohrbach's. She bought Chrysler stock at $2.75 and sold it at $36? That's because she made a good home for Max, and never *once* told her mother-in-law that her chicken soup and matzo balls couldn't hold a candle to what her own mother had taught her to make.

So what was I to make of the fact that the only reward I could see for myself here was meeting the handsome Lieutenant Russo, who suspected me of theft?

I had *tried* to be a good person, damn it. I hadn't wanted the letter. I hadn't asked Skripnik to come to my house. And I *had* schlepped all over the five boroughs—well, two of them, anyway—doing my best to do what seemed right. Wasn't three days enough? Did I really owe it to a man I'd never met—never *wanted* to meet—that I should schlepp all the way out to Kennedy to pick him up? And what then? The Skripniks who had houses and money had made demands enough on me; how in God's name was I going to defend myself against one who was blind, penniless, and spoke no English?

I wasn't, that's how. At that second I understood with perfect clarity that I could either get up now and walk out of Phyllis's apartment, or be prepared to have blind Shmuel share my apartment until the end of time.

So I stood up and opened my mouth for a firm, and final, farewell.

Which I never got to say, because a key scraped in the lock.

9

"MOM! Phyllis! Midge!" we all shouted more or less together.

Jason leapt up as though we had just been found in his bed, and I suppose that the pink I turned would have supported a similar conclusion. Phyllis, key in hand and arms full of parcels, looked confused.

I had spent most of the day fuming that Phyllis Smolensky was playing me for a fool, and I had stormed over to Manhattan to give her hell. Which I remembered as she came into the apartment, then immediately forgot, because how can you be mad at anyone who is wearing an ankle-length dress of pleated brown wool, in which the toe of her shoe is tangled? To say nothing of her purse, which was hooked over the doorknob, making it impossible to bring her two shopping bags into the room, so that, hunched over and hopping, she peered perplexedly and in mute supplication, with eyes that I realized in a second looked strange because she was wearing contact lenses.

As a rule people wear contacts to improve their looks; conceivably that was Phyllis's intention too. Her glasses, though, at least kept the two wings of hair away from her eyes, and somehow disguised the fact that the two sides of her hair were of uneven length, probably because the left side was curly, while the right was straight. When she was wearing contacts, her head seemed to be permanently tilted, as though she were listening attentively.

"Here, let me give you a hand." I leapt up to help untangle her.

"How did you get in, Mom?" Jason was wrestling to take a bag from the other arm but got himself tangled with the purse and the door.

"I was over in Jersey, doing some shopping, and I stopped at Mother's, to get Shellie . . ." Phyllis was trying to untangle herself from her son and the door without taking her eyes off me, which didn't help.

"Who is this person, Phyllis?" someone said from the corridor, in a voice which made all three of us drop the straps of Phyllis's purse and stand up straight.

"Uncle Shellie!" Jason sounded surprised, but not pleased.

It took me a moment to realize that the man standing behind Phyllis was familiar not just because he had been my own personal nightmare since I was about seven, but also because I had seen him recently.

"You're from the funeral, right?" He stepped around

Phyllis, extending his right arm. I thought he wanted to shake hands, but in fact all he did was point a bony forefinger at me. "The one that Leon, that schmuck, was involved with." My hand, which was halfway up, dropped back to my side.

"They weren't involved, Shellie," Phyllis said timidly, still attached to the doorknob. "Were you?" she asked me, double-checking.

I opened my mouth to shriek my now familiar line about not knowing Skripnik, which I intended to follow by storming out of Peter Cooper Village forever, but then I shut it again, because it dawned on me that this Shellie person was the first person I had met so far whom I agreed with.

Leon *was* a schmuck.

And I had come into Manhattan because I was convinced Phyllis was framing me as Skripnik's mistress, which she had just denied I was. Numb, I just shook my head finally remembering to shut my gaping mouth.

Shellie said, "Whatever," and went into the kitchen. "You got any club soda, Phyllis? My stomach is giving me hell again."

I watched, awed, because Shellie Smolensky is the man that I have been terrified I might one day have to marry, ever since my father first took me to the bathing club out on Sheepshead Bay. You know the Woody Allen movies where he tries to act suave with girls? That's Sheldon Smolensky, except that Woody knows what his character and Shellie don't, that he isn't even in the same zip code with suave, that what they really are are skinny little guys with hair that won't stay down over their bald spots and accents that get dragged through so much nasal tissue that their voices make the hairs on the back of your neck stand up. You go out on a date with one of these Shellies, you had better be prepared to learn that where most human beings are 92 percent water, these guys are 92 percent arrogance.

How do I know this Sheldon was like that? Tortoise-shell glasses, a polo shirt so expensive it didn't have a logo on it, Italian silk slacks with the pleated, almost baggy waist and the pinched-in legs, bare, tanned ankles, loafers, and a sweater tied casually over his shoulders; all this gave me a hint, because they didn't go with Sheldon's looks any better than Phyllis's clothes went with her. Where her clothes though said "In theory I know how to dress like a person," his said "I'm rich, and fuck you."

He didn't make a good first impression. Nor did he seem to care. He came back out of the kitchen, glass in hand. He sipped, then belched.

"You got no limes, Phyllis." Then he looked at me. "So what, you just leave your door open or what?"

Which seemed to require *some* explanation from me.

"No, I was . . . Jason let me in. I was looking for Phyllis."

"She a friend of yours?" Still addressed to Phyllis, as though I was perhaps a new houseplant that had just been discovered to have aphids.

Phyllis finally got disentangled and came into the room, setting her parcels down. "I'm sorry, Shellie, this is Midge Cohen. She . . . we met when . . ."

"I did some translations for Dr. Skripnik."

For the first time Sheldon looked interested in me. "Translations? How?"

"How?"

"How did you do the translations?"

"What do you mean how? I know Russian, that's how."

"No, what I mean is, how did you do the translations?"

Thoroughly mystified, and getting angry, I said severely,

"I put my dictionary on my left, the letter on my right, and a yellow pad in the middle. Then I got a nice sharp pencil, and turned on my desk light. That give you enough to go on?"

The interested look in his eyes disappeared, and he waved a hand. "Feh, mechanical still. You see what I'm up against, Phyllis?"

I must have looked lost, or angry, or both, because Phyllis scurried to my side to explain. Taking my arm, she glanced at her brother, then at me, then at her brother again. "Shellie is in artificial intelligence, and he does a lot with machine translation. In fact—can I tell her, Shellie?"

"No," he said shortly, and went over to the television in the corner, which he switched on. "How come you're not watching the Mets game?" he asked Jason.

Phyllis still had my arm, which she released slowly. "Well, anyway, Shellie's got a business interest in translation."

There followed one of those silent tableaux, like directors who don't get to work in real theaters with curtains use to indicate that the act is over. Then, as if recovering, we all started to move again. Jason went back into the depths of the flat, presumably to flush the evidence of how he had entertained himself while his mother was away, and Phyllis and I went over to the shopping bags.

"You go to Jersey to shop?" I looked at the bags, all from expensive clothing stores.

Phyllis nodded, seeming preoccupied. "I grew up there, so I know where the stores are. I visit my mother and shop."

I held up a Bloomingdale's bag. "You go to Jersey for *this*? You know they opened a branch here in the city too?"

She snatched the bag away, seeming embarrassed. "I always get lost going uptown."

For a moment she looked like a child forgotten during hide-and-seek, who emerges while the rest of the birthday party is eating cake. Then she pulled herself together. "Jason isn't supposed to open the door for people he doesn't know."

Which was a polite way of asking why the devil I was there. The problem was, I wasn't sure what to answer. "I came over to give you hell because I thought you are framing me" is a poor conversational gambit.

"Oh, I was just around, and I was . . . wondering about the painting! Did you hear any more about—"

At which Phyllis put her hand on my lips, her eyes round with alarm. Then, her voice loud and phony, she said, "No, I decided to keep the bathroom the same color. You know how much the man wanted, just to paint *one* bathroom? Come on, you want to see what I bought?"

Doing my best to look like an eager, if mystified, girlfriend, I followed Phyllis into her bedroom and, as she gestured I should do, shut the door.

"Thank *God*." Phyllis sagged onto her bed, relieved, though still whispering. "You almost let the cat out of the bag."

"Why? *Is* it a Chagall?"

Even though I was whispering too, Phyllis said *"Shh!"* sharply, and jerked her head in the direction of her brother. "Look, I'm sorry, but Shellie is . . . well, he's having a bad time."

"Is it real?"

Phyllis shrugged, impatient to be discussing her brother. "I don't know, it was only yesterday, and you know how the police are. Poor Shellie. He's been telling me . . . his *problems*."

I had had enough of Skripnik problems. "Look, Phyllis, I just dropped in, and your brother and I just met, so, uh, maybe you shouldn't tell me, you know?"

Phyllis looked urgent. "No, no, it has to do with . . . *the picture.*" This last she didn't even whisper, but rather mouthed, so exaggeratedly that I could see all her back molars, and even so she glanced over her shoulder again. "See, Shellie is in the computer business—he's such a *genius,*" Phyllis interpolated fervently, with all the awe of a sister who's always had to play "the good one" while Shellie got to be "the smart one." It is a proven fact of medical science that all Jewish families have a pretty but dumb child, an ugly but good child, and a black-sheep uncle; this comes, I think, from inbreeding, like Tay-Sachs disease. "Fourteen years old, he was putting together radios, and he built, he actually *built* his first computer, gosh, clear back in the sixties or something. And he did really well at Stevens, so he started his own software company. Did fantastically at it, too."

"That's that artificial intelligence stuff?" I remember some of the AI types—that's honestly what they call themselves!—from Ithaca and Cornell, and I remember too that the real problem with artificial intelligence was the number of cheap jokes it seemed almost to beg for. I mean these guys were the sort that automatic doors don't open for, with their pockets full of pens, their thick, thick glasses, and the complexion you get from a diet of Twinkies, Coke, and too much exposure to fluorescent lighting. All of them had strange hobbies, too, like designing bicycles you had to ride lying down or inventing musical instruments that needed a large room full of electronics and a computer keyboard to play. A lot of them made fortunes with their gadgets, but one of the things money won't buy you is a way out of geekdom. I must say too that of all the AI and computer types, the ones that drove me the battiest were the machine translation crowd. I used to run into a lot of them, because they were all trying for Star Wars money, and the big bucks were naturally in Russian-to-English computer translation. They would appear in my office beaming with pride at their latest triumph, some scanning and programming combination that allowed a television that had gotten above its station to take some standard Russian phrase and turn it into a standard English sentence like "Persons in process of labor in all lands become one!" for which achievement they wanted my praise. *Me,* who had spent a fair chunk of my life actually *learning* Russian!

Phyllis shrugged again. "I don't exactly know, because it was all classified. But he had high hopes for it, he was really excited. See, the thing of it is, he's younger than I am, so when he was starting up, well, he came to us. For money."

"Us?"

"Well, Leon really, because he was a doctor. Not that we had much. I mean, people always assume doctor, you've got maybe *millions,* but . . . Well, anyway, we did have a little something, and Shellie convinced Leon. So we put some money in."

"Like a loan?"

"No, stock. We bought stock. Leon and I were one-third owners."

"And when the divorce came . . ."

"Right, we split it. I have a sixth, Leon had a sixth. And believe me, there were times I was very glad I had that! Shellie's company was doing *great,* with all the Star Wars money." She fell silent and began picking at her skirt.

"Was?" I prompted.

"Well, it's been a hard time for the industry. Congress got picky about the money, and then when Reagan started going to Moscow . . . And I guess there've been some problems with the product too."

"So what's that got to do with the painting?"

"Well, if it *is* real . . ." Phyllis picked harder and harder at her skirt, until she managed to pull a thread loose. "*Damn* it!" she snapped, and sat erect. "If it is real, then I think I know where the money was going to come from. To buy it, I mean."

Suddenly I understood. "Leon was selling his stock!"

Phyllis shrugged glumly and nodded. "Sort of."

"But what's wrong with him selling his stock? It wasn't like the house, was it? He didn't need your permission?"

"No, it was his. But see, that stock, it's not like GE or something, it's not traded on Wall Street. Shellie's company is mostly just him; a secretary, a couple of programmers, and what's inside his head. There weren't any other shareholders, and it wasn't really spelled out what happens if someone wants to sell. I mean, it was all in the family."

Until the family fell apart, I thought.

"Shellie doesn't have the money to buy Leon's shares back, not without liquidating, and when Leon tried to sell them outside the family, Shellie tried to get an injunction. But Leon was very insistent that he had to have the money, so they compromised: he could use his shares as collateral."

"For a loan?"

"Mm-hm. Except that when he applied, the bank naturally wanted to know more about the company, and . . ."

"And they decided the stock was overvalued!"

Phyllis nodded again, looking miserable. We sat in silence as I mulled this over, trying to fit this financial muddle in with the confused bits I already had. Why Sheldon should call Leon a schmuck was now clear, and I had some inkling why Phyllis had not wanted the painting mentioned. After all, it might not sit too well with her brother that all this trouble was for a *picture,* and besides, who knew how deep her feelings of sororal duty might go? Would she feel obligated to consider the painting Shellie's if it did prove to be a Chagall?

"Well, was the stock actually sold?" I asked, really meaning, was the Chagall actually bought, and if so, for how much? Because it still didn't make sense to me that a man like Skripnik, whose idea of valuable collectibles seemed to be a box seat from demolished Ebbets Field and a wad of Gary Carter's chewed gum would suddenly plonk down a large sum for a painting.

Phyllis shook her head, speaking as if she hadn't heard me.

"The real fault though is Uncle Herman's; his bank gave Shellie the loan in the first place, using the company as collateral. But now that the other bank is examining the books, Herman says he has no choice, he has to re-adjust the collateral."

I had a sudden and very vivid picture of Uncle Herman from the bank, who had given his bright nephew lots of money that belonged to other people and who now could feel federal inspectors breathing down his collar. So he needed something more to cover the loan, because the other bank had said the company's liabilities exceeded their assets, which is the polite way that banks have for saying your business has gone belly-up.

Not something that someone whose brains and Uncle Herman have let him build up a comfortable little business wants to hear. But how *much* would Sheldon not want to hear this, I started to wonder, because it didn't take long to figure out that this little financial glitch of bankruptcy would disappear if the stock were returned to the company, which then would no longer be subject to public scrutiny.

Which would happen, for example, if Phyllis inherited Leon's stock.

Which suddenly made Skripnik's death look curiously convenient.

It *could* have been coincidence. People *do* get beat up during burglaries in New York.

But . . .

The afternoon had made very clear that there was no shortage of *motives* for murder.

Jason Skripnik hated his father, but then every fourteen-year-old hates his father. If that were motive enough for murder, Manhattan would be ankle deep in blood. On the other hand, though, read the papers; teenage boys kill their parents all the time, right? Heavy metal music, dope, plus lots of hormones, a stunted sense of responsibility, and that Freudian nastiness can all combine to form a murderous monster, which maybe had blinked at me a half hour ago through young Skripnik's sudden rage. That glimpse had startled and confused me, because Teen Beast, if indeed he had been there at all, had immediately slipped back beneath the spotted surface of young Jason.

Phyllis? The first couple shelves of her books made me think I was nuts to suspect her of *anything*, let alone murder. People who read things like *Wanderings* and *My People* don't go around clobbering their husbands, correct? Still, if anybody would kill for a Chagall, wasn't Phyllis a good choice? Frankly, such a Phyllis Skripnik was not easy to picture, with the long ill-cut hair, the large nose and buck teeth, the mismatched clothes and air of inability, all right in front of my face—except that this wet noodle had also tied devious doctor Skripnik up in such contracts that she now owned every nickel he ever possessed. So Phyllis was a wet noodle with brains, and sound instincts of self-preservation.

Or maybe she was a dutiful sister, who would do anything to keep her brother's bankrupt company going.

But why let Shellie off so light? That self-righteous bastard out in the living room, making all of us listen to the Mets game, would *he* scruple at taking Leon's life?

Actual physical capabilities for murder not as abundant as motives, but they weren't lacking either. The boy was certainly tall enough to hit his father, Phyllis was not. Shellie was a close call, maybe two inches shorter than the doctor. But then, height wasn't so important if you were standing on the stairs. The boy certainly had the strength, but I was reasonably sure Phyllis did too; when I had grappled her into bed that evening, she had proven a lot more wiry than she looked. And all that baseball stuff around, there had to be a bat, so means wouldn't be much of a problem.

I brought myself up sharply right there. It's an easy thing to say maybe so-and-so murdered so-and-so, as though murder were as easy as sneezing. Which it is, in the movies and in books. We novelists make people do all kinds of incredible things, to keep our plots rolling along. But what I was trying to do, sitting beside snuffling Phyllis in that frilly pink bedroom, was to imagine someone physically, actually killing Leon Skripnik, for real.

Sure, I say it a hundred times a week, just like you do, "I could have *killed* him!"—but could you really *do* it? Really truly *kill* someone? Take a living human body and turn it into *meat*?

It's not just a matter of physical ineptness, either. Sure, it was hard to imagine Phyllis getting through a revolving door without problems, let alone breaking into Skripnik's home and clobbering him with something big and ugly, and Shellie looked more likely to bore you to death than anything else, but I was thinking of something else.

Have you ever killed?

When they tore down the building next door to mine, to put in an even bigger building, we suddenly were overrun with mice. I put out the regular traps at first, but I couldn't bear to throw away the victims next morning, with their eyes bugging out like lumps of caviar and blood congealed on their little noses. So I bought another kind of trap, a tray of some sticky substance that doesn't kill but just mires mice down. The next morning I found I had one little captive, absolutely stuck fast, exhausted from struggling, pathetic as can be. And very much alive.

I had no idea what to do. How do you clean off a sticky mouse, especially if it is likely to misinterpret your intentions? And even if you *do* get it clean, what do you do then? Drive out toward JFK and release it in the garbage dump there? Set it free in Prospect Park?

In other words, I had to kill it. That was what I had put out traps for. So *how*?

I finally decided that drowning was the most humane way, meaning it was least likely to make me vomit. I filled an old coffee can with water and dumped the mouse in, tray and all. What I had not reckoned on was how much life wants to live, even if it's only in a mouse. That exhausted little animal struggled and fought so hard that I finally had to hold the whole tray under water, where the struggle continued for a few fierce moments longer, finally to end in two tiny bubbles which slipped from the little nostrils, danced upwards through the water, and popped silently on the surface.

I dreamed about those two bubbles every night for a week.

So who of this family had whatever it took to batter a father, husband, or brother-in-law to death?

I stood watching Phyllis unpack her shopping bags, smiling at my own foolishness. *None* of these people could have killed him! I mean, maybe the painting wasn't a Chagall. Or maybe it was, and Skripnik had just made a lucky guess in an antique shop. Or won the lottery. Or had a lucky year in business. Followed by a not so lucky decision to walk in while someone was in his house. Okay, his son hated him, his wife hated him, and his brother-in-law was going to be put out of business because of him. That didn't mean that they had killed him, did it?

Except he was dead.

And the police were investigating.

Then I remembered there was one more suspect, who I kept overlooking.

Me. His mistress. The one who had apparently stolen his address book.

10

"JEEZ, Midge, first say hello at least!" Russo looked amused, a lazy smile on his face as he leaned back in the booth. "Go right to the heart of things, don't you?"

We were in a coffee shop about a block up from Russo's precinct house, where he had agreed to meet me when I phoned from the first booth that I could find after dashing out of Phyllis'. Peter Cooper Village is a rent-controlled island in a murky urban lagoon haunted by lots of creatures who don't look particularly cheery even in bright sun; now that dusk was drawing in, and I had just come to the suspicion that someone was trying to frame me as Skripnik's killer, the whole place was positively creepy.

Which is probably why I gave Russo the impression that meeting with me now—*right now*—was a lot more important than merely life-and-death.

He had suggested this diner three blocks from the station house, one of those places that has a mirrored revolving dessert case right by the door, slices of cakes and pies so big and gooey they could be ticket booths at Disneyland.

By the time I got up to the West Side it was dark, and the coffee shop was empty, except for a couple of pensioners, one at the last booth in the corner, one at the counter, both noisily slurping from bowls.

Russo looked a lot more rumpled than he had that morning. His tie was pulled so loose that the knot was nearly at his second shirt button, and his undershirt was showing. There was a soft curl of blond-gingery hair peeking over the neckline that I found very distracting.

All the long way uptown I had been rehearsing offhanded, subtle questions, how I would tease more information out of the lieutenant as if in passing, and how I would finally pounce, pointing out all the logical fallacies in his case, which would prove that I couldn't *possibly* be a suspect.

Which is probably why when I saw Russo in the back of the diner, head bent over his coffee, I swooped in, slid into the booth across from him, and screeched, "The housekeeper, lieutenant! How about the housekeeper? Since when do housekeepers work Sunday?"

My trump card, my ace. The one inconsistency I had been able to recall from Pearl's description of the article in the *Times*.

Russo looked me over for a moment, stirring his coffee and smiling faintly. Then, just as I was about to either pound on the table and demand an answer or get up and walk out in total embarrassment and perhaps join the Foreign Legion or something, Russo slid lithely from his side of the booth, stood by the table. He gestured with his right hand that I should do the same.

"What? Get up? Why?" I slid out, confused.

When I stood, he took my denim jacket from my shoulders with a ceremony that would have done justice to Pearl's mink stole and a tenderness that gave me butterflies. He hung it on the tree at the end of our booth, and, smiling that devilish grin of his, indicated I should sit again. When I did, he sat opposite me, smiled, and signaled for the waiter.

"Business? At the *table*? The street is for business; the table, that's pleasure. You have a bite, you catch your breath, *then* you talk. Okay?"

Which reminded me immediately that I had had nothing to eat since that gyro, about three murder suspects ago. I ordered the brisket special, while Russo just had seconds on the coffee.

I did some unladylike wolfing, wiped my face, and asked my question again, this time with some explanation.

Russo, still smiling, looked at me levelly. "That's all you want to know? You hoping maybe the cleaning lady has a free time slot now?"

I blushed, remembering the condition of the apartment I had forced him to search this morning. "No, but, well, I was reading the newspaper, and, I mean, this murder—"

"Hold it, hold it!" Russo sat forward, suddenly intent. "Who says it's a murder? You know it's a murder?"

Which sounded a lot like the accusation I had come up here to make sure wasn't leveled at me. "Of course I don't know if it's a murder. I mean, why would I know whether it's a murder? But if it's not a murder, then how come you answer the phone, 'Homicide'?"

Russo studied me with an attention that made me uncomfortable before he asked quietly, "So what's it got to do with you?"

"What do you mean, what's it got to do with me?"

"Just what I said: What's this guy's death got to do with you? How come you're so interested?"

"You hinting maybe *I* had something to do with it?" I sputtered, my anger magnified because I had spent most of the afternoon imagining myself saying those words to Russo, with the stress on different words.

Russo waved his hand. "Did I say I thought you had something to do with it? All I ask is how come you got so interested. You claim you don't know this guy, you only saw him once in your life, and then every time I turn around, bump, there you are. At the funeral, at his house, and now this, with some cockamamie question about a housekeeper."

"Well, don't you think that's *fishy*?"

Russo laughed. "There's something fishy about every death. Usually people aren't supposed to be dead. That's how come I get a paycheck, 'cause people are always being dead when they're supposed to be alive."

"No, no! I meant fishy about the housekeeper!"

Russo studied me for a moment, then shrugged. "You say you didn't know the guy."

"Yeah, well, until last Saturday I didn't, but I know a lot about him now! Like that he had stock in a company his brother-in-law owns because he needed money and he was going to cash it in, only he couldn't, because it was overvalued, so he was mad!"

"Who was, Dr. Skripnik?"

"No, the brother-in-law. Skripnik was selling the stock, and the bank found out the company was overvalued, and now the brother-in-law has to come up with a lot of money or his business folds."

"And you're saying somebody killed Skripnik for that?"

"Well, it's a reason, isn't it?"

Russo sat up, his face no longer amused. He turned his coffee cup this way and that in the saucer, like someone searching for the proper combination of words.

"Look, you're a writer, you said, right? So you think this is all very interesting, and maybe you want to write about it someday, and us cops are a bunch of flatfoot oxes, right?"

"I never said any of that!" I pushed my empty plate away angrily.

He shrugged, looking weary and sweaty. Rumpled. "Nobody ever does. But that's what it comes down to. Look, you live in the big city, you got crime all around you, you read about it in the papers, you see it on the TV. You think you know something about it. Am I right?"

He paused, looking at me until I shrugged and nodded.

"Bet you this is the first crime you ever really been involved with, I mean, where you know the people?"

I was about to shoot back that my purse had been picked and that I knew someone who had almost been mugged, but then I felt ridiculous. I shut my mouth, glaring at him, and waited for him to finish so I could tell him what I thought of his superiority.

Which I have to say didn't seem to bother him. "You're like everybody, or at least everybody who lives in a nice place in Brooklyn or down where that Mrs. Skripnik lives, and who's got some basic smarts and a little bit of luck. Death just isn't something most of us have to get involved with, until our natural time comes around. So it seems exciting. You want to play junior cop a little, learn all the new developments. No, no, don't apologize," he said, waving his hand, even though I hadn't been about to. "You think you're the only one? I go home at night, everybody's an expert, telling me how to do my job." He fell silent, still examining the cup. Then he looked up, his eyes now colder than I had yet seen them, the yellow-green glittering almost with menace. Russo suddenly didn't seem so genial.

"Let me tell you something, okay? Murder isn't glamorous. It's bloody and it smells and it's stupid. People kill other people to get money for drugs, or because it's hot and somebody stepped on somebody else's Air Jordans, or because they've had maybe a little too much to drink. You've got kids running around now, they watch cartoons all their life, cops-and-robbers-shows, that kind of thing, where guys are blown up or machine-gunned all the time. All kinds of nasty stuff. And these are *kids* watching it, so then some crack runner gives one of these kids fifty bucks and a pistol, says go do so-and-so, he's trying to sell on my corner, you think the kid is going to say no? There's kids out there don't even *shave* yet, they've killed somebody. And for *what*?" He thumped the table.

I was startled, by his tirade and even more so by his intensity. So was he, I guess, because he suddenly grinned and sat back in his chair. "Listen, I'll tell you a story, okay? About why my grandfather left his village. This is a man, when he came to America the Depression was just begun, he doesn't even know real Italian, let alone English. Just some dialect from this mud-poor village. Struggle? I remember as a kid, family picnics, we'd get him to take a hot coal out of the barbecue with his fingers. Like a trick, right? Because his fingers were that calloused from how hard he worked all his life. And every time he talked about Sicily, he would get a tear, right here." Russo put his finger next to his nose, at the corner of his right eye. *"But he wouldn't go back."* Now Russo tapped his forefinger on the table to emphasize. "You know why?"

I shook my head.

"Because he was the last cousin."

I waited. Russo had that same lazy grin, like he didn't really care to move his lips and jaw too much, but his eyes made plain that what he was telling me came from somewhere deep inside. He was leaning on the backrest, hand gesturing indolently, looking so handsome that I finally realized my mouth was hanging open.

"Okay, so?" I sat up, grimaced peevishly, and did some industrious crumb-brushing, so as not to keep gawking into those yellow-green eyes.

"So, about fifty years before my grandfather was born, this like great-great-uncle or something of mine, he had made a contribution to the village church. Four hairs from Santa Rosalia's head!"

I decided I'd better straighten the sugar packets too, because if there's one thing that us nice Jewish girls have difficulty keeping a straight face about, it's the little bits and pieces of saints that Catholics keep around to venerate. The thought that a prayer works better because you said it to the blackened leathery finger bone of some saint induces a certain, well, skepticism. So, you ask, what about when I went to Jerusalem and pushed the little piece of paper bearing Aunt Dora's prayer into a crevice in the stones of the Wailing Wall, because "that's the one place God is always listening"?

That's different, okay?

"Santa Rosalia, the patron saint of Palermo, who miraculously stopped the plague! You think such a relic was cheap? Four hairs cost this man—well, you can't say everything he owned, because peasants owned nothing. It cost him his freedom, I guess, because to pay for it, he indentured himself and his family to the local baron."

"Indentured? You mean . . ."

"This relative of mine basically sold himself as a slave, and his kids, and their kids."

"My God, why?"

Russo shrugged again. "That part nobody remembers. It was a vow of some sort that he had made to the saint." Russo played with the coffee cup, looking thoughtful. Then he chuckled, without real amusement. "Anyway along comes Garibaldi, Sicily becomes part of the Republic, and suddenly everything is modernized. Including the church. Palermo gets a new bishop, young guy, forward-looking, who wants to cleanse the church of dubious practices. So he sends commissions out all over the western part of the island, to make them verify the art and document the relics, and in general make sure that what the peasants are worshipping isn't idols. And of course my relative's contribution—he's an old man by now—turns out to be four hairs from the tail of a horse, and so they strip the silver off the box and chuck the rest out with the rubbish."

"And he had made himself a slave for that? So what did he do?"

"Two days later the son of the relic dealer had a hunting accident. Shot himself with his own shotgun, one barrel in the chest, the other in the back of the head. A week or something after that, this great-great-uncle, he slipped and fell, broke his spine."

"A feud, in other words."

"A feud. I've tried over the years to get Grandpa to count how many of our people we lost, but . . ." Russo pursed his lips. He sat up straighter and smiled, as if apologizing for boring me. "Lots anyway. Dozen, couple of dozen. And think how many widows that meant, and orphans, with no father to feed them or raise them. The only way out for my grandfather was to come here, before the feud passed to him."

I shivered. "That's a horrible story."

Russo nodded. "That's my point. How many people dead, and for what? Horse hairs. Pretty glamorous, huh?"

I didn't answer, because I was thinking about his story. Not *thinking* thinking, but ruminating, letting my brain show me scenes of Sicily and mountain villages, crones in widow's weeds and lots of young men, like Russo here. The diner was beginning to get busier, and outside the sky had turned the sodium yellow of night in New York. I pulled my brisket plate toward me and was pushing the pickle around in my cole slaw, watching the three fine muscles that ran along the tanned curve of Russo's cheek, now shadowed with the day's beard, the texture of buttered toast.

I had come to Russo crazy, tense, jangly, and now, overcome by some drowsy lethargy, I didn't care. I was happy, I was interested.

Which is probably why I let myself be driven home.

I hadn't expected Russo to give me a ride home, and I would have refused if he had offered; no matter what he had said that morning, Brooklyn is *not* on the way to the Bronx. Problem was, Russo never offered. We just left the diner, talking, went down the street, talking, and got into his car. Talking.

Even so, I might still have refused as we came up to his low red car; it was the sort you usually see with little red lights running blip-blip-blip across the back and maybe a license plate frame that says "Italian Stallion," and you just *know* the driver's name is Vinnie. I even opened my mouth to ask Russo where his furry dice were, but then he switched on the engine and the radio began to play.

"*Classical* music?"

Russo looked embarrassed. "You don't mind, do you? WQXR is doing a Scarlatti thing tonight; it's his birthday."

"His birthday? You know when it's Scarlatti's birthday?"

"Well, he was from Palermo, you know."

So we rolled quietly down the West Side, watching the Hudson slide past the new towers in Jersey, and then hammered over the chunks of pavement by Battery Park. Russo drove fast but calmly, sliding confidently in and out of openings, never braking or accelerating too hard. I let myself sink into the bucket seat, trying not to think about me and a cop and Scarlatti and what Pearl would think if she knew.

We talked about Sicilian celebrations, which led us to Sicilian monstrous family occasions, which sounded a lot like monstrous Jewish ones, and not just because we both had an uncle who wasn't really an uncle who always got drunk at weddings, bar mitzvahs and first communions and would get up on the bandstand and make them play "Hava Nagila" or "That's Amore," depending. But that's family, what can you do, look at the people we grew up with who never left home, but on the other hand you can't be like the ones that moved out to the Island, so far away you're always on the Long Island Expressway to come visit, and who'd want to live on the Island anyway, I mean how many Pathmarks and Toys-R-Us does a person really *need*? As for the friends who had gone the other way, into the city and the gray-pinstripe-suit-with-tennis-shoes life, who needs that rat race either? What kind of money did they have to be making, just to live in their tiny apartments, and what kind of life was that anyway, that you couldn't raise kids in? We agreed that the boroughs were better, and the ethnic neighborhoods especially, because of all the interesting food you could get, but then we struck out on comparing restaurants, because we had never been to the same ones, and anyway who can afford to eat out on what *we* make, except for some take-out place, like my beloved Chinese around the corner?

I must admit that by the time we were passing under the Brooklyn Heights Esplanade, with lower Manhattan shimmering across the East River, questions were starting to have the strained quality of conversations where you really only have one thing you want to talk about but you can't, so you talk about everything else but barely listen to a word either of you is saying, other than to stay alert for the slightest hint as to whether or not Russo was single. Like this was a date or something. Which it wasn't, right?

Russo fell silent as we pulled onto the parkway and started looking thoughtful as we turned out onto Cortelyou Road. He parked in the No Parking in front of my building, staring straight ahead, drumming his thumbs on the steering wheel, making about as much noise as my heart was, throbbing up my neck. The Scarlatti was still playing softly, one of those intricate keyboard pieces where you have to cross your hands over, and the night air was as soft and clean as the air ever gets in Brooklyn. My mouth was dry, my palms were wet, and I knew I had to say something. So I did.

"Look, you never answered me. What about the housekeeper?"

Russo looked puzzled. "Housekeeper? What housekeeper?"

"The Skripnik murder, what I came to the diner to ask you about. How come the housekeeper that found him works Sundays?"

"You've convinced it was a murder then?"

I didn't like the mocking in his voice. I started feeling around for the door handle. "You didn't come all the way down here to Midwood to ask me about that address book because the guy slipped on the stairs."

Russo acknowledged this with a shrug, then laughed, beating a quick tattoo on the steering wheel. "Actually, way things look, he might have." Then, serious, "But like I asked you before, what do you care? You wanta write about this or something?"

"No, what I want to do is *forget* it, instead of having policemen waking me up to ask about address books! But what do you mean, he might have?"

Russo moved his head slightly, which put the top half of his face in shadow. After a longish silence, as if he had been thinking, Russo said softly, "The housekeeper said there was blood on the stairs, but she cleaned it up. Before she found Skripnik. Some outside too." I saw him shrug, his shoulder disappearing for a moment into the gloom hiding his face. "But that still doesn't make it murder. Fact, find that guy thirty blocks north of there, nobody would even bother to ask, but he's a rich guy, good neighborhood, so . . . Got to ask all the questions, you know. Like about the address book. It was missing, I had to ask. That bother you?"

"Bother me? Of course it bothers me! You're running around checking *me* out, and meanwhile the housekeeper and Sheldon Smolensky—"

Russo chuckled. "What do you have against Sheldon Smolensky?"

"Have you *seen* Sheldon Smolensky?!" I flared. "He's

a *creep*, one of those guys at school dances, they'd only do the slow dances, you could feel them trying to work up the courage to touch your butt but never daring to, so the whole time they *sweat*, getting grubby marks all over the back of your dress, their hearts beating so hard they can't even *talk*, you're afraid they'll have a coronary and die. And afterward, they lie to their friends about all the places you'd supposedly let them touch you. They all grow up to be rich gynecologists and oral surgeons and divorce lawyers and stockbrokers, which is supposed to make them irresistible, because all us girls want out of life is a nice Mercedes station wagon to cart our children around Westchester in, taking Whitney and Fraser Smolensky from ice skating lessons to judo."

Russo waved his hand. "Hold it. Sheldon Smolensky proposed to you?"

"No!" I slammed my palm down on the dashboard. "NO God damn it! I'm not Skripnik's mistress and Smolensky didn't propose to me!"

"Who said you were Skripnik's mistress?"

"YOU did!" I almost jabbed him in the chest with my finger. "This morning, with that address book!"

Russo's lips grew thin and straight; I wished I could see his eyes. "I told you, it's my job. We've got a guy who's dead, cause of death unknown and suspicious, I have to check out everything that might have something to do with the case."

"What do you mean 'cause of death unknown'? The paper said he had head wounds."

"The papers, the paper." Russo made a noise of something between exasperation and amusement. "So that makes it murder? It couldn't be suicide?"

"*Jee*-sus, Lieutenant." I so was angry I yanked up on the door handle, turning on the interior light and making both of us blink. "How many suicides do you guys get who beat themselves to death on their own heads? It's not exactly the best method for doing yourself in, is it? Maybe you cops ARE as dumb as everyone says!"

"The gas was on," he muttered.

"What?" I shut the car door again, putting us back into darkness.

"I said, the gas was on. In the kitchen." He said it a little louder, but still with the air of a man who wished he could take the words back. "The papers don't know about that."

"You've got a dead man with a housekeeper who works on Sunday, a brother-in-law that he's putting out of business, a doped-up son who maybe hates him, an ex-wife who's hysterical, the gas is on in the kitchen AND SO YOU INVESTIGATE ME?" I think I hit the dashboard again, because Russo reached up and took my hand, which I immediately snatched away.

"That's what an investigation is." He sounded uncomfortable. "You try to find out everything about everybody who turns up. I mean, that address book *is* missing, you know."

"Everyone?" I was falsely calm. "So you've checked out Shmuel Skripnik too, then?"

"*Shmuel* Skripnik?"

"Ha! You didn't know about him, did you?" I pulled up on the door handle again and started to get out. Russo put his hand on my arm again, which I jerked away from so hard that the seat belt caught.

"Okay then, you want to play detective with me, do you? You want to tell me how you figure Eleanor Walters, then?"

I slowly sank back into the deep bucket seat and looked over at Russo, whose face looked bizarre with the dome light shining straight down on him, making deep shadows of his eyes. "Eleanor Walters?"

Russo's smile looked almost devilish in that light, his eyes invisible in shadow. "Ahha, see? The nurse at Skripnik's practice. You checked her out?"

I vividly recalled the funeral, a stiff blonde with a tight bun and a grim expression. "My god! She's a suspect too?"

"I didn't say that." Russo's voice was severe, and he put up both hands, as though in self-defense. "All I said, you want to collect suspects, you ought to put her on your list too, right?"

"Why?"

"Well, you figure it out. Small practice, not one of your big clinics. Just Skripnik and her, and receptionists, but those Skripnik has trouble keeping, they quit on him. Walters, though, she's there eight, nine years. Then the doctor gets divorced. . . ."

"My god." I shut the car door again and swiveled right round to face him. "Skripnik and his nurse were having an affair?"

"Did I say they were? I just say you want to play detective, you think about everything, right? So here's this lady, single, not so young anymore. Not old exactly, but that old biological clock is ticking, you know? So what's to keep her from whacking him one on the head, he won't marry her? You know how women can get, a certain age and not married yet."

Okay, *maybe* that biological clock business wasn't pointed at me—what I had seen of Eleanor Walters at the funeral didn't make it hard to believe she could be a hormonal time bomb—but nobody was going to sit in front of *my* house and tell me that being single could drive a woman to murder. I smiled my best society smile, opened the door again. "Gee, I guess you're right. Us single women get so desperate."

"Hey, I didn't mean that!" He once again grabbed my forearm, which I didn't resist this time but didn't react to either. "Or maybe it's the other way; she spurns him, he gets uh, despondent, and turns on the gas."

I plucked his hand from my arm like it was a little distasteful. "I'm quite sure you're right, Lieutenant. Turns on the gas, hits himself on the head a couple times to make sure." I swung my legs out of the car. "And Skripnik's cousin suddenly turning up from Israel like that, obviously it would have nothing to do with it. Thanks for the ride, good night." I got out of the car.

Russo leaned across, nearly impaling himself on the gear shift. "Wait a minute, what's this about a cousin from Israel?"

I bent down. "Gee, I'm just a writer, you know?" For punctuation I slammed the door, spun on my heel, and strode toward the apartment building.

I must have hit Russo's head. He shouted. I turned around, halfway to the front door; he was standing by his car, rubbing his head. "She's a Jew," he shouted after me.

I stalked back down the sidewalk, ready to punch him. "WHO'S a Jew?"

Still rubbing his head and looking angry, he said, "The housekeeper. She doesn't work Saturday, she works Sunday."

"She's a Jew?" I was trying to figure out whether this was some sort of tasteless joke. "She's black."

Russo smiled, like he was in control again. "Miriam Mizrahi, belongs to a group calls themselves Black Hebrews. Mrs. Skripnik hired her about ten years ago, because she understood about all the kosher laws and stuff. You see, Midge, that's what I'm trying to say."

"What's what you're trying to say?"

"You don't cut your own hair, am I right? You don't take out your own appendix, and you don't do your own taxes. Or come to that, you don't collect your own garbage on barges and ship it out to sea, do you? You get people who are professional at it to do it for you, am I right? So why should you do your own police work? Better you keep the mysteries for those two girls of yours, let them worry about solving things."

"My girls?"

"In your books. Let's see, *Mystery at Indian Rocks* and . . ."

I blushed. "How do you know my books? You have kids?" I was surprised how much my stomach clutched as I asked that.

He laughed. "Hey, I'm a cop, I'm *supposed* to find things out, right?"

I turned away and stumbled up the steps into my building. Phyllis, Shellie, blood on the Chagall, the missing address book—and Russo was investigating who I was. I started to shiver.

11

THURSDAY broke gray and rainy, one of those days that looks colder than it really is, so you put on too much clothing and feel clammy all day. I had woken up early, a dull throb somewhere back of my eyebrows, and made a cup of coffee you could float a spoon on, which I drank as I stood by the kitchen windows, listening to the cars squish by on the parkway, watching the old ladies trundle slowly to the avenue, their grocery carts squeaking.

The night before, for the first time since Aunt Dora had left me her apartment, unlocking the front door had failed to give me that little zetz of delight, that this is *my* door, *my* home, *my* life. There were dishes still in my refrigerator, the Sunday *Times* was still in the shower, the bed was still unmade, my bathrobe thrown over the pillows, a dustball stuck to its lapel, and chapter eleven was still waiting for me in the Selectric.

There are those, like my mother, who claim that a bit of vigorous cleaning is just the thing for moods like that one. Straighten the living room, and you straighten your mind, the theory goes. A little sweat, a little polish, and before you know it you are humming like Snow White in the Seven Dwarves' cabin.

The problem is, this only works if you have something a little lighter to think about than I did that particular evening. The load on my brain was distinctly on the chubby side, like was I *really* a suspect in Skripnik's murder? If it *was* a murder. But how could it be anything but a murder?

Blood on the stairs, blows on the head, gas on in the kitchen, and the painting upstairs. It was like something out of *Alice in Wonderland,* where I was Alice in front of the Red Queen, subject of court proceedings that would give "sentence first, verdict afterwards!" I knew that I had not committed this murder, but how many TV shows, movies, and murder mysteries have I run across about the Wrongly Accused Falsely Imprisoned? In all of those stories, the situation is always like this, a swirling cloud of messy evidence, lots of people who *could* have committed the crime, and one poor schmuck around whom, with the connivance of the *real* villain, some clever detective or prosecutor weaves all the random bits and pieces, until the role of perpetrator fits the innocent person like a glove.

"You say you didn't *know* Dr. Skripnik, Ms. Cohen, and yet you were present at the inventory of the deceased's apartment?"

"You claim you have no interest in Dr. Skripnik's affairs, and yet you went to Brighton Beach to search for these supposed relatives of his?"

Whoever was doing the prosecuting there in my imagination talked a lot like the prosecutor in *Rumpole of the Bailey*, with that supercilious British voice that makes absolutely clear that you are a liar from birth and beneath contempt besides, which only made the answers I tried to offer seem so feeble and contrived that I began almost to *believe* I was lying.

Especially about the letter. The letter was the hardest to explain.

If I wasn't a suspect, then why didn't I tell Russo about that damn letter? That letter was *evidence*, you stupid bimbo! In fact, four or five times I even went to the phone to call and tell him about it; twice I even began dialing. Each time, I put the receiver back. In the first place, I lectured myself as I carried newspapers to the garbage chute, washed the dishes, and changed the sheets on my bed, You only have his work number, and he won't be there now.

And in the second place . . . well, wouldn't he take the call as a kind of apology? A come-on, almost?

I do not like to admit this, but only part of my brain spent the rest of the evening worrying about whether or not I was going to Sing Sing for murdering Skripnik. There was another and very insistent part that kept reconstructing the evening, trying to decide whether or not Russo had been working up to something physical.

In fact, by about one, that part was winning, keeping me staring at the ceiling as I reran the scene, the Scarlatti, bucket seats so low and deep you were practically lying down anyway, that fast smooth ride with the nighttime lights of the Big City twinkling through the T-top, followed by that wonderful, heart-thumping pause that I was pretty sure I hadn't felt since I stood with Paul Blank wondering what was so special about this little black cow and why didn't this weird guy kiss me.

He's a *policeman*. How the hell could Russo have been going to kiss you, let alone anything further? He thinks you *did* it, for crying out loud!

So I punched the pillow and flipped onto my stomach, determined to relax even if it killed me. Except it really *had* seemed like he was about to make a move of some sort, before I had to go and open my mouth. Maybe it was a trick? Soften me up, turn my head, and then I'd confess, or make some fatal error?

Jesus, Cohen! NOBODY works like that!

Along about three A.M. I decided that I was pretty much absolutely certain that Russo *had* been about to kiss me, but instead of putting me to sleep, that conviction worked like one of those video games where you've killed all the evil gnomes only to have the screen go *blip* and now you've got a roomful of fire-breathing wizards to contend with.

Such as, was Russo single? Would I ever see him again? What did I *care* whether I ever saw him again?

The sky was beginning to go gray when my brain got around to what was really disturbing me, which is what always disturbs you at four thirty in the morning after a night of insomnia. Life, and what I was doing with it.

I wonder, when you're just about to check out, do they give you some sort of performance score card? Like you made 83 percent correct choices in your life, so we can give you a B− on this? Or do you go to wherever it is you go still wondering, *should* I have let Russo kiss me good night?

I mean, why was this such a problem with me? I had let Sasha kiss me almost without thinking; in fact, I'm not entirely sure I wasn't the one who kissed first. Why did the question of whether or not Russo kissed me lead so rapidly into wondering what I was going to have to look back on, when I got to be as old as Aunt Dora had been? Did I *want* to be writing the eight hundredth installment of Tammy and Tanesia? To be just one more old lady, squeak-squeak-squeaking my cart to the market, the high point of my day when I caught the deli boy trying to sneak me whitefish salad after I'd clearly asked for herring?

But then why did that seem so terrible, if I had fought so hard to be single *now*? I had *been* married. To Paul Blank, with his round little head and his hands pink from milking and the big country house outside Ithaca, where even though the forced air from the furnace blew notes off the message board by the phone and peeled the oak veneer from all our furniture, the cold drafts *still* slithered about your ankles like turgid snakes.

But maybe not married to Russo, with his slow lazy smile, his beard like grains of wet sand on a golden Sicilian beach, his eyes the color of sunshine filtered through a canopy of trees . . .

Was I wasting my life?

When your brain is batting that sort of question around, the telephone sounds like a bomb. I must have jumped four feet in the air and was still quivery when I got to the receiver.

"Hello?" I croaked, mouth dry, then tried again. "Hello?"

"Excuse please, I am searching Meedge Cohen?"

The woman's voice was unfamiliar, but the accent wasn't: the mechanical, textbook English of a native Russian who hopes that volume will accomplish what fluency can't. Telephone solicitation, I figured; with all my Russian friends, the petitions I've signed to support refuseniks and dissidents, the money I've given to émigré organizations, I have wound up on some very weird solicitation and mailing lists. You'd think after the nutty calls that I've gotten before, most of them starting just like that, I would have had the sense to hang up. Instead, mustering asperity, I said, in English too, "I am *Margaret* Cohen."

"Friend Leon Skripnik Margaret Cohen?" The woman's voice rose hopefully. "Leon Skripnik?"

"Well," I began, "*friend* is a little . . ." then "OH MY GOD! You're the cousin!" I squealed, understanding. "You're Leon's cousin! Finally! Listen, Phyllis told you, right? To call, I mean. God bless her, she half scared me to death, I thought . . . Well, no matter what I thought, she found you." It was incredible how much that voice rearranged my mood. Because Phyllis *had* called, which meant she *wasn't* trying to frame me, which meant even if Russo *had* suspected me, he couldn't, not now, and *that* meant . . .

Maybe he could try to kiss me again?

"Yes, cousin." The woman sounded confused, so I switched into Russian. "Look, when can we meet? I've got—"

"Ah, you speak Russian!" she squealed herself.

"Sort of. And I've been trying to find you all week, I've got something of yours . . ." I had the word *letter* on the tip of my tongue but then remembered how many times already I had presented this letter to various Skripniks, only to have them give me the dead-fish look and hand the letter back. Pique a little curiosity, I told myself. Slyly, I added, "Leon left it here."

"Excellent!" the voice cried, then, more soberly, "I may get it?"

"Sure, but I think maybe the best thing would be if we

met. It's a little complicated, and . . ." i stumbled, acutely conscious that my fish was not yet firmly on the hook, and I wasn't about to have this woman disappear again, leaving me with Shmuel.

Fortunately she seemed to grasp the reason for my hesitation. "There's something you want?" She sounded weary, but resigned.

"Well, frankly, there is." I felt embarrassed, a little, but grateful too that it looked like finally this would be easy. My desire to wash my hands of poor blind Shmuel may not have been the most charitable emotion I've ever had, but no question it was genuine. Shmuel and the Skripniks had cost me a week's work, several nights' sleep, and a chance with the best-looking man who had ever sat outside my apartment maybe deciding whether to kiss me.

"Okay, understood," the woman said with a sigh. "Where and when?"

I gave her my address, repeating the numbers three times to assure myself I'd made no mistake and then almost hung up; just before I did, I remembered one thing more.

"Your name! What's your name, please?!"

"Faina." There was a pause, then she added, "Bender. Faina Bender."

You've heard me make fun of the émigrés, the way they dress, their inability to keep appointments, their chutzpah about what you should do for them. You've also listened to me kvetching about how I had lost this entire *week* to looking for this woman, so I can see how you would wonder why I spent the next two hours showering, tidying my apartment and . . . Well, why hide it? making cookies. I even wondered whether I ought to go out and get some flowers, before I remembered that where the florist on Ditmas used to be there was now a video rental place.

Why the fuss? Well, some of it was guilt, as I said; I was being pretty calculating in my determination to hand off Shmuel, so I felt I had to do something to pretend I wasn't. And some of it was just sheer giddy relief. How else could this Faina have gotten my phone number, except through Phyllis? So Phyllis *must* have taken that address book and just never bothered to tell me. And rightly too; it was her letter, Faina *should* call me. Why should I have to waste more time running her down?

The biggest reason, though, was, well, I kind of like émigrés. Most of them, they're sweet people, the same kind of schleppers as your Uncle Izzie and your Aunt Rose, except that bad luck got them born in the Soviet Union instead of the Bronx. Born in the Bronx, your Uncle Izzie starts maybe as a shoe clerk, works hard, moves out to the Island, then buys himself his own store in a mall near where the Sunrise Highway intersects the Cross-Island Parkway, and now he has a boat, he sends his daughters to Barnard in the winter and France in the summer, and he goes to the Holy Land for Passover, where he can visit the three benches he donated for Liberty Bell Park, his name right there in brass. He remains a schlepper to the end, but a comfortable, secure, and productive one, whose children feel a God-given right to go to expensive restaurants wearing the big jewels and loud clothes that make WASPs grind their teeth, and they always send the wine back, with loud complaints.

You take that same Uncle Izzie, though, and start him out in Russia; first thing he has to live through is the famine of 1918–1922, then the famine of 1932–1934; after that there's the purges, then World War II, and if your Izzie is *still* alive after the Doctors Plot of 1953, when Stalin didn't kill the Jews that remained only because he died before he got the terror machine completely cranked up and running, then all Izzie has to worry about is that his daughters can't get into any form of higher education and his sons get beat up after school and in the army because they're yids. You know what accomplishment is, in an environment like that? Not the house, not the overdressed, overindulged daughters . . .

It's just being alive.

And besides, about accomplishment, for anybody born in the USSR, what could ever sound more impossible, more unreachable than living in New York? Izzie from the Bronx, back with the shoehorn and the Brannock device, might occasionally have let himself dream about the store he would one day own. Any time between 1917 and 1970, a Russian Jew could maybe dream they would send him to the moon, but *America*? That's *insanity*, not ambition.

Then suddenly, one incredible day—Khalloooo Brodvay! An achievement like *that* makes the Donald Trump story look pretty small potatoes.

Not that there was much of the tycoon about Faina Bender, when I opened my door to a short woman with dyed blond hair and dull gold lower incisors. She was perhaps an inch smaller than me but stockier, with the shoulders and arms that you get from a lifetime of lugging string bags full of potatoes and tinned fish on buses with no empty seats. She had on a cheap cotton print dress that was really a little too short for her thickish and somewhat veined legs and that didn't look right with her shoes—black, open-toed spike heels. Soviet life is hard on women, so her age was impossible to figure; she could have been my contemporary, or she could have been Pearl's.

"Hello? May I come in?" She peered from the hall, smiling in a diffident way. "I am Faina . . . the cousin of Dr. Skripnik?"

"Come in, please, welcome!" I was feeling exuberant, elated that my quest was so nearly over. "Come in, sit down. May I give you tea?"

"Oh, I don't want to trouble, please. Just I'll take our property, and then I'll go. You are already too kind."

By now I had invested a week in this, and it didn't take more than a glance at Faina to know that the butter was already spread pretty thin in her life, making it doubtful that she was going to be excited at the prospect of inheriting her cousin Shmuel, especially if Shmuel was arriving expecting an operation and some rich-cousin coddling. Meaning I was going to have to put some real enthusiasm into my entertaining, if I was to avoid being left holding the letter again.

"No, really! The tea is all made! And I can't tell you how happy I was at your phone call! I searched and searched—I even went out to Brighton Beach, but I didn't know your name, and people thought maybe it began with an *L*." I was shooing her toward the sofa, where I had cookies and tea already set out on a painted tray I had schlepped all the way back from Moscow one January when I had taken a group of Ithaca students there on a tour.

"You were looking for me?" She appeared almost frightened, huddled against my sofa, darting glances around the room. Then, "Brighton? Why Brighton?"

"Something the doctor mentioned, that you were a singer. Sit, please, have some tea, and some cookies!" I held up the plate of my tollhouse, which had turned out unusually well, with almost none of the bottoms burnt.

No Russian turns down a sweet. Faina sat, still in her

raincoat, clutching her oversize purse to her knees; she would have looked just like that, sitting on the Moscow metro. She shrugged, eyebrows raised, and took two cookies, looking away. "Singer? The doctor said that?" Cookie crumbs scattered across my coffee table as she munched. "What else did the doctor tell you?"

"Please, take another." I laughed, a little shrill. The relief was getting to me, I think. "*Nothing,* that was the problem! Dr. Skripnik said very little, actually, so it was the only way I had to try to track you down."

Faina took another cookie, and sipped her tea. She appeared a little more relaxed, sliding back into the couch a little. Her raincoat stayed firmly on, however. She shrugged. "Singer? Singing, maybe, but singer? It was a dream, back there. At weddings, parties, that sort of thing, people always begged me to sing. Faina, they'd say, you have the most beautiful voice! Folk songs, Beatles, classics, you name it! But the stage? Back there, to do *anything,* you've got to have connections, you've got to have the right papers—and what Jew ever gets the right papers? So when we got here, I try, but . . ." She smiled, her face looking very pale, almost washed out in the rainy light. She sipped tea, letting the silence tell me about how she had learned it was lack of talent, not lack of Russian blood, that kept her off the stage.

Rostropovich, Brodsky, Baryshnikov, they missed this part of the emigration, but a lot of the rest didn't. The part where you learn that maybe it's better to have your poetry not printed for political reasons instead of because no one wants to buy it, or to think that you didn't become head doctor because you're Jewish, instead of what you find out here, that your medical skills are about two notches above those of a medieval bloodletter.

So some émigrés go back, and some spend their time

whining about the false promises of America the golden, but most take a long sober look at their skills, their talents, and their possibilities and set about building lives out of what they are, instead of what other people say they are.

Growing up, it's called when we demand that others do it, but when it's ourselves, we call it growing old, time running out before our ambition does, so that we will leave undone more than we will have done. For many émigrés, after a lifetime of cursing Soviet circumstance, this is the last disillusionment, which gives them the look of Faina—timid, watchful, and quick to grab at the cookie plate when it passes by, half-convinced that her hand will get slapped for doing so.

"Well!" I laughed brightly, then took three cookies myself, to show Faina that it was all right. "We can't all be Galina Vishnevskaya, can we?"

Faina shrugged and wriggled on the sofa, studying me with eyes that didn't look so timid anymore. "Listen, sweetheart, who are you, anyway?" Her gaze narrowed. "I insisted to Dr. Skripnik, and he promised, nobody else was to . . . take part. And where's my, uh, property?"

I opened my mouth, then shut it again, because suddenly I began to wonder whether Faina knew the doctor was dead. Meaning I had to be the one to tell her? I stared at Faina, who was getting suspicious and excited. "My God, you didn't know?"

"Know what?"

"About Le—Dr. Skripnik. See, he left it here, Saturday night." My voice was squeaky, because I was tense. What do I tell her first, that I wasn't Skripnik's mistress, or that he was dead? Damn it, I had spent my entire *week* telling people I wasn't Skripnik's mistress. "That was just before he . . . uh . . ."

"*Saturday?*"

"Well, Saturday night, almost Sunday morning. And then—"

"Saturday?" she interrupted to repeat. "This property, he left it Saturday?"

"He wanted my help, that's all. He was supposed to pick it up, but—"

"I don't like games, you tell him that. It's *Thursday* now, and my son and I, we've been looking all over. I don't have a car, you know, so I have to get my son to leave work." Faina was getting angrier and angrier, punching at the air with her right forefinger like Mussolini giving a speech. "This is no way to treat—"

"Your son came with you?" I interrupted. "Where is he?"

Faina lost her thread for a moment. "In the car, outside. Why?"

"Well he shouldn't be out there, in the rain! I mean, bring him in, we'll give him a cup of tea."

Faina pulled herself to the edge of the couch, glaring at me. "He gets all the tea he needs. Just give me what Skripnik left here!" She slapped her knees with her vinyl purse, as if suddenly overcome with exasperation.

I was puzzled by Faina's anger, and a little hurt that my tea party was such a disaster, but looking at things soberly, it was best to do as she said. Give her the letter, tell her about Leon's death and the arrival of Cousin Shmuel, then let her son take them out to Kennedy in his car. And I, Midge Cohen, would retire from the world of Skripniks forever.

"Okay, it's in my bedroom," I said, trying to make my voice businesslike. I got up and headed for the other end of the apartment, where I had left my purse with the letter in it. Put out with Faina, I was simply going to hand over the letter and show her the door. Seeing the envelope, though, scrawled all over with Shmuel's myopic handwriting, the leaking ballpoint and the cheap kraft-paper envelope, I felt a pang of guilt again. Mad or not, I was about to saddle Faina with a relative who was expecting a rich American cousin, not a down-at-the-high-heels émigré as impecunious as himself. No matter how put out I might be with Faina, that didn't seem fair. Not without warning.

"It's too bad, isn't it?" I put the envelope on the table near Faina. "Here you all were about to be reunited, and then . . ."

Faina looked at the letter, puzzled, but made no move to pick it up.

"It's for you," I urged her.

"From Dr. Skripnik?" Faina looked at the letter as though it might bite her.

"For him. For you, now, I guess. It's from your cousin Shmuel, to Leon."

Faina still looked blank.

"Shmuel, from Chernigovka? Then he emigrated to Tel Aviv? You *do* know Shmuel Skripnik?" I asked sharply, because I had the growing sensation Faina was about to bite me. You know the expression "gimlet-eyed"? I don't think I ever really understood what that meant until Faina looked at me just then. Kind of like someone running an awl through your breastbone, except instead of an awl Faina used her faded blues.

"Very convenient," she hissed. "The big hurry, then this *cousin*, just like that. And you, and this—this *letter*." She waved her hand contemptuously, then threatened me with her finger. "This is not Russia, you know, that poor working people can be robbed! America, there is justice here!" She stood, so abruptly that for a second I thought she was maybe going to sing the national anthem.

"You don't remember cousin Shmuel?" I asked, surprised, with the now familiar sensation that I was about to lose another round of Musical Skripniks, a defeat in which I was damned if I would be gracious. "He's coming. Today, as a matter of fact. He needs medical care, and I guess he was hoping, Leon being a doctor and all, that—"

"Sure, a cousin," Faina repeated venomously. "I don't know what you are trying to work here, sweetie, but you can tell Doctor Skripnik that in the first place, I wasn't born yesterday, and in the second—"

"Look," I interrupted hurriedly, "I don't know what you think I'm talking about or what you're talking about, but there's something I think you don't know."

"What?" Faina asked, looking like some sort of scruffy, plump lizard backed into a corner.

I took a deep breath. "Skripnik's dead."

"*Gospodi,*" Faina whispered after a long moment of silence: *Lord.* Exclamation or prayer, I wondered, watching her deflate back to merely bedraggled, pale blue eyes round in her white face. "He died?"

"Saturday or Sunday," I murmured, unable to think what more to say. Outside I could hear the rain pattering down through the mulberry leaves, and the car tires on the parkway. There were distant thumps and knocks, the sounds of the building, which seemed to make the silence in my apartment even deeper. I looked at Faina, the Soviet émigré, faded, worn, exhausted.

And I had just informed her that her only tie to America was dead.

"He was found dead, so everything is all tied up in legal formalities."

Faina clenched her fists, the rough knuckles turning redder. Her jaw was knotted, and there was a flush high along her neck. She looked at me with defenseless, watery eyes. "That means lawyers and wills?" she asked in a strained voice.

I nodded, looking over at the letter, which was still in the middle of my coffee table. How could I force blind Shmuel on her *now*?

We probably would have been sitting there still, had there not been a knock at the door.

I leapt up, grateful for anything to break that heavy silent gloom, thinking that must be Sasha, because I had heard no buzzer from the outer door downstairs. Russo had warned me it's a mistake to make that kind of assumption, and in the future I think I'll remember. Because when I opened the door, there was a man standing there. Thickset, with a broad chest bulging out into the kind of gut men get from holding their gut in, pretending it's really chest, all this emphasized by his wide red suspenders. Big hands, with short fingers, their backs sprouting black hair. A bandage on his left hand, gauze looped around his thumb. He wore a short beard that was supposed to disguise his double chin but didn't.

"Yes?" I tried to look as forbidding as possible, wishing I had left the guard chain on.

He put his hand on my stomach and moved me to one side as though I were a bead curtain. He smelled of sweat and garlic, and something sharper, like turpentine or Pine Sol.

"Faina? What's the holdup? The whore give you the rabbi or not?" he growled in Russian.

"She speaks Russian, Vitka." Faina was at the door, eyes wide with alarm.

I wasn't overly pleased myself. "Yes, the whore speaks Russian, and now the whore asks you to get the hell out of her house!"

The ape-man shrugged. "Happy to. Just give me what's mine."

"I don't know what you're talking about." I was furious now. "Are you getting out of my apartment or am I calling the police?"

Grimace. "More games. I am growing tired of games. Listen, girl, Dr. Skripnik *told* us you have it!"

"I have *what*? Anyway, you mean Mrs. Skripnik." I was getting a little disgusted myself. "I don't know what she told you, but the only thing I've got that belongs to you is right there on the table. So why don't you take it and get the devil out of my apartment, all right?" I pointed from where I stood, trying to maintain some kind of authority by hanging on to my doorknob.

Vitka looked where I indicated, but Faina said, fairly sharply, "It's just a letter."

"Damn it, that letter is the only thing of Skripnik's that I have! Now will you get out of my house!?" I even pushed against the man's shoulder, with about as much effect as if I was trying to move my refrigerator.

Vitka plucked my hand from the knob and shut the door.

"You're lying," he said, with a little smile I didn't like one bit.

The click of the latch went up my spine like electricity. I stood in the corner, trying to control my panic. This was my own apartment!

"I am giving you three seconds to get out of here, and then I'm calling the police," I said switching to English, because you can't be icy cool and imperious if you're also worrying about using the wrong genitive plural.

"Picture first, then we leave," Vitka said indifferently. His English had that nasal quality in the vowels that even the best Russian speakers of English never seem to get rid of, so they sound whiny, even when they're not. He looked around my apartment indifferently, then went to Dora's couch and sat. After a moment's impassive silence, he wriggled forward to fill his meaty paw with a handful of cookies, which he shoveled into his face, sitting back to chew and dropping crumbs on his shirtfront.

Speaking with all the nastiness I could muster, I said, "The only thing of Skripnik's that I've ever had is that letter. As for this *picture* of yours—" Then, suddenly, illumination! Excited, I shrieked. "My God! You want the Chagall!"

The two of them glanced at one another. Vitka nodded, and relieved and excited, Faina took my arm and began pumping it. "Yes, yes! Chagall! You *do* know our painting! You know where it is?"

"So it *is* your Chagall then?" I sat down opposite Vitka. "Is it really by Chagall?"

Faina and Vitka exchanged glances again, then Vitka began to fiddle with the teacups, avoiding my gaze. "Yes, it's by Chagall," he finally said.

"And you just *lent* it to Skripnik?" I tried to look stern but could not suppress a grin at the simplicity of such people. A painting worth *millions,* that they lend out like you or I would lend maybe a cup of sugar.

"He is family," Faina said, making *family* sound like something off Moses' tablets.

"It's a long story." Vitka shifted uncomfortably on the couch, still rearranging teacups on the tray.

"Yes, but a *Chagall.* What's something like that *worth?*" I couldn't help wondering about these two, who walked around in clothes that could have come from a rummage sale and possessed a painting worth maybe millions. A painting which they had *lent.*

Vitka waved dismissively. "Money, what is money? That picture belongs to our family. It was a gift, from Mark Zakharovich to my great-grandfather; a gift from a genius! Do you talk of the *price* of such a gift?"

"Your great-grandfather knew Chagall?"

"My great-grandfather *studied* with him! Grew up with him!"

"I remember him well," Faina cut in, in Russian again.

"Chagall?" I tried to remember when Chagall had left Russia. Sometime in the early twenties. Which would make Faina seventy?

"No, no, my grandfather. Solomon Skripnik." She shook her head, smiling at the memory. "Even as an old man, in Leningrad, he would paint, his hands all gnarled from arthritis. My mother would put a brush in his hand, and such magic! Roosters, and cats, and little mud huts!"

"Your grandfather was a famous painter too?" I had never heard of Solomon Skripnik.

"No, no, just a painter. A dreamer, when he was young, but he stayed in Vitebsk, got a job. Not like Chagall. Grandfather said that Chagall was a bad boy, a scandal. At the painting academy he made fun of the others—even of the teacher! And he wore makeup, too, like Esenin. Rouge." Faina mimed dusting her cheeks. "So no one was surprised when he ran off to Petersburg. But my grandfather, he was a good boy. He helped his father in the shop, went to school. And then came the Revolution and the civil war and the world war. Grandfather was in Leningrad through the whole blockade. He used to talk about how they put on plays, to cheer people up, the actors so hungry that they fainted reading their lines. He painted scenery. There was no oil paint, so he used candle wax dyed with beet juice and grasses and saffron to get colors. And it worked, until one of the actors learned that these dyes were edible, and then they began gnawing the paint off the scenery." Faina was smiling, admiring her grandfather. "Can you imagine such a world?"

Now Vitka growled. "It was in such a world that great-grandfather held on to that painting. You said yourself he could have sold it, traded it for bread or meat. Famines and more famines, the bombing, the war, and he preferred to look at that painting and starve, rather than sell it and eat. And *you* were going to sell it!"

"For *you*, Vitka, for *you*!" Faina said, and burst into tears.

"That money I don't need." He turned away from his mother, his face thunderous.

Faina wept almost soundlessly, while Vitka chased the remaining crumbs around the cookie plate, trying to pick them up with his thick fingers. The rain continued, a steady drizzle that sent drops zigzagging erratically down my dirty windows. Surrounded by books, feeling damp and chill, listening to someone describe horrors from Soviet history, I might have been back in Leningrad. Gently, I asked Faina what she had wanted to get Vitka money *for*.

"To start a video shop." She looked up sharply, as though I were going to take Vitka's side. "In Jersey City. For the emigrants, and other people. There is good money in video shops!" This to Vitka, apparently part of an old argument.

"Akh, mother." Vitka twisted in disgust.

"It's a good business, Vitenka," she cooed, as though she were trying to get him to swallow a bitter medicine. "You don't need a lot of money to start it, and everybody watches the movies. I talked to Sofi; her cousin's good friend has one, not for émigrés, just English, but out in

Ronkonkoma, and they take in *thousands*. Every week *thousands*!"

"I'm not saying it's not a good business." Vitka was slapping the back of his left hand against his right palm, making an unpleasantly loud noise. "What I'm saying is it's a sin. You hear me? A SIN! I will find the money. Somewhere is *someone* that will lend it."

Faina flared up, shaking her finger at her son. "What bank is so stupid? To lend twenty thousand dollars to a Russian émigré who doesn't even own the shirt on his back?"

"Bank?" Vitka waved his hands in apparent despair. "Who said *bank*?"

"Wait a second!" I had been drifting along, uncertain what I was supposed to do in this mother-son argument, which for some reason was being carried on in my living room. The mention of money, however, caught my attention. "Twenty thousand? You were selling the picture for that little?"

Faina turned on me. "Twenty thousand is such little money to you? Happy woman! *You* may not respect such money, but do you know how many floors I must wash to make twenty thousand? On my *knees*, with the hot water turning my fingers into the hands of a drowned corpse."

"No, no," I waved my hands defensively. "That's not what I meant; what I mean is, that's all you wanted for the painting? Twenty thousand?"

Unexpectedly, Faina sat, her face very sad. She sighed, spreading her hands wide in helplessness. "It was not a sale. I could never sell it." She glanced at Vitka, who was still glowering away like some Moloch devouring firstborns. "I kept thinking of what grandfather had said, like

Vitka here told you," she went on, her voice very small, "how they had preferred to starve and look at the painting, and what it cost us to get it out of that place."

"Russia, you mean?"

"If they had found it, we would still be there," Vitka growled. It was hard to tell whether this was accusation or admiration. He looked at me. "She didn't tell me where it was. I thought we were leaving it there."

"You *smuggled* it out?" I looked at Faina, astonished. She smiled shyly and shrugged. "There are ways."

I could bear it no longer. I stood up, walking about the living room, waving my arms. "My God, you have this painting, this real Chagall, that has been in your family for *years,* through wars and famine, and that you smuggled out of Russia, that you could be maybe in the Gulag now if they caught you—and this painting you were going to sell to Leon Skripnik for a crummy *twenty thousand dollars?*"

"*Not* sell. It was, what you call it, *collateral.*" In English. "On a loan." Faina was embarrassed again.

Vitka, attempting to be funny, but too bitterly, added, "Anyway, she asked twenty-five thousand."

"I just said that that was what you needed to open a shop." Her halfhearted attempt at self-defense fizzled miserably away. "But Dr. Skripnik said twenty was the most he could loan us." Faina now drew herself up with dignity. "We are not wealthy, we have nothing to get a loan with, to start our future. Vitka, he wants to go to the loan sharks, but I'm afraid, I hear things where I work, what they do if you don't pay. So I asked Dr. Skripnik. He was very good to offer to help us, and the painting he can hold until we pay him off." She turned to Vitka. "That's not selling it, and besides, it is not with a stranger. Dr. Skripnik is *family.*"

Some family, I barely restrained myself from spitting, too mad to wonder at Faina's choice of tenses. For a moment I wondered how loathsome Skripnik could possibly have been. Even if he couldn't tell art from a box of cereal, Skripnik would have had to have known that that painting was worth ten times what he was loaning to Faina, if not a hundred. Even having known the doctor but one short evening, I could easily imagine the kind of a loan Skripnik would draw up, and the chance timid little Faina had of ever paying it off. That son of a bitch! I looked at poor pale, washed-out Faina, a rag wrung almost empty by life in the Soviet Union, from whom Dr. Skripnik not only was perfectly content to just about *steal* a valuable painting, for a fraction—a decimal point!—of its real value, but the man had had the brass-bound, oak-hearted CHUTZPAH to offer a counterbid that was twenty percent lower!

Then I felt a kind of guilty glee; Pearl is quite right that you should never be glad about anyone being dead, but it was hard not to feel a certain justice had been done in the case of Dr. Leon. Here was a man who was maybe an eyelash more ethical than the mustached villain who ties beautiful orphan girls to railroad tracks, but instead of him snatching up the Chagall, the Angel of Death snatches *him*.

Then I remembered that maybe Skripnik was going to have the last laugh anyway.

"Oh my God!"

"What?" "What?" Vitka and Faina, startled, both looked at me.

"I just . . . I mean . . ." They both looked so tattered and downtrodden sitting there that I didn't have the heart to point out that Skripnik might be dead, but he still had the painting. In his house, among his effects. Phyllis maybe didn't know where the painting came from, but I doubted that would stop her from accepting it once it passed to her.

"Look." I tried to sound as calm as possible. "Is there . . . do you have any proof that . . . of ownership?"

They both brightened. "So you do have the painting!" Vitka said.

"No, but I know where it is, and I think I can help you get it—if we can prove that it's yours!"

12

VITKA pulled himself up to the edge of Dora's bottomless couch, so that he looked like a bullfrog on a lily pad. His legs were spread wide, his belly stuck out, and his hands were on his knees; his face was serious and glum. "Prove it's mine? I have to prove that my property is my property?"

I opened my mouth to explain about Russo and the blood, then shut it again and waved my hand, meaning explanation would come later. It was nearly noon, and somewhere out over the Atlantic Shmuel was right now fumbling through an El Al kosher lunch, trying to tell salt from pepper by touch. I was attempting to sort out some ideas, which was not easy in the jumble of the last few days. The Chagall belonged to the Benders, and Skripnik had all but stolen it: that offended my sense of justice. My initial flood of forgiveness for Phyllis was also ebbing away at the thought that she was going to benefit from Skripnik's smallness of soul, to the tune of a Lower East Side apartment, an Upper West Side brownstone, *and* a Chagall big enough to eat breakfast on. Maybe putting up with Leon Skripnik for years had earned her the first two, but certainly not all three.

Especially since that would mean that Faina and Vitka got the rented walk-up in Jersey City and the clean patch of wallpaper under where the Chagall used to hang.

And I got cousin Shmuel.

Which gave me an idea: if I had any hope at all of somebody other than me picking blind Shmuel up at Kennedy, it was Vitka here, the drawback being that so far he hadn't seemed exactly the soul of charity. But maybe he wasn't such a bad businessman,—meaning that if I did something for him, such as getting him his picture back, then maybe he would do something for me, to wit, pick up Shmuel and let me get on with my Skripnik-free future.

Not a bad plan, except for the fact that I was far from confident I could talk Russo around to agreeing that the painting rightfully belonged to these two and should be handed back.

"You have nothing, nothing at all, that proves the picture is yours? A copy of the agreement with Skripnik, or a bill of sale that shows you owned it, or, I don't know, insurance papers?"

"Insurance papers? Do you think we could afford to insure a painting like that? And bill of sale? Chagall *gave* that to my great-grandfather, and *we* smuggled it out of

Russia!" Vitka stood, waving his arms. "The picture is ours! My great-grandfather *starved* for that painting! Why must I prove that my property is my property?"

I was half listening to Vitka, my heart sliding into my Top-Siders. But I was also thinking, remembering . . . There was *something* there, with Russo. The way he had listened to me in the diner the night before, and then in the car, and our parting, with him maybe almost kissing me, me almost inviting him up . . .

Russo seemed to like me, didn't he? So wouldn't he kind of give me the benefit of the doubt, if I asked him the favor?

Except, did I want to ask him the favor? How much I liked him I hadn't even started to sort out yet, because I was only just letting myself believe even a little bit that someone as handsome as Russo would ever like me. And if he did like me, and I liked him, well, that made a lot of problems. Like that he wasn't Jewish, and I'm not Sicilian. And he was just a cop, who talked like a cabbie. Which Pearl would *certainly* point out to me, after I introduced him to her.

And besides, was I going to do that? I didn't know if I wanted to get married again, which I didn't know why I was worrying about it, because no one had mentioned *dating* yet, and anyway, I didn't even know whether Russo was single.

Faina was still staring into space, pale and worried. In the gray light of the rainy morning her face was wrinkled like a drying apple, crow's-feet clutching deep into the skin around her eyes. Her face powder stood out against her skin, making her look grainy and air-brushed, like a Soviet photograph. It was easy to imagine her standing up to sing before a roomful of drunken strangers, struggling to overcome their roar with her breathy, watered-down little voice. A woman who had never had a real life, just something always a little ersatz, in which she was never quite pretty, never quite well off, never quite happy, never with a man she truly loved.

Faina suddenly brightened. She dug in her satchel and came up with a piece of paper, a much-folded letter. "Would this do anything?"

I took it from her and opened it, smoothing the creases in the heavy, very expensive paper, which Faina had wrapped around a Polaroid snapshot of the painting. I glanced briefly at the picture, the Hasid dancing with the Torah, and looked at the letter, which had an embossed, two-color logo, CULTURE RESEARCH ASSOCIATES, with an address in the East sixties between Park and Lexington. It was dated about two weeks previous and addressed to Skripnik. "Re: Watercolor, photo of same attached, submitted for our appraisal. In the opinion of our staff, the work submitted is consistent with early works of Marc Chagall and there are no grounds for ascribing the work to another artist. The conclusion of the staff is that the work submitted is quite probably a genuine Chagall." Signed by someone whose signature was illegible, with big curling underletters.

I looked up, confused. "How did you get this?"

Faina looked at her son, who shrugged and looked away. "It was . . . when we were making arrangements. Dr. Skripnik, mm, gave it to us."

Vitka turned back from the window, angry. "He was afraid that Mother might be cheating him, taking his money and leaving him nothing, because he doesn't know anything about art!" Vitka indicated his mother with a wide-flung arm, a gesture that looked almost contemptuous. "And *she* agreed to pay for it!"

"Vitenka," Faina remonstrated softly. "He didn't trust. It wasn't so unreasonable. And the loan was for you."

Vitka snorted again and once more looked out onto Ocean Parkway, while I looked down at the letter again, my contempt for Skripnik now so large that it had become a kind of wonder. Not only was the man willing to cheat his own relatives out of this painting, and for pennies at that, he was so damn cautious he made them get the painting examined before he would risk a cent! And he made them pay for the examination!

"I'd be afraid even to *ask* what percent he wanted on this loan," I muttered to myself, in English, as I fingered the paper, which was as crisp and stiff as those brand new twenty-dollar bills the money machines give you. Instead of mucking with Dr. Leon, Vitka would have been better off going to the loan sharks.

I was idly rereading the letter, trying to imagine how Russo would react to it, when gradually I realized something was wrong. It took two more readings before I figured out what it was.

"Hold it!" I must have shouted, because the other two snapped around to stare at me; they had been huddled together by the window, muttering to one another. "Hold everything!" I repeated, waving the letter. "What are we talking about here? This letter says 'watercolor'!"

Vitka grabbed my arm, hard enough to make bruises, the gauze digging into the bend of my elbow. "Listen, sweetheart," he said suddenly in English, and also loud, like for some reason he thought I had moved two rooms away, "you got lots questions, how about some answers now? You can't play me for an idiot, say you don't know about the watercolor. Skripnik *told* us."

I jerked my arm away violently. "Told you *what?*" I

hissed, ready to hit this Neanderthal who had pushed his way into my apartment.

"That the sketch is here," he said, for the first time sounding not quite so confident. "It is, isn't it?"

"HERE?"

" 'It is at girlfriend in Brooklyn,' " Faina whined in what I guessed was an imitation of Skripnik, while Vitka, impatient and disgusted, said, "You are Midge Cohen and this is Brooklyn? Then this is where my watercolor is supposed to be."

"HE TOLD YOU THAT I WAS HIS GIRLFRIEND AND THAT THE PAINTING WAS HERE? HE GAVE YOU MY **ADDRESS**?" It hurt when I shrieked that; I wondered whether I hadn't ripped something.

Vitka shook his head. "Of course not, why do you think it's Thursday already, that we didn't come sooner?"

Faina finished the explanation for him, with that downtrodden, washed-out smile of hers. "Telephone. It took a long time. There are a lot of Cohens in Brooklyn."

I felt stunned, overwhelmed by too much information, none of which fit together very well. I decided I might as well start with the little stuff.

"You keep saying watercolor," I said, feeling the soreness of whatever I had done to my throat. "But I saw a big oil painting ..." I held my hands out vaguely, the letter flapping.

The two of them looked at one another, hesitating, and then began talking at once. Faina silenced her son by patting his arm. She smiled at me, shrugged. "That's just it, it's a very big painting."

Vitka stepped around her, glaring. "There is a watercolor study, about so large"—he indicated something the size of a large book—"of the main figure in the picture."

I looked at the Polaroid snapshot in my hand more

closely and realized that the photo indeed showed only the large central figure, with none of the smaller ones behind.

"And that's what you took to this Creative Whatsit?" I rattled the letter. "There are *two* Chagalls?"

Faina nodded, then looked at her glowering son.

It made sense, I guess. I had started with one Skripnik, and now I had a whole zooful. Why shouldn't the Chagalls begin multiplying too?

"Skripnik has *both* pictures?"

"You understand." Faina came over to look at my arm, which she massaged gently, speaking in a low voice. "That was the arrangement. The picture, the little one, it was like a guarantee. Dr. Skripnik agreed the big one was too large to carry around the city, and besides . . . well, anyway, I let him have the watercolor checked, and then when he was satisfied, we were going to give him the big one."

I understood in a rush, almost stunned by Skripnik's behavior. Not only is he willing to cheat his threadbare Russian relatives, not only is he too cowardly to risk having anyone find out about the big painting, but he also insists upon that mean-spirited verification, after which he . . .

"He refused to give you back the watercolor?"

Faina winced, glancing at Vitka, who was leaning against my windowsill, thick, hairy arms crossed over his chest, a look of deep displeasure on his face. "No, it wasn't like that," she objected quickly. "Things were just, mm, very sudden. He wasn't sure, he wasn't sure, and then suddenly, he decided." She looked abashed again. "But he didn't have the money."

That was the last straw. "Skripnik told you he didn't have the money? He robs you, he cheats you, and then he asks for your *sympathy*?" My contempt was so great that my lips were trembling, which made it sort of hard to talk.

Vitka looked like he was about to explode, so Faina put her veined, rough hand on his shoulder. "Money, he had the money." She looked shrunken, apologetic. "Just, it was a check, and I asked him the whole time, no check." She smiled as though expecting me to laugh at her. "Crazy émigrés, right, don't trust paper? But that wasn't it, it's the taxes, the government, what happens to our benefits from the Jewish immigration people if all of a sudden I'm cashing checks for twenty thousand dollars."

That they wanted cash to get around taxes didn't faze me; most of the émigrés would do the same, because where they came from the only taxes there ever were were so arbitrary and steep it was like a fine, not a civic duty. But I suddenly saw a glimmer of light here. "Wait, let me guess! This was Saturday, right? And he was in a big rush, but he didn't have the cash, and he promised he'd get it to you Monday?"

Faina and Vitka looked at one another; after a shrug, Vitka nodded once, furious.

Obviously Skripnik had been dithering, maybe hoping to beat the price down a little more, or maybe just reluctant to part with that much money, even if he was getting the art bargain of the century. Or maybe, I don't know, he really *didn't* have that kind of cash, maybe it was all tied up in certificates or something. Maybe that was why he had tried to cash in Sheldon's stock, instead of just because he wanted to make Sheldon's life miserable, as I had been suspecting.

But whatever the reason, there came that Saturday morning when Shmuel Skripnik dropped out of a clear blue sky and into the mailbox.

As the philosophers teach us, things change.

Another cousin, another Skripnik. Somebody who *might* know of the painting, or might even have a claim on it, and maybe wouldn't even let Skripnik have it at all.

Skripnik wouldn't know, because he couldn't read the letter.

What he *could* do though is worry, which he must have done pretty heavily, because suddenly he had decided this loan nonsense had better be hurried along.

"When he didn't have the cash, why didn't you just take the painting back?"

The two Russians looked uncomfortable, as though I had put my finger on the very thing they had been kicking themselves for all week.

"Well, it's—" Vitka began, then looked at his crossed arms, because Faina had also begun talking. "Such a *big* picture, and he is family."

"No, no, the *little* picture, the watercolor! Why didn't you at least insist on getting *that* one back?"

Again they looked at one another. Then Faina stared at me, saying in a flat voice, "Because he said you have it. That's what we came for."

I am reasonably certain that it was at this point that I stopped getting mad and began to think about getting even.

"Come on, put on your coats." I shooed both of them toward the door.

Faina looked at me suspiciously. "Where are we going?"

"To get your pictures back," I said grimly before going into the kitchen to make a few calls.

It wasn't easy to convince Phyllis that she should let me back into the brownstone. The locksmith was finally coming over to her Peter Cooper place for sure, and then she had to go back over to her mother's to return the set of keys she had borrowed from her, and anyway, she didn't want to go to the brownstone ever again, the last time had upset her too much. Once she admitted that she had keys, though, I knew she was going to let me in, because I kept hinting around that I knew something about the painting that I couldn't tell her on the phone. Finally curiosity overcame her, and she agreed to meet me there at two o'clock, though with no particular grace.

Convincing Sasha to pick up Shmuel was even harder.

"Why must *I* go to Kennedy to get this man?" he roared into the telephone, indicating his irritation by refusing to speak Russian with me. At the moment he sounded so much like this ox Vitka who was cluttering my apartment that it did not improve my mood any.

"Because I *can't,* and *somebody* has to!"

"Meeeedzh," he said, giving my name the most alien, Russian mangling he could muster, "there in this city are ten millions who can go to airport, and only one who promise to unplug Karla Braverman's kitchen sink."

"Karla Braverman? You refuse to do me this one little favor because of *Karla Braverman?*" I erupted. Karla Braverman lives on the sixth floor, in the back. She is tall, single, and a little too skinny in most of her places except for the boobs, which she usually displays so bouncily in some tight spandex exercise suit that she looks like a picture from the neon edition of *National Geographic*. She is an aerobics instructor, a job I always figured girls took because they weren't bright enough to be career car rental clerks, and she has bouffy processed hair that makes her look like a Jewish Barbie doll and her eyes are too small and she chews gum, and I never used to think about her at all, until one day when Sasha happened to remark that she sunbathes in the nude. Since he also refused to tell me how he knew this, Sasha's discussions of what he is going to do for Karla Braverman tend now to irritate me.

"It is little favor to go all the way out to Kennedy and then to bring this man who I never met all the way into Manhattan?" Sasha finally capitulated, with what seemed even less grace than Phyllis had shown. "All right, but Midge, please, never ask me *big* favor."

Which made me so mad that I was even nicer to Russo than I had planned to be.

"I've got a surprise," I purred, when they put me through. "Can you meet me?"

He laughed. "Hey, funny coincidence, you know? I was planning on calling you later. A surprise? What is it?"

"If I told you—"

"Yeah, yeah. It wouldn't be a surprise. But hey, I can't just leave work."

Either I was a lot madder at Sasha than I thought I was or considerably more worked up, because suddenly I heard myself dropping my voice down into a register as close to Lauren Bacall as my throat can get. "A lady asks you to meet her in the middle of the afternoon for a surprise and you say you're busy?"

Russo laughed. "So okay, maybe I'll have a surprise for you too," he said. "Three o'clock?"

"At Skripnik's apartment." I waited just long enough to be certain he had understood where I wanted him to meet us and then hung up. Let him wonder about *that* for a couple of hours, I thought, trying not to think about what else I might have led the detective to think about.

Faina and Vitka were still in the living room, where I could faintly hear them muttering to one another. I apologized as I went back out that I had kept them waiting; both looked up, wary and puzzled.

I must have sounded a little hysterical, or perhaps my excitement garbled my Russian, because they continued to look dubiously at one another as I tried to explain what we were doing. On the third or fourth try, Vitka suddenly relaxed and sat back in the couch, grinning.

"All right, I get it. Let's go!"

At which, I confess, I got a real thrill, from doing something I don't often do: lie and get away with it.

Don't get me wrong. I don't like to lie, and I'm not very good at it anyway, but *sometimes,* well, there is no alternative. I mean, if I had explained that I was only pretty sure the watercolor was still at Skripnik's, and that even if it was and we found it, we were *still* going to have to get it away from Phyllis, and even if we managed that, it *still* didn't mean Russo would agree the big painting was theirs . . . Well, with all that uncertainty, why would Vitka and Faina agree to schlepp all the way back into Manhattan? Which if they didn't, then who was I going to give Shmuel too?

So it wasn't really *lying* when I told the two émigrés that I had an idea where the watercolor was, and how to get it. Think of it as good salesmanship.

It wasn't a perfect plan, but given what I had to work with, it didn't seem bad. Going out the door I felt so clever and pleased with myself that I decided I would allow myself one final pleasure when this afternoon was all through.

I would finally tell Pearl *exactly* what I thought of her meddling in my social life!

I went back into my kitchen to telephone, but she wasn't home; I redialed, to leave a message with the doorman, that Pearl should meet me outside Skripnik's apartment at six, because I was taking her to Rumplemeyer's.

Which ought to tell Pearl how angry I really was.

Family code. When I was a teenager, the way my parents used to handle *really* serious subjects, like that I shouldn't date this guy, or I couldn't go to the country to camp with my girlfriends, or the new bathing suit I had just bought with my baby-sitting money, that if I wore it out of the house, they would kill me, was to get out the ice cream, maraschino cherries, and Reddi Wip and make me a big huge sundae, which I would sit meekly at the kitchen table and spoon into myself as they yelled at me. The ice cream was supposed to make it clear they loved me, in case their words gave me the opposite impression. Over the years I learned to judge the seriousness of the upcoming talk by the quality of the ice cream. With what I wanted to say to my mother after *this* week, about the only ice cream good enough had to come from the only ice cream parlor on Central Park South, where I figured I would buy her a sundae they serve in a bathtub.

And then BOY was I going to let Pearl have it!

Vitka's car was a big nondescript Chevrolet that he drove like he'd learned at the Smolensk Tank Academy, as witnessed by the snaggled front left fender and a bashed-in right taillight, the kind of car that when you see it on the highway you slow down and change lanes, because God knows what the driver might do. All the way out on the parkway and onto the Brooklyn-Queens Expressway, Vitka kept pushing his thundering car right up on someone's bumper and then suddenly swerving into the next lane, more often than not to pass on the right. The rain was steady, and the asphalt glistened with a rainbow skin of oil. It was the sort of day when driving, you notice the tire fragments, carcasses of dogs, and bits of clothing—one shoe, someone's underwear—that accumulate in the median, for no reason you'd care to think about.

I sat in the back, feeling greener and greener, cursing myself for not taking my car. When I bounced down the stairs after leaving that message for my mother, it made perfect sense that Vitka should drive—they couldn't come with *me* and still take Shmuel home, and I *certainly* couldn't take him home if I had no car. And, yes, maybe somewhere in the back of my mind was Russo and that low-slung red car of his, the two of us settling down in the bucket seats . . .

Faina must have been feeling just as green, because she began muttering to Vitka to slow down, which made him snarl and jerk the steering wheel even more sharply, his big bandaged thumb hooked over one of its spokes. In the middle of the Brooklyn Bridge, slithering around on that iron mesh roadway, I decided it was prudent to move into the middle of the back seat and brace myself as best I could, because I doubted Vitka would be Americanized enough to buy tires; those are so hard to come by in Russia most people drive theirs until the air shows through. God knows his wiper blades didn't inspire a lot of confidence; they were so worn they mostly just slapped mud around.

Someplace around Tenth and Fiftieth we stopped at the light and a skinny black kid in a bright orange slicker squirted soap on the windshield. Before the kid even got his squeegee up, Vitka was out of the car and had him by the arm, hustling him toward the sidewalk.

"Vitka! Don't! What are you doing? STOP!" Faina screamed.

The burly Russian had already thrown the kid against a parked car, where he landed awkwardly, purple Keds flailing in the air. Vitka stepped toward him menacingly, but the kid was already scrambling away, Faina and I were shrieking, and the cars behind us began to honk. Vitka bent down, picked up the squeegee the kid had dropped, and snapped the handle in two, like you or I might do to dry spaghetti. He threw the two pieces after the kid, got back in the car, and accelerated away savagely.

"Damn black beggars!" Vitka snarled about two blocks later, in what I guess was supposed to be an explanation. The racism didn't surprise me; blacks, gays, feminists and other things they don't have in Russia. These surprise and frighten most émigrés. The violence though, that was a surprise. Not an encouraging one either. Our last thirty blocks were silent, except for the rumble of Vitka's big engine, the rain hissing off the street, the squeak of vinyl as Faina kneaded her shopping purse, and Vitka grinding his teeth and muttering.

It wasn't just the car ride that was giving me a sick stomach, as I sat wondering whether my plan was going to work.

Skripnik's street was one-way away from the Park, but instead of going the one block north and swinging around, Vitka just turned left, wheeling the car into a pay garage halfway up the block on the other side of the avenue.

The block and a half back to the brownstone I made like a writer, trying to dream up convincing explanations of why Faina and Vitka's picture should be in Skripnik's apartment, and why Phyllis should let us look for it; as soon as I saw Phyllis, though, I knew my audience was not in a buying mood.

Which, frankly, made me mad. Mad that with two houses and all the credit cards and everything, this woman could think of herself as a victim of life, when there was Faina here, who really *was*. Mad that *I* had spent all this time coping with the mess her husband had made, about which she felt no responsibility. And damn it, just plain mad that right at the moment she had *two Chagalls!*

Which reassured me that it wouldn't be so terrible to take at least one of them away.

"You said two o'clock, and it's almost half past! I told my mother I'd be over no later than four!" Today Phyllis was wearing a green A-line raincoat with huge brass toggles and an upside-down yellow plastic tulip of a rain hat that pushed her hair into a curly wad and emphasized her glasses and nose. She would have looked like a picture on a box of fishsticks if not for the pinched displeasure about her mouth.

"Jeez, Phyllis, I'm sorry. There was traffic, and the rain, and listen, this is really sweet of you, to meet these people and help them out."

"Help who?"

"Remember I told you about your husband's relatives, how I was looking for—"

Phyllis shook her head vehemently, spraying me with drops. "Oh no, I thought it might be something like this! I've got enough problems, I'm not helping anyone."

"They're not asking for anything," I hastened to reassure her, wholly illogically, since we had come to get a couple zillion dollars worth of paintings. "See, Leon had something of—"

Phyllis was still shaking her head. "Go see the lawyers, they should go see the lawyers."

At which point Faina and Vitka caught up with me, to stand just behind me, one at each elbow.

"Phyllis Smolensky, this is Faina Bender, and her son Vitka," I burbled, enunciating so clearly that I almost shouted. "They are cousins—"

"Of your husband," Vitka bellowed. He shook the hand which Phyllis had automatically extended in response to his and went up the stairs to wait at the door. The three of us looked stunned for a second, then Faina hastily shook the hand Phyllis had not yet withdrawn and followed her son.

"What have they come for?" Phyllis finally gathered her wits enough to stage-whisper at me.

"Inside, I'll explain everything." I took her elbow and pushed her up toward the door. I could feel her stiffness, her tension, and so smiled even wider, determined that when this day ended, I would be through with these people forever.

Phyllis fumbled with the key, but we finally got in; the alarm that Russo had ripped loose had not been reconnected. Phyllis and I started shrugging out of our wet coats; Faina stood irresolutely, looking about like a country mouse out visiting. Vitka headed for the stairs, like a guy who's not used to people who own entire houses and not just rooms in them.

"In here," I said brightly. "Why don't we all go sit in the living room—if that's okay, Phyllis." I was beginning to get that giddy sensation you get when blowing on a fire that won't start. "We can sit, and you and the Benders—come on, right in here—can talk."

I have been in oral surgeons' waiting rooms with folks more convivial than the little cluster settled about Dr. Leon's glass-topped coffee table. Vitka had humphed down in the recliner, and Faina was huddled on one end of the sofa with Phyllis on the other, her expression flickering between the superior *femme du monde* that she had frosted me with at the funeral and the weak-eyed, sharp-beaked Phyllis who was ready to take a bite out of the Benders. And me.

For lack of anybody I wanted to sit next to I remained standing.

"Phyllis, about the painting," I began.

She looked around at me, watery blue eyes as close

to blazing as they would ever be. "My husband's painting?"

"MY painting!" Vitka set the recliner upright with a resounding *sproing.*

"Your painting?" Phyllis asked with a sweetness that a newborn would have known was false. "A painting in my husband's house, on his wall, locked behind his lock. This you call yours?"

Vitka glowered, the cords of his neck swelling.

"Meesus Skreepneek," Faina began, putting her hand on Phyllis's leg.

"Midge, get these people out of my house." Phyllis brushed away Faina's hand and started to stand, so I squatted, also to put a hand on her knee.

"Listen, the painting isn't Leon's, it's theirs, and Leon was trying to . . . well, he had borrowed it." Talking as fast but as soothingly as I could manage, I told her the story—Chagall, the grandfather, the blockade, and Faina. Figuring that there was no point, I went kind of light on how Leon had been preparing to cheat his relatives out of hundreds of thousands of dollars, instead putting everything I had into my finish, the business about the sketch.

Phyllis looked interested. "This sketch is also by Chagall?"

"That's why Leon had it, so he could authenticate the big painting. And the letter"—I gestured at Faina's purse, where the expert's opinion presumably rested—"says it is really a Chagall. So, what I was thinking—"

"Then where is the sketch?" Phyllis was showing a narrowness of focus that should have told me prospects were looking dim.

"That's . . . somewhere here, in this house." Both hands raised like the little exorcist in *Poltergeist,* I rotated through the room.

"Probably in the study upstairs." Vitka jabbed his short, thick index finger in the direction of Skripnik's room. "In a file or something. It's about this big." He gestured.

"That's what I was thinking too." I turned back to Phyllis. "Since it's not on the walls or anything."

Phyllis had the distracted look of someone doing mental arithmetic. "So you want to look around the house?"

"Well, Phyllis, it is theirs, and Leon *did* kind of mislead them, about it being at my house."

"So I should just let these people, whom I've never seen before, rummage through my house?" Phyllis's voice was acquiring a distinct edge. "So they can help themselves?"

"Phyllis, the pictures were never his." I tried to be as gentle as I could, but firm too. "Look, be reasonable; you said yourself you didn't know where the painting came from."

"We were divorced," Phyllis reminded me sharply. "Does that mean that anything he bought after we separated that I don't know about, he doesn't really own? It isn't really mine now?"

"See, that's the thing, he didn't *buy* the paintings," I said, trying to sound as convincing as I could, as I launched into the last unexplained part of this mess. "It was a *loan*, to these people." I indicated Faina and Vitka. "And the big painting was collateral. He was supposed to give them the money and return the sketch and keep the big one, except . . ." I paused, trying to think of a diplomatic way to say, except your late ex-husband was a four-flushing snake who would steal the Pampers off a baby's tush.

At which Faina broke in, to argue with *me*. "No, is not true, money he gave!" Then, smiling, to Phyllis. "*I* refuse. Silly émigré woman, wants cash." Then she burrowed a moment in her handbag and brought out a piece of paper, folded over. "Not this check."

"You mean you *have* the check?" I was flabbergasted.

Faina smoothed the paper on her knee, and held it up. Citibank Money market account, for twenty thousand dollars, payable to Faina Bender.

Hand trembling, Phyllis reached for the check, touched it, but Faina did not let go. "It's his check, but . . ." Phyllis murmured.

"Come on, Mama, let's just do it like I say, all right?" Vitka snapped impatiently. "Give to lady the check, she'll give us our pictures, and we'll go. Great-grandfather *starved* for those pictures!" he added vehemently.

"My grandfather was touched." Faina tapped her forehead with her finger and clicked her tongue. "Are we museum, that we have to keep such paintings? When I was little girl, *hungry* little girl, I hate that painting! Every day Grandfather says, that painting I could sell for *heaps* of bread but I refuse! And my hungry little belly, it asks, for why do you refuse? For colors, squashed on cloth, we starve?"

"Chagall was great man!" Vitka thundered. "Soviet pigs spat on him, they drove him from the country! They called his pictures alien, decadent, *trash*! And Great-grandfather *saved* that painting."

"Vitka, Vitka! Vitenka! Calm, calm." Faina had shed her timidness, and was now in charge. "Save that painting for *what*? That painting, it is not person, it is not child! When Dr. Skripnik offered loan money, to help, I think to myself, Vitka deserves life, he is in the new country, he is young. We have nothing but this picture, why should we hang it on our necks like millstone? The doctor is family. If Vitka makes money, we pay him back; if not, let the doctor have!" She turned to smile at Phyllis.

"Family, even if divorce." She reached across the no-man's-land of sofa they had put between them and patted Phyllis's hand.

"I say we take the pictures, give the lady her money back." Vitka was prowling restlessly, like one of those nasty, shaggy bears in the zoo, back and forth. "You've already caused enough problems for everyone."

Faina reached for Phyllis's arm again. "This woman is person too, Vitka. Two complete strangers come in, say give me pictures she maybe doesn't know she has. But she looks like nice lady, who can understand what means two people, we get out of the Soviet Union with *nothing*, they take almost the string from around our parcels! It's not so much for you, the loan, but for Vitka . . ."

Phyllis was wavering, or at least listening. Nor was she shrinking away from Faina anymore, who now had a solid grip on Phyllis's forearm.

Faina added after a moment. "Okay? You give us little picture, you keep big picture?"

"That's right!" I leapt in behind Faina, "You keep the—wait a minute!" I realized that I had just missed a sudden bend in the conversation. "You said she could have the *big* painting?"

Faina waved both hands dismissively, the most Russian of gestures. "Feh, you could see my little apartment, you would know. I need painting so big it covers my window? The little one, we find it, I put it on wall, I look at it, I remember Grandpapa. And one day it goes on *your* wall, Vitenka. And in between time, you also have your video shop. Real first-class video shop, hey!"

I was beginning to realize that I was very confused, when Phyllis, talking as though her mouth were very dry, said, "Uh, the check."

All three of us froze, looking at her.

"It's no good. That . . . that account is—"

"CLOSED?" I finished for her, astonished that we *still* hadn't plumbed the slimy rotten depths of what Leon Skripnik was capable of.

Vitka seemed to agree with me, because his face grew dark and turgid with blood. Even Faina looked worried when he growled, in Russian for the first time since we had gotten there, "My picture, Faina, and then we're *gone!* Understood?"

But Phyllis, hesitantly, was continuing. "It was, well, that's an old, a joint account. Leon should have thrown the checkbook away, but . . ." She looked from Vitka to Faina to me. "Maybe I could give you a check? On my account?"

Vitka and Faina glanced at each other; then somehow seemed to spring back a little, like grass that's been under a huge rock. "And little picture?" Vitka asked cautiously.

"Well." Phyllis pushed the glasses back up her nose, a gesture which made her seem even more helpless than she normally did. "If that was the arrangement . . ."

And Vitka and Faina smiled.

I should have too. I mean, the Russians were so happy they surely couldn't begrudge taking Shmuel off my hands, and God knows Phyllis would have nothing to complain about. We would all go up and root around in Skripnik's study, find that sketch, and then go our separate ways forever, Vitka to his video store, me to my typewriter.

And Phyllis to her beautiful Chagall, that she was getting for twenty thousand dollars.

Which is why I had the distinct taste of ash in my mouth when I went to answer the front door.

"Hi." Russo grinned, after a moment of being startled

by my dour face. "This your surprise? That you're going to yell at me?"

I did my best to smile. "I don't know, I think you're a little late for the surprise. Better you should give me yours, maybe." Doing my best to be lighthearted, I took his arm and pulled him inside, not really thinking what I was saying.

Which was too bad, because life would have been a lot simpler if I had told Russo my surprise first.

Instead, the detective shrugged and let himself be pulled toward the living room. "Okay." He smiled again, though his eyes questioned me closely. "We'll do it your way." He handed me a folded piece of paper from his breast pocket.

"What's this?" I had been about to introduce him to the Benders.

"Lab report on that big painting we took out of here. Good people down at the Museum of Modern Art telling us, if that's a Chagall, then I'm Kojak."

13

I STOOD behind Russo, blinking and gaping, trying to put together a sketch that the Creative Associates people said was real with a painting that somebody at MOMA swore was a fake.

If both were gifts from Chagall, how could one be real and the other one fake? Had the experts made a mistake? Well, they're human, and anyway, God knows, most of the mess the world is in, it's the experts who got us all in it. But the problem here was that if you have to choose which experts are more likely to screw up, you'd have to go with the people at Creative Whatsit, right? Because the MOMA people, they're doing the evaluation for the police, they've got some reputation on the line, they probably see lots and lots of Chagalls. Plus they don't stand to make any money. But if the folks down at Evaluations-R-Us were mistaken . . .

That meant *both* pictures were phonies?

For which Faina's grandfather starved through three years of the Leningrad blockade and Faina herself risked Soviet jail, smuggling them out?

Some grim scenarios glimmered in my head: an echoing Leningrad apartment building, dark because there is no electricity, slops frozen on the stinking staircase, dull thud of distant guns.

A small group huddled around the single candle. "We must sell father's painting, we *must*. Otherwise our children will starve!" A woman speaking, more skeleton than flesh, lips blue with exhaustion and cold. "It will kill him!" says another. "Not if he doesn't know!" answers the first, smiling bravely. "We will copy it!"

Or, same building, same war, the apartment door is found open, swinging crazily on shattered hinges. "My God! They've taken . . ."

"The picture! Quick, we must have it copied, before father finds out!"

Or the father, ribs sticking so far out of his chest he looks like a broken Slinky toy, lovingly ponders his sleeping children, shivering beneath one thin blanket. He tucks the big painting under his arm and heads for the door. "Oh, how can you sell the painting?" whispers his wife. "You have held on to it through so much! And what shall I tell the children?"

"Don't worry," Papa whispers back sadly, "they will never know. I will have it copied."

All of these scenarios had the common problem, that in wartime Leningrad, or peacetime either, you couldn't

exactly take your wall-size canvas down to Kopies On
The Korner to ask them to make one life-size repro, natural colors please.

Faina was huddled on the couch, gripping the armrest
with her right hand, clutching her purse to her breast with
her left. Vitka was pulled forward to the edge of the
recliner, examining his bandaged hand under the light of
Skripnik's Mets lamp, legs crossed beneath him, exposing
black nylon socks and white, hairy shins. Both of them
looked ill-kempt and hard-done-by, with none of Russo's
glowing health, or Phyllis's prosperity—which she ra-
diated, even if her taste made it look like she got her
clothes out out of a Goodwill bin behind Henri Bendel's.
God, what if they *didn't* know? Those Chagalls were all
they had!

But even as I looked at them, my brain began to throw
up some other considerations it had not bothered to ask
me about before, such as how could this pair of sad sacks
smuggle a painting the size of a table out of Russia? I've
been through Soviet customs myself, and I couldn't have
gotten out the *snapshot* of that painting. And why had
Faina and Vitka argued in English just now, and why was
Faina so generous leaving the big picture for Phyllis?

Come to that, I couldn't remember that I ever told Vitka
the address of the brownstone, and how did he know
about where to park? And why had Vitka started immediately upstairs? Where he said the sketch probably
was, in the study he shouldn't have known was there.

The answer, that Faina and Vitka were not the nice,
befuddled émigrés I had taken them for, was pretty obvious, once I got it.

What was unfortunate about that realization was that
it had come kind of late.

Russo had his hands in his back pockets, his shoulders

hunched forward as he approached the couch. "Miz Skripnik," I heard him say, then he looked at the two strangers.

Phyllis, putting her checkbook back into her purse, said more equably than usual, "Smolensky, Lieutenant. *These* people are more Skripnik than I am. This is Faina and ... mm ... uh, relatives of my husband." I saw her pat her purse contentedly and smile nearsightedly at the room. "Lieutenant Russo is investigating the circumstances of my ex-husband's—"

"Jesus, Midge, these the Russians you were telling me about?" Russo said, turning to me, astonished.

Unfortunately he had come expecting sweet nothings, so Vitka changed gears a little faster than the Sicilian did, taking two quick steps and jamming both thumbs hard into Russo's gut, then clubbing him in the back of the neck when the cop doubled over. Russo slid flat and lay still.

Phyllis shrieked, and I suppose I did too. I know for sure I ran over, I guess to kneel by Russo, except that Phyllis grabbed me first, to pull me down onto the couch. Faina was shouting too, in Russian. "Vitka! Stop it! Don't be an idiot!"

Vitka was already frisking Russo in a businesslike way. He stood up, grinning, Russo's revolver small in his meaty paw.

"Hey, look, Ringo Kid!" Vitka spun the gun clumsily on his finger, dropping it. He bent over quickly to retrieve it and looked at us darkly. Thank God neither of us had laughed.

"Stop playing the fool," Faina said sharply, still in Russian, stepping over Russo to take the gun away from Vitka. "What in the devil did you do that for, you brainless monkey? You've put us in the shit now."

Vitka snatched at the pistol, which Faina had put behind her back, out of reach. Sounding aggrieved, he said, "This is a *cop*, Fainochka, you didn't hear the lady? And who you calling brainless? You've cunted up every fucking step of this thing."

"Shut up," Faina said preemptorily. "You forget *she* understands Russian?"

Which I did, of course, but not nearly as well as I did before they started with the Russian they were using right now. My Russian is nice polite classroom stuff, with just a sprinkling of the more conventional curses, not much use for understanding their rapid thieves jargon.

On the other hand, you can pick up a lot from the context of the situation.

Take Faina. The same strawlike hair, the same acetate dress blotched with unnaturally colored flowers, the faded, powdered face—and yet she'd become a totally different woman: the person in charge. She studied Russo, then Skripnik's living room, then Phyllis and me, who were huddled together on the couch, Phyllis quivering like a hammered gong. "This number has been dog vomit, start to finish," she muttered. "Let me think."

"What's to think? Find the fucking picture, stop at the bank, and we're gone!" Vitka looked around happily, rubbing his hands.

"Gone? What do you mean, we're gone? They've seen us, they know about the picture, and you're up to here in shit!" When Faina said this, as thoughtfully and calmly as if she were discussing the weather, all the hairs on my spine stood up, because I'd just remembered something else.

Though she was surprised—even upset—that he was dead, Faina had never asked how Skripnik died.

Phyllis must have gotten the same idea at the same

moment, because she dug her nails about an inch into my arm. "It's them, isn't it? The ones who killed—"

"*Shut up!*" I pinched her right back, saying through clenched teeth, "Just shut up! We don't know anything!"

"Midge, it was *them*, they ... they're ..." she was screeching, making the hiccuping noise that on Monday night had turned into hysterical sobbing spasms. "They're the—"

"You want to end up the same way?" I hissed, squeezing her elbow so hard my fingers hurt.

Too late. Faina was looking at us in a way that washed sheets of fear down into my belly. I began talking loudly, blithering the first things that came to my lips. "Don't worry, Phyllis, nothing's happened, they're just angry, your ex-husband was trying to steal from them, they'll take the picture and *go*. He was cheating them, Phyllis, taking unfair advantage—"

"That picture's worth money, damn it! It's got to be here someplace!" Vitka shouted in Russian at Faina, grabbing her shoulder. "Maybe we can't do business anymore, now they've seen us, but we can't walk away from money like that!"

Faina was still looking at us. "Wrap them up," she finally said.

Vitka looked at her. "What do you mean, wrap them up?"

"What I said, tie them up. Or you want *they* should spend some time on the telephone to the bank while we look around for the sketch?" Faina looked at Vitka with barely restrained impatience, pointing at us on the couch.

"Tie them up? With what? Where?" Vitka still seemed furious. "Just do them with the gun, and—"

"Vitka!" Faina's voice was not so much loud as final.

Vitka submitted sullenly. "Okay, you two, take him out

in the kitchen." His eyes were sunk about two feet behind his shaggy black eyebrows, where a malevolent gleam of intelligence flickered faintly, like a campfire in a cave. I swallowed, to discover that my mouth had welded itself shut.

Phyllis was still shaking. "But they're monsters . . . and *you* brought them here!" she hissed, suddenly turning on me. "I *told* you not to come over today!"

For once, I wished I had listened to her, but rather than argue, I got up and tried to lift Russo. I could hear him breathing, at least. I grunted and tugged, trying to lift him by a right arm and shoulder that felt like it was made of warm rock. I got his shirt untucked and the carpet all wadded up but otherwise didn't move him.

"Motherfucker," Vitka spat in Russian, and took Russo's belt in his free hand, by which he half carried, half dragged Russo across the dining area and into the kitchen.

Once in the kitchen, Vitka looked around, making us stand in the corner between the window and the breakfast bar while he rummaged in a drawer. My heart stalled when he pulled out a carving knife, but all he did with it was slice the cord from the venetian blind. The blue metal slats collapsed with a clatter, watery and sunlight stabbed in.

"Rain is finally ending," he told us after glancing out. Then, taking the cord, he indicated that we should hold Russo's hands together; we did so, and he quickly bound them, passing the rope around a pipe of the radiator and back to Russo. A few more quick knots, and a slice of the knife took off the excess cord. Vitka considered a moment, the knife tucked under his armpit, and then bound Russo's ankles, passing the rope through the handle of Skripnik's restaurant-size gas oven. Then, grunting again, but this time with satisfaction, he said, "Okay, over there you two."

"There" was the stools at the breakfast bar. Vitka pulled two away from the breakfast counter and made Phyllis and me sit on them, back to back. He tied us elbow to elbow, lashed our wrists, and finally tied our ankles to the legs of the stool. The sash cord was not uncomfortably tight, but there was also no question of pulling it loose or breaking it; instinctively I tugged at the rope, and just as instinctively Phyllis pulled back, nearly dumping both of us onto the floor.

"I wouldn't wiggle around a lot," Vitka said, amused, stepping back to check his work. "It makes the knots tighter." As he nodded to himself, satisfied, apparently, a sunbeam sliced through the breaking clouds, catching him and us for a moment in a lovely clear gold light. Which only emphasized the incongruity of the tranquil, well-appointed kitchen; cabinets granite gray, handles and knobs a glistening hi-tech black to go with the stools, on which sat two bound women, with a hog-tied police-man sprawled at their feet.

The kitchen. Where Skripnik's body had been found.

Chuckling at his own wit, Vitka said, "So, don't see me out. I have to go look for that damn picture."

"What about us?" Phyllis wailed, turning around so violently she almost knocked me off my stool again. "What are you going to do to us? If I'm not in Jersey by five my mother will be *frantic*!"

In *High Water at Lake Poncatoncas* Tammy gets tied up by the bearded stranger who has stolen the canoe from the camp boathouse to row out to Indian Rocks. She knows two things: that she will not be found until at least the next morning, because Tanesia has taken a group of Brownies on an overnight to Wild Horse Meadows, and that the stranger is making his secret rendezvous with the one-eyed pilot as soon as the nearly full moon sets. Meaning that everything depends upon her. As soon as the bearded stranger's heavy steps recede, she wriggles and worms herself over to an old soda bottle she can see shining in the moonlight coming through the broken boathouse window and pushes it down the stairs onto the dock. It breaks. Tammy squirms down the flight of stairs and, working by feel, wedges a sharp fragment into the space between two boards; then she saws the rope against it, to free her hands. She unties her legs and takes cabin four's rowboat and cuts across Big Moose Inlet, to beat the stranger to Indian Rocks.

You know, until Vitka forced me to do this actual research on the subject of being tied up, I was pretty proud of that scene. Now I was beginning to doubt that Tammy could have done all those things.

God knows *I* couldn't do the sort of wriggling that was going to get us out of this mess. I mean, if Phyllis were to agree to flop up onto my back while I wriggled down far enough to touch the floor with my toes, *maybe* I could sort of hop on my tiptoe across the kitchen still tied to the two stools and Phyllis, then tip sideways so she could rummage for a knife, which *maybe* she could wedge into something, so we could cut the ropes.

A plan which should work just fine, provided I wasn't crushed under Phyllis when we fell off the stools, or didn't suffer a heart attack when I tried to hop across the kitchen with her and two stools on my back, or get fatally stabbed by Phyllis, who I wouldn't trust to put cream cheese on my bagel with a plastic knife, to say nothing of how I felt about her wielding a Sabatier butcher knife upside down and with her hands tied behind her back and mine.

Not to mention the additional problem that Phyllis was so mad she wouldn't talk to me.

"You shouldn't have laughed!" she had screeched. "It's not funny!"

"Phyllis, for crying out loud! It's a nervous reaction! Somebody ties us up in your own goddamn kitchen, and then *you* say it's going to make your *mother* mad—"

"Yeah, ha-ha. Just like the rest of them. You pretend to be my friend so you can break into my house and let your horrible friends—"

"They're *not* my friends, damn it!"

"I suppose you're saying *I* asked them to come here and ruin my house?"

"I thought I was doing you a favor, for Christ's sake!" Which wasn't quite true, but our conversation was well beyond such niceties. "So you'd know about the painting—"

"The painting! The painting!" Phyllis sounded almost beserk with rage now. "You didn't even KNOW about the painting, you just wanted the address book, because you were worried that you were in the diary part, like everyone else! Well, you know what—"

"Wait a minute." I forgot we were tied up and tried to turn around, my turn to nearly tip us both off onto the floor. "What do you meant the diary part? You took—"

Phyllis snatched herself back, jerking me too. "Don't play Little Miss Innocent with me! The diary! Where Leon wrote down all his . . . his . . . TRYSTS! *With my so-called friends!*"

"He was seeing your girlfriends? And writing about it?" I repeated, dumbfounded at Skripnik, whose loathsomeness seemed inexhaustible.

Instead of answering, Phyllis was silent, doing all she could in our ropes to pull herself away from me.

I pressed the point. "He was actually writing out *descriptions?*"

After another longish silence, Phyllis said icily, "When I opened it, there were days with little stars, and initials. That I recognized some of them. A nasty childish kind of a thing, which Leon . . . shouldn't be remembered for. So I threw it in the incinerator."

"It couldn't have been like an appointment book or something?" I asked, unable to square the Leon Skripnik I remembered with a black book full of salacious stars. "There were just initials? No names?"

"L.S.: Leah Segal, who I know from kindergarten; B.G.: Bambi Goldberg, who collects for the UJA bonds from the temple," she snapped back, with slashing sarcasm at my naïveté.

"But even if it *is* those women, couldn't they have been seeing him professionally?" I was now defending Skripnik, which I had no desire to do, but neither could I believe that Phyllis could be so paranoid as to interpret a few initials in her husband's appointment book as proof of her wholesale betrayal by everyone she knew.

"I know what I know," Phyllis said with that massive dignity she had tried to crush me with back at the funeral service, giving a final flourish with a shake of her bony shoulders. "And I know something else too: When we get out of this, I never want to see you again."

I almost shot back that I had never wanted to see her again before I even met her but then decided that if I was going to die, I was not going to do so squabbling like a third-grader. We sat there back to back, our sweat mingling, both maintaining absolute, demonstrative silence, even when the bumps and thumps of the search party

upstairs began to sound more like the crashes of a wrecking crew. Phyllis would start at each new crash, then
tremble violently for a moment, shaking me too, but she
really didn't say anything.

On the whole, I think I would have preferred being
yelled at. One of the problems of being tied up like that
is that it gives you a lot of time to think, and to wonder
things like whether we were really going to die.

I made a real effort to convince myself that all Vitka
and Faina wanted was us out of the way, not dead. After
all, they could have killed us right away, correct? Instead
of going to all the trouble of tying us up?

Unfortunately, underneath the part of your brain that
does the talking there is also the part that secretes skepticism, the part that makes you understand things even
when you don't want to, such as that this blind date may
be kind of good-looking, doesn't pick his teeth, and owns
an apartment in Brooklyn Heights, but he's still a creep,
or that the five little pounds you'd have to lose to fit into
the absolutely *gorgeous* Diane von Furstenberg that is
now only twenty-eight dollars at Loehmann's is really ten
pounds, and you'll never lose it anyway. That helpful little
layer of consciousness was now busy finding flaws in my
consolations, such as that *truly* nice people don't tie other
people up, and besides, why kill us anyway, if all they
had to do was leave us in this big, solid, empty house,
where we could all scream our heads off unheard, slowly
starving to death?

Which is why it took me a while to realize that it would
be worth killing us only if *one* of the Chagalls was real.

Do you ever do the Hirschfelds in the Arts & Leisure
section in the Sunday *Times*? A caricature of Al Hirt that
is supposed to have *Nina* hidden in it? You look and you
look, your coffee turns to ice and your lox curls up at the

corners, but still you can't find all of them. Finally some-body points out one you've missed—it's right there!—and you can't believe how blind you were.

I lacked some details, like where they had gotten the real Chagall, but suddenly I understood what Faina and Vitka were up to. It was a line of work dating back to the serpent, when the snake wanted Eve to make a little applesauce. More up-to-date variants include selling the Brooklyn Bridge, peddling snake oil, and dealing in du-bious Chagalls.

Finding customers would be simplicity itself, because they actually came looking for *you*. Vitka and Faina could locate all the suckers they wanted in the ads in the Jewish newspapers, the sort that Skripnik had placed to find his relatives. How they decided who would make a good "relative" I don't know; maybe the address to contact, like in Scarsdale, or the name, as in "please contact Dr. So-and-so," or maybe even they chose victims from the right part of the old shtetl, close enough to Vitebsk to make it believable that some distant relative would have known Chagall. But after that, the rest was easy.

Faina, with her broken English and her poor but proud émigré shtick. Talking about the hard times in Russia. What the heroic family—*your* family—accomplished in spite of all those hard times. How hard it was to get started in a new country. Thank God for the one treasure the family had managed to hang on to.

You mean someone in *our* family was friends with *Chagall*?

Not just friends, Faina smiles. He gave my grandfather a painting, even!

It puzzled me for a bit how they would get enough information to pretend to be relatives, but then I remem-bered Skripnik. *Nobody* talks as much as family-tree nuts;

two hours with him that Saturday night, and I had heard so much about his family that if I had been listening to him I could have pretended to be his *mother*. And with the ads to begin with, what could be easier. "Seeking relatives of Mandel and Minny Moskowitz from Minsk," so all Faina would have to do is ask in her weepy little voice whether *this* Mandel was the older brother or the younger.

And as for the Chagall, have you ever met anybody who was surprised that his relatives had been friends with famous, important people?

Just then Russo, who hadn't budged, groaned and tried to roll over, tugging hard on his ropes. "Jeez, one hell of a surprise, Midge," he mumbled.

"You're okay!" I jerked around savagely, nearly dumping both of us again, and proving what a slow learner I am. "God, he didn't hurt you, I was *terrified*."

"Those're nice friends you got." Russo's legs were thrashing; he flopped energetically for more minutes than I could have, but he finally subsided, still tied. "I feel like a sausage here," he muttered.

There was an especially loud bang from upstairs, like a bookcase tipping over.

"STOP THEM!" Phyllis shrieked. "Aren't you going to stop them?" She twisted towards Russo, jerking me the other way. "They're tearing my house to shreds!"

Russo strained to twist his head around so he could look at us. "Don't think they'll hear me over the racket," he grunted, "but soon's they come down, I'll be sure and mention it to them, okay?"

I couldn't believe it, but I was grinning. Like I felt better. There was Russo strung up like a mozzarella in the deli, and I felt *secure*? Or whatever you'd call that warm wet feeling that blossomed under my sternum when I heard that dumb-boy voice and saw his slow, lazy grin, which made me remember that exuberant Scarlatti and the Brooklyn Bridge at night, the lights of Wall Street and Brooklyn Heights dancing on the East River.

"But you're a policeman!" Phyllis shouted.

"I'm a cop, lady, not Batman! What do you want from me, like maybe I'm gonna chew through the ropes or something? Who are those people anyway?"

Phyllis, in a voice like I can imagine maybe the Prophet Jeremiah had, said, "Them? They're Midge's friends. The ones who killed my husband."

14

PHYLLIS had tried to say that already, before I shut her up, but this time something clicked when she called Vitka and Faina killers, and I began to wonder . . .

Faina feeds the newfound family member a little borscht and bullshit, then squeezes out a few tears about hard-working Vitka, who for want of a few bucks isn't becoming video king of the émigrés. And her with nothing to her name but this enormous painting by Chagall . . . maybe—*sob*—she should sell it?

My father was given to maxims, most of which he made up, so not all of them made sense. One that did, and I remember him saying it every time some peddler appeared at our doorstep with a Bargain You Don't Want To Miss—aluminum siding, easy-to-replace storm windows, electrical arthritis cures—was that you can't swindle a man who wouldn't swindle you. If Faina had made her pitch to you or to me, we'd offer perhaps to go around to the banks with her, to help her get her loan, or maybe we'd even help to locate a reputable art dealer.

Which is one of the reasons why the Fainas of the world are always on the lookout for a fresh Skripnik. Skripnik, his voice breaking from the tension, says no, no, don't sell it, it's a *family* piece. Maybe he could do a little something to help instead, but he's not a rich man, just a simple hardworking urologist, with an ex-wife and a kid to support. He wouldn't be able to live with himself, if he didn't take something as collateral. Is that painting *really* by Chagall?

At which point grateful Faina becomes fastidious. Well, I don't know for *sure*, everybody always *said* it was, but, tell you what . . .

And out comes the sketch, which you may take to the picture checker of your choice, because Faina and Vitka know *this* picture is the absolute genuine article. One dancing rabbi from the pen of Marc Chagall.

How it should probably work after that was, reassured by the evaluator that the picture was real, you'd pass over your money and return the sketch, she'd bid the big painting a tearful good-bye, and "Faina" would disappear forever, because she had twenty thousand easy bucks, and you thought you had the art bargain of the century.

Such a beautiful swindle, I thought.

Only what part is there in it for Vitka? Sure, Faina would *talk* about Vitka and his video shop, but . . .

Their search had moved downstairs. I could hear Vitka

in the front hall, swearing steadily, mechanically, under his breath, like some kind of machine for wrecking houses. Glass shattered—pictures being broken; a tearing sound—the wallpaper coming off; a rapid clattering—books being shoved off the shelf. I kept picturing Vitka's glower, his shoulders round and plump like hams, the neck he didn't have. He would kick open the swinging door, and there we would be, three chickens trussed on a platter. Was this how it had been, that Saturday night? Skripnik in the kitchen, and Vitka kicking in the kitchen door . . .

But the blood on the stairs? The head wound? The gas?

And then I remembered one more thing. Faina had never told Vitka that Skripnik was dead. I decided it was time to do something.

"Russo," I interrupted imperiously, "the blood on that picture frame. Was it Skripnik's?"

"Midge, you're tied to a kitchen stool and you're still playing lady detective?" He sounded more irritated than amused now, but a little time with Phyllis has that effect on people; she had been being awfully insistent that the hog-tied detective should DO something.

"Damn it, I'm not playing lady detective, just answer me, would you?"

I guess my urgency must have gotten through to him, because Russo shook his head. "No."

"HEY, VITKA!" I shouted, as loud as I could, in the Russian I heard Sasha use when he stubbed his toe. "YOU RUSSIAN MUSH–HEAD, GET IN HERE!"

"Midge, what the devil?" Russo thrashed around, sounding alarmed.

Phyllis echoed the question, with some strangled, panicky noises.

"Phyllis's mom is expecting her," I said sweetly, in English, then in Russian again, "HEY, VITKA, YOU PENCIL-NECK!"

The racket beyond the door stopped, the silence dropping on the house like a rock. I could almost hear my pulse thundering at my temples, the second thoughts circling like hungry buzzards. So I shouted again.

"VITKA, YOU STUPID SON OF A BITCH, YOU WANT TO GO TO JAIL FOREVER?"

He came through the swinging door slowly, his face sweaty red, streaked with dirt. His hair had flopped the wrong way, revealing that he cultivated a long side lock to hide his baldness. His shirt was all rumpled, and he seemed to have opened his cut again, because the bandage around his thumb was blood-soaked. He looked hot, angry, and mean. Phyllis was trembling so hard that our backs were making moist little slapping noises.

"You have decided to tell me where my picture is?" he growled at me, in Russian.

"No. Because I don't know."

"Then keeping your fucking mouth shut, slut." He stalked toward our stools, his hand raised as if to give me a whack; Phyllis shrieked and ducked forward, which left me sort of lying on top of her. I felt incredibly vulnerable and powerless, like at the gynecologist's.

I cranked my head forward as best I could, so that I was looking down my belly at him, knees apart because of the stool, shoulders thrown back because of Phyllis. It was not the best position for type A behavior, but it was all I had; I made my voice as hard but reasonable as I could, trying to project the authority that being tied up with Phyllis was denying me. "But I *do* know something you don't know. You let us go, right now, you might get away cheap. You *hit* me, though, or hurt any of us, es-

pecially *him*"—I rolled my head in Russo's direction—
"you're going to prison *forever*."

Vitka snorted, too hot and dirty to be really amused.
"You are threatening me? It is you who is tied up, not
me." His face growing more fierce, he stepped nearer.
"Where's my picture, you—"

"HEY!" I yelled up at him; he was now almost leaning
over me, stinking of sweat and dirt and turpentine. "You
think all they can send you up for is fraud, don't you?"

He smiled down, but not in a friendly way. "I do nothing illegal, that I know. Fraud means to lie about what
you are selling. We don't lie, and we don't sell." Then,
more menacing, "Besides, it is the doctor who has taken
my painting! It is he who should go to jail!"

"Vitka, sweetheart," I said, trying to be as authoritative
as I had ever been, "he's not going to any jail."

"Ha! America!" Vitka waved his arms angrily. Then,
in English, "Land of free and brave!" he said. Back to
Russian: "Free for rich doctors, maybe, but—"

"It's not because he's a doctor," I cut in flatly. "it's
because he's dead."

Vitka paled but otherwise didn't react, still staring at
me, his face too close, so I could see all the grizzled little
whiskers on the elephantine skin.

"Faina didn't tell you about that part, did she?" I
crowed, trying to rub it in. "And you know who they're
going to get for doing it? . . . YOU!" I yelled, when I grew
tired of his lack of response. "Murder," I said softly,
looking him in the eye. "They'll put you in *real* jail."

Vitka smirked, apparently regaining his composure.
"This you can scare a Russian with? American jail is better
than most Soviet vacation places."

I smirked back. "Maybe, but then you don't find any
black poofiks in the Gulag, Vitka. They put you away for

murder, you'll be in there with those types a long, long time. I hear they like big strong sweaty men." That's the nice thing about bigots; there's a lot of ghosts to scare them with.

He paled again, then looked up as the door swung open. Faina also looked hot and rumpled, her face grim. "What's all this noise, Vitka? Why aren't you working?"

"Murder, Faina. Vitka's finding out that you're trying to set him up as a murderer." I said.

Vitka turned. "Faina is this true, what she says? That the doctor died?" He sounded worried. "You said—"

"Shut up." She crossed the kitchen and put her hand under my chin, squeezing the sides of my jaw. I was startled by how strong her grip was, and even though her hand was positioned the wrong way to strangle me, I was painfully aware of my helplessness, so I swallowed—and kept right on talking, even though Faina had squished my lips sideways. "Vitka, ask her why she didn't tell you about that part, huh?"

"Faina," Vitka began again.

The woman let go of my jaw but didn't back away. "She is his girlfriend, Vitka," Faina said flatly, implying that nothing I might ever say could possible be trusted. "Besides, there is no proof we were here," she added haughtily.

"You think nobody's going to notice two people carrying a great big picture down the street, even in the middle of the night? The police ask around, I bet they'll find *thirty people* saw you—"

"Vitka, go finish tearing open the cushions," Faina interrupted me.

Vitka waved her away. "I want to hear this."

Faina put both hands on his chest, as though she were going to push him. "Thirty people, *fifty* people who says you can't bring somebody a painting? That doesn't mean you killed him."

"Vitka, it's your blood on the picture frame, isn't it? That's how you cut your hand—and I bet your blood is on Skripnik too!" I tried to catch the big Russian's eye, but he was still staring at his mother. I was pretty sure, though, that he was listening to me. "How come you never asked what he died of, huh, Faina? Because you *know*, don't you? Skripnik wouldn't give you the money, so you had Vitka come in to threaten him, and there was a fight, wasn't there? Vitka hit Skripnik, didn't he? Vitka, they're going to say *you* killed him."

"I never hit anybody," he said angrily, looking like a baited bear. "We were arguing . . ."

I closed my eyes, almost faint with relief. I had guessed right. I had been sure I was right, but . . . well, you know the expression "dead wrong"?

"Shut up, Vitka," Faina now hit her son with both fists, not hard, but not gently either. "When we left he was alive. Now come on, we get the picture and we get out of here."

Pushing my luck, I kept hammering at him, replaying the only ace I had. "Vitka, your blood is on the picture frame, Vitka; how are you going to explain that?"

He looked at his bandaged palm. "I was going to take the painting, and the doctor grabbed it out of my hands and tried to run down the stairs with it. When he pulled, something cut me. The sketch is mine, damn it." Vitka's voice was low, almost bestial. "That greedy lying doctor. He said he was going to get another checkbook, and then he grabbed the painting and ran. Halfway down the stairs he slipped and cut his head open on something. He was out like frozen fish, so I hung the picture up in his study and then carried him down here. Faina made him tea. The devil take all of you, we *saved* him, we didn't kill him!"

"He's dead, Vitka, and they're going to prove you did it. Vitka, you're a swindler, a thief, a crummy little émigré, and *he* was a—hey, Lieutenant!" I said, switching languages. "What's the maximum penalty in this state for fraud?"

"Christ, Midge," Russo snapped, "chattering away like that to those two, what kind of craziness . . . ?"

"Just work with me, Russo, work with me, damn it!" I stage-whispered, hoping I'd said it too fast for the Russians to catch and trying to keep eye contact with Vitka. Then, louder and more distinctly, "Just tell me, some people selling paintings say they're real but they're not; what's the maximum penalty in New York state?" I asked.

"God damn it, Midge, I'm not a lawyer and this isn't a court!" I could hear him hammering his heels on the kitchen floor.

"GOD DAMN IT YOURSELF RUSSO JUST TELL ME! FRAUD, HOW MANY?" I yanked around so hard I finally tipped Phyllis and myself over. The reflex to cover my face with my bound hands almost dislocated my elbows, and my face smashed against Russo's knee. Phyllis shrieked, but I figured she couldn't have been hurt badly, because she clobbered my shoulder with her head. I gasped. I thought I could feel a tooth wiggle, and I tasted blood.

Russo said "Ouch!" and then he chuckled. He honestly CHUCKLED. "No need to get excited, Midge. I'll tell her, I'll tell her: it depends on the money involved, but fraud normally will get you, oh—"

"Twenty thousand dollars," I mumbled into his leg, feeling my lip puff up. "That's the money, that's all it was."

"Just twenty grand? You might do a year, a year and a half."

"Tell him where." My lip felt like a hot and pulsating sausage and my mouth was full of bloody saliva. I wondered whether my tooth was broken.

"Minimum security someplace, probably. Maybe even work-release, if it's a first offense."

"Hear that, Vitka?" I yelled in Russian again, but muffled, because my face was pushed into Russo's leg. "Compare that to what you get for killing a fancy New York doctor. That gets you life imprisonment, you stone brain! You want to spend your whole life locked up with a bunch of poofiks, guys who try to fondle your tush every time you go to lunch? Because of a *picture*?"

Faina was silent. Had it not been for the noise of Vitka's breathing, I might have thought they had left the room. I tried to ease the pressure on my neck; my cheek had become one enormous throb. What a sight we must make, the three of us tangled together like fish in a net! How easy to shoot us, or even just to smother us. I had to keep talking.

"Skripnik knew you weren't really relatives, didn't he? He didn't believe your story anymore, about the grandfather and Chagall; he just told you that it was too bad, didn't he? That you had the money and he had the paintings? So you had Vitka come in and scare him, didn't you, Faina? That's what Vitka is for, scaring people. But this time Skripnik laughed in your face. He told you he was keeping *both* pictures, didn't he?"

"Vitka," Faina said, switching back to Russian, "shut her up and get on with it."

"How come she didn't tell you he was dead, Vitka?" I strained so hard I was almost surprised the ropes didn't burst. "Vitka, *she's* not going to go to prison for this! Nobody will believe it! YOU'RE the one they'll believe did it!"

"The sketch, Vitka," Faina said in a flat and wicked voice. "I'll take care of her."

"Ask her why she didn't tell you!" I was frenzied now, fighting the bonds but scarcely able to move. "She wants *you* to take the fall, Vitka!"

From the corner of my right eye, looming far above me, I could just see Faina's face, mottled red and white with fury; it terrified me, but there was no going back. I braced myself to be kicked—

And blinked in surprise when I saw that Vitka had grabbed her shoulders, and turned her around. I was staring at the worn-off heels of her muddy shoes.

"Go get the car, you said. You'd make sure he's okay, you said." His voice was insinuating now, building toward a fury. "What'd you do, kill him in here?"

"Of course not." But Faina's voice sounded as though her control was finally beginning to break. "Why would I kill him? He was breathing, you saw that—"

"TALK ENGLISH!" Russo shouted unexpectedly, making us all jump. My cheek burned against his jeans, and I could feel saliva drooling from my swollen lip. It didn't seem like he had much leverage for this request, but for some reason he didn't need it. Faina turned in the lieutenant's direction. "He fall on stairs, Vitka bring him in here. I put tea water on stove." She paused, as if weighing her next words. She shrugged. "Pull cord from phone just in case, to go look upstairs quick for sketch, but all I find is letter about it."

Sighing, she went on quickly, as if she didn't expect to be believed. "But when I get back in kitchen, doctor not here, and back door is open."

"SEE!" Vitka exulted. "He was not dead! I did not kill him!"

"Lady," Russo said, "it's a nice story, but—"

"I am not finish." Faina shifted her feet, pulling her worn and muddy spike heels a little farther from my face. "Gone for police, I think. I look everywhere. I am terrified, police will come any second. Then suddenly I hear feet, coming to the front door. I run, maybe it is Vitka, maybe it is the police. But key goes into lock, then I hear shout."

"What . . ." Phyllis's voice, squeaky and strangled, startled all of us. She cleared her throat, and tried again. "Excuse me, but you wouldn't know, about . . . what time this was?"

"Ask those thirty neighbors you say you find, because I don't stop to look." Faina sounded irritated by Phyllis's interruption. "All I know is door swing open, doctor is lying on stairs, with blood and siren! Like end of world! I was more frightened than ever in my life! I pull doctor in and close door."

"*You* put the keys on the table there!" Russo interjected, in the voice of a man who had just solved a puzzle.

"Yes, they were in door. Doctor is not awake, is bleeding, I take him in kitchen, again" Faina sounded more lively, as if encouraged by Russo's apparent belief, but then she faltered. "But this time I am very very frightened. The alarm is still going. Then I hear Vitka honk, so I run outside . . ." She trailed off. Then, fiercely, "We did not kill the doctor Skripnik!"

Which we scarcely heard, because Phyllis began to wail, a desolate keening like a February north wind scouring the dead countryside upstate.

"I really think you better untie us now," Russo said after a minute. The rest of us were stunned by the banshee wail. It was a horrible sound, half the denizens of hell clawing at the devil's chalkboard, which somehow obviated the need to persuade. Vitka leapt to cut us free, Russo first, then me, then, very gingerly, Phyllis. If Phyllis had not been in spasms on the floor, getting untied might even have been comical, because all our limbs were dead. Russo and I tried to stand staggering clumsily on our wooden feet, which were utterly without feeling, until the returning blood began to course, millions of little explosions of pain against the numbness.

Russo immediately took my arms, looked me up and down, peered in my face. "You okay?" he muttered, close enough to my ear that the words were warm, moist puffs, close enough that I could smell his skin. A sharpish smell, like curry, but something like new leather too. I nodded, brushing my hair back behind my ears. I noticed the mess I had made on his jeans, and blushed; *God*, what I must look like!

As soon as a pale and very somber Vitka managed to cut Phyllis's ankles free of the stool, Phyllis sat up against the kitchen counter, curled into a fetal ball, and rocked, moaning a bubbly, wet noise.

"Come on, Miz Skripnik, it's okay now." Russo, kneeling, put his hand on her shoulder. "It's over, it's okay."

If Phyllis responded at all, it was only to knock her head the harder against the cabinet.

"Pick her up, bring her in there." I pointed at the living room.

To whom this order was issued was not entirely clear, since Faina had already disappeared. Vitka stood by the kitchen door, which hadn't yet swished to a complete stop, with a confused grin on his face.

"I'll . . . help Faina."

Russo, still kneeling by the thrashing Phyllis, looked up and said sharply, "Hey, just a second, I've got to talk to—"

"Faina . . ." Vitka grinned even wider and backed

through the swinging door. Russo stood up, dropping Phyllis.

Who began to bawl, flailing now like a just-landed trout. Her glasses flew across the floor, her head was making nauseating thumps on the linoleum, and her feet were churning like those of some character in a video game, only turned on her side.

Which is why when Russo stepped over her he tripped and fell heavily against the breakfast bar.

I was stunned by the power of Phyllis's despair, which totally mystified me as she rolled onto her back, her skirt half-way up her legs, her hair a stringy tangle of curls, her face blotches of rose and chalk white, eyes glittering, unfocused, nose streaming, mouth open in horror like in that woodcut of Munch's.

"Russo, do something, or she's going to hurt herself," I finally said, when Phyllis started banging her head again. Russo gave a sharp tug at the hand I had put on his elbow, looked at the kitchen door, looked at Phyllis, then glared at me. Muttering something under his breath that I don't think I want to know what it was.

He hoisted her easily and almost ran with her out to the living room, where he put her down on the sofa just gently enough that you couldn't quite say he had thrown her, and then raced off upstairs. I immediately wrapped Phyllis in the raincoat she had left lying there. It is one of Pearl's articles of faith that tears are best treated with blankets, and even if a wet plastic poncho wasn't exactly warm fleece, at least it would help restrain Phyllis a bit.

So I sat down and put my arms around her. Her first reaction was to pull angrily away, but I held on, and Phyllis collapsed against me, clinging tight and shivering. From somewhere deep in my throat, and even deeper in my past, I began to sing. Nonsense words, or not even words, just sounds, the soft bubbles of noise I recalled drifting through approaching slumber as Pearl rocked me out of my bouts of childhood insomnia. We rocked, Phyllis sobbing, me singing low and stroking her hair.

Bit by tiny bit, Phyllis relaxed.

When Russo came back into the room, his face was like some carved stone idol that would require the sacrifice of your first-born.

"They're gone," he said with a glare that made it pretty much my fault. I shrugged, as well as I could with my arm around Phyllis.

She gave one mighty sniffle, then let go of me and sat up. Russo squatted in front of her.

"It *was* you at the front door, wasn't it?"

"*Russo! Jesus!*" I pushed him away, "The woman's hysterical—"

But Phyllis, after a high sob that seemed to have slipped out on its own, inhaled. And went on inhaling. The intake went on so long she might have been trying to make her lungs pop. Then she breathed out, and met Russo's searching look.

"I didn't know it was him. I thought it was a bum." Phyllis hesitated, then looked at me. Her eyes without glasses looked blurred, but her face was growing calmer. "It was dark."

"But what were you doing here?" I had spent three days suspecting this woman of killing her husband, and now that she was confessing she had, I was stunned.

Phyllis smoothed her skirt across her knees, then raised her slightly receding chin. "I came to see Leon."

"Why that late, Miz Smolensky?" Russo sat on the coffee table across from her. I could tell he was trying to keep her calm and talking. "You often come that late?"

"Is that a crime, too, Lieutenant, to come so late? He was my husband." Phyllis's voice broke on the last word, but otherwise she seemed in control again.

Russo shook his head. "No crime. But he was your ex-husband, and two in the morning is, well, kind of an unusual time."

Phyllis looked at me blindly. "The money . . ." she said very softly. "I was afraid he wanted the money . . . to remarry."

Russo looked questioningly at me, and I mimed that I would explain, so he patted her hand. "No, what I mean, weren't you afraid?" he asked, his voice more human.

"Of course I was afraid!" Phyllis snapped. "I was terrified. That's why when . . . when he . . . the man . . ." Her lip was trembling, and her hands rattled like bare shrubs in a blizzard.

"Phyllis . . ." I put my arm back around her shoulders, but she shrugged me away.

"No, it's okay. I was terrified, jumpy. I *never* go out at that hour." She waved her bony hand weakly. "When I was on the stairs, in front, something . . . somebody suddenly came *running,* from the trash tunnel, and tried to grab me." Phyllis was staring through Russo, her voice growing softer and softer until it merged into silence.

We sat, staring at her, willing her to go on.

When she didn't, I prodded her gently. "You thought it was a mugger?"

"I was wearing my good fur and jewelry." Her voice was just above a whisper.

"What, you'd been at the theater? Out to dinner?" I asked.

Phyllis looked up so sharply that for a second I thought she was going to attack me; then a pink blush suffused her face. "No, I was . . . I was going to Leon. I had decided

... I would ... do those things he ..." She waved her hand weakly, then buried her head in her arms.

For a moment I was puzzled, but then I remembered why Skripnik had divorced her, remembered the books at Phyllis's bedside: *Any Woman Can!*, *Joy of Sex*, *The Sensuous Woman*. I hugged Phyllis, overcome with pity. My mouth against her ear, I whispered, "You had nothing on underneath?"

Phyllis shook her head, so violently she might have been trying to make it come off. Then she shrugged and looked at me. "Stockings. Does that count?"

I sat back on the couch, overwhelmed by the vision of Phyllis as Lady Godiva, tripping down that Upper West Side block at two in the morning. Dressed like a urologist's wet dream: fur coat, gold chains, high heels, stockings, and garter belt. Making her last desperate gamble, ready to eat her last morsel of crow to get back her marriage, because she was terrified her husband was remarrying. What Phyllis must have *felt*. . . . Strange shadows, weird noises, wild hope battering at her heart, that horrible nightmare sense of being on the street without your clothes . . .

And then somebody grabbed at her from out of the dark.

"God, Phyllis. What did you hit him with?" I held her tight.

"My big Pyrex pan. I figured if the . . . other thing didn't work, maybe my Leon would like my kugel, and would remember he used to love me. Onion and potato, his favorite. I had it in my hands, and when he grabbed me, I just *hit* him." She mimed banging something down with both hands. Then she looked at Russo and me. "I didn't know it was Leon. He loved my kugel. *Honest!*"

15

"MIDGE, what in the name of God *is* this?" someone asked in Russian from the open door. Russo and I looked up to see Sasha, who was indicating the living room with one of those broad Russian shrugs that extend out to the fingertips. "You have a party or something?"

The bookshelves had been dumped out, the credenza had been gutted, and all the picture frames were broken. Chairs were tipped over, rugs rucked up, and potted plants pulled out of their pots. Leon Skripnik's house looked like the Jets and the Giants had just held a scrimmage there, and the quick nervous hand I ran through my tangle of hair and the tingle of swelling in my upper lip made me suspect that I probably looked like I had been at least a water boy.

Russo stood up angrily. "And who in the hell are *you*? And where's that Vitka guy?"

Sasha came into the room, treading gingerly through the debris. "Who am I? Who are you? And who the hell is Vitka?" he growled in his best just-off-the-boat English.

"Never mind that, how did you get in?" I ran up to him, surprised that I had forgotten he was coming, and even more surprised that I wasn't so glad to see him. I mean, what if I had to tell Russo who he was?

"The door was open. I guess Tolya Shlapentok left it like that." Sasha grinned at me. "I never knew you knew Tolya."

To which of course Russo and I chorused, "WHO THE HELL IS TOLYA SHLAPENTOK?"

"What do you mean, who is he? You don't know who is in this house? With the beard, the fat guy. And his wife, Faina. Son of bitch, I don't see him maybe twenty years, I'm coming up the street, and first, at the corner, Faina. Hi, how are you, can't talk, got to run, like this is Leningrad and I see her yesterday at the store. I finally am closing my mouth from surprise, I am walking two more steps down this street, and who comes out this door? Tolya Shlapentok!"

Russo swung round on me, his face icy. "You told me his name was Bender."

"Bender!" Sasha hooted with laughter. "Like Ostap Bender, the great combinator?!"

I slapped my head, and if I could have, I'd have kicked myself too. Ostap Bender, the greatest con-man in Russian literature! I should have *known* that, damn it!

"You see which way this whatever-his-name-is went?"

Russo cut in, with a voice like one of those things they cut bolts with.

Sasha looked at Russo with blank contempt, then asked me in Russian, "And who's this type?"

I opened my mouth to answer, closed it, opened it again, then just waved my hand. "Police, Sasha . . . just answer him."

"So that's why Tolya and Faina didn't want to take time for a chat, eh?" Sasha grinned. "Did somebody take too close a look at one of his 'masterpieces'?" The grin, more wolfish, was turned toward Russo.

Who took a step forward. "I asked you a question."

Sasha squared his shoulders and stuck out his chin, before saying in the most fractured English he could muster. "No Englitch spik maybe, hey, policeman? Need interpret!"

Now Russo glanced at me, back at Sasha. Sasha was doing the same, from me to Russo and back. Crackling sparks of supposition and jealousy and suspicion were beginning to arc about the room.

"For Christ's sake," I snapped, "Just tell him which way they went, Sasha. Russo's got to get somebody after them."

Instead of a reply, Sasha shrugged his shoulders, then waved at the street, away from the park.

"And you wouldn't know where this Tolya guy lives either, of course." Russo glowered, just before a short, powerfully built man in a dark green leather coat, with a smooth-shaved head and a Taras Bulba mustache the same color as his smoke-stained teeth, stepped from around Sasha, grabbed my hand to crush in his, and bellowed in Russian, "Mrs. Skripnik, I am delighted. I am your cousin, Shmuel Skripnik. But please, call me Slava!"

Russo was the first to recover from stupefication. Inside of ten seconds, he turned into Supercop and headed for the kitchen to phone.

I was just drawing breath to shriek at this new arrival that I was not Mrs. Skripnik, when Sasha laughed, and tapped me on the arm, to whisper in Russian.

"So Tolya finally got his fingers in the fire, eh? He never was much of an artist on his own, but for *faking*? Our teacher used to say Tolya could copy the tattoo off the devil's backside!"

Sasha turned a lot less jolly when Russo came stomping back into the debris of what had not long ago been Skripnik's living room, and said in a gruff, growly Bronx so thick that Pearl's eyebrows would have gone through the brim of her hat, "Sorry, pal, but I'm going to have to ask you to come down to the station and tell us what you know about these Shlapenwhatsits."

Sasha's angry glare suggested my social life was about to go on a diet, but for the moment at least, I was too tired and sore to care. Anyway, what right did he have to be mad? All this had cost him was an afternoon with Karla Braverman, and a few bucks in tolls. I shrugged, trying to look sorry.

Then, his voice much softer, Russo informed Phyllis that she too would have to come down to the station.

She had been slumped on the couch like one of those empty beetle skins you sometimes find, still the shape of Phyllis, but the insides long ago flown on. Now she protested feebly, saying she couldn't, her son, her son was alone at home . . .

I put up a more spirited defense, even placing my hands on Phyllis' shoulders. "Hey, come on, lieutenant, give her a break! It's not like she's *dangerous* or anything, why lock her up? It was an accident, she didn't mean to kill her husband!"

Russo's face, when he finally looked at me, was a complete cipher, with that lazy half smile below those totally unamused sandy green eyes. I could feel little bits of my insides curling up and turning black, like impatiens when the frost hits them.

"She didn't kill her husband."

"What do you mean she didn't kill her husband?" I could not believe how angry I suddenly got, particularly since a second before I had all but mother-henned her under my wing. "Of course she killed her husband!"

Even Phyllis turned around to look at me quizzically, that I was now trying to get her locked up. I wasn't, but still . . . You know the expression, getting away with murder?

"She didn't kill her husband," Russo repeated firmly, taking Phyllis's arm, to help her off the couch. "You're the big mystery writer, you didn't figure that out?"

"But you *heard* what she just said, with the pan of kugel!" I brought my fists down hard, as if a reenactment might make my point more convincing. "On his head!"

"Skripnik died of asphyxiation. Natural gas."

And then I understood, but it was too late to impress Russo, or comfort Phyllis.

Faina's kettle, put on for tea. Frightened by Skripnik's disappearance and then the door alarm, dragging him back into the kitchen again, she had forgotten about it. The kettle had boiled over and put out the flame, leaving gas leaking out into the kitchen, where poor battered Skripnik lay dazed from his two blows to the head.

I felt an enormous relief as I watched them troop out the door to Russo's car. Phyllis *wasn't* guilty. . . . And then I remembered that she was on her way to precinct headquarters, to explain why she had been at Skripnik's stoop that early Sunday morning, and what she had—or hadn't—been wearing.

But then I understood with a sobering wrench that any punishment or humiliation Phyllis might ever get, or even deserve, nothing could ever be worse than the fact that Leon, her ex-husband, was dead, and there would be no reconciliation.

Which left just me and Shmuel.

"I thought you were Mrs. Skripnik," he essayed, broad smile beneath inquiring eyes. Inquiring *seeing* eyes.

"And I thought you were blind," I said, sourly enough to curdle milk.

Pearl was late. The sky was still thick with broken clouds, and anyway the setting sun barely penetrated down to those depths, so the street was in that thick half-gloom that sets in just before the streetlights go on. Puddles shimmering with oil rainbows were black against the asphalt, disturbed only by the drip of water from the rain-soaked tennis shoes kids had flung over the streetlamps. Leaning forward into the bow window I could just see Central Park West, where the cars were a solid ribbon of yellow headlights and red tail lights, but in front of Skripnik's it was quiet. Surrounded as we were by the debris of Vitka's search, the house felt shattered and eerie, like something out of an old war movie. Even the few words Slava and I exchanged had a strained, hollow ring, as though we were spies, addressing each other in code.

Compared to some of the frauds I had been party to this week, Slava's slight exaggeration of his vision problem was pretty mild stuff, but for some reason it left me absolutely furious. Some distant part of me kept trying to point out, okay, so he lied a little, but it's his fault the U.S. consulate will only give him a visa for a medical emergency? And besides he has just arrived from a long flight, he must be tired and hungry. And puzzled.

But it was no good. Maybe if he had really been the emaciated Talmudic scholar that I had spent an entire week picturing him as, I might have squeezed a few dabs more sympathy out of myself.

Maybe not, though. I was doing too good a job of pitying myself.

Finally, I saw a tiny figure in a black-and-white pleated skirt, walking so rapidly that the pleats bounced instead of swayed and she had to hold down her hat with her right hand.

Pearl. In a hurry, as always; going to arrange something, fix something, give someone advice.

I opened the front door for my mother.

"My God, *look* at this place!" she exclaimed even before she got her hat off. "Such a beautiful house, and to keep it like *this*!" She took the hat off, shook her hair, then looked suspiciously at me, and cautiously at Shmuel. I could see her wondering what connection he might have to the house, and whether she should congratulate him on his beautiful home, or offer him the name of a good cleaning service. Then she glanced at his hand, looking for a ring.

"*Mother*," I began too forcefully; then, restraining myself, "This is Mr. Shmuel Skripnik. From Israel." I told her.

Skripnik beamed, bent over her hand, and even clicked his heels. "Delighted! You are sisters?" he asked, in Russian.

Pearl managed a strange little bob, like a remote ancestor of the curtsy. "What'd he say?" she asked through a smile.

"He asked if we're sisters."

"Ohhh!" Pearl giggled. Grinning, Shmuel smoothed his mustache with the back of his thumb, and I swear to God there was a twinkle in his eye.

I groaned. To lose Russo, to see Phyllis shattered, to end up with Shmuel—and then to have this ponderous flirtation to translate.

It was more than flesh could bear.

Pearl snatched her hand back, focused on me. "Baby doll, what's the matter? You look . . . Is there a bathroom, maybe you could go freshen up a little?" She looked around doubtfully, as though a house this poorly kept might only have the shack out back.

Freshen up? My teeth were intact but still felt loose, my lips were bruised, and swollen, and my clothes were bloodstained. I had rope burns on my elbows, my hands, and my ankles.

I didn't need to freshen up. I needed to be rebuilt, starting from the ground floor.

"Let's just go, Mother."

"But what about *this?* What happened?" Pearl clutched my elbow, making me wince.

I gave her a quick and not very coherent rundown.

"My baby!" She hugged me, her head not quite coming up to my shoulder. "My poor poor BABY!" Then she held me at arm's length, making significant eye gestures in the direction of Shmuel, who was hovering around behind her looking supernumerary. "Id-day ey-thay ind-fay e-thay icture-pay?"

"He doesn't speak English, *Mama*." I had to laugh, because if Shmuel had spoken English, then this whole week need never have happened. "And no, I don't think they *did* find it."

"Did they look in the freezer?" Pearl said, in English at least, but taking no chances, she whispered.

"The freezer? Aw, come on, Mamma, let's just go home." I started for the door, but Pearl stopped me. With a bright smile and insistent gestures, she sent Shmuel upstairs, miming that she wanted him to put water on the snowy little handkerchief she pulled from her sleeve. Looking mystified but anxious to please her, Shmuel stepped around me and gingerly began to ascend the badly littered stairs.

Pearl gave him a little pat on the shoulder as he went. Then she gave me a conspiratorial look. "The kitchen?" she whispered. "Where's the kitchen?" I pointed. She disappeared. I followed, to find her at the refrigerator, holding the freezer door open. I could see some foil-wrapped packages, some prepared foods, a pizza box.

"Mama," I began.

"How big is this painting? So big?"

"I guess so, but—"

"So okay, then!" Pearl pulled out the pizza box, ripped open the top, and underneath the pizza . . .

"How did you *know?*" I ran over to grab the thing in my hands. Skripnik had wrapped the watercolor in aluminum foil and, I saw as I pulled back a foil strip with trembling hands, plastic wrap. A terrible knot of dread in the bottom of my stomach made me wonder whether this was any way to treat a watercolor; refrigerator frost had crept inside the plastic, white needles which spread over the surface like some horrible mold, through which I could just see the rabbi grinning.

"That's it, baby doll? What you were looking for?" Pearl held my elbow; in a minute I knew she would feel my forehead.

"But Momma, how did you KNOW?" My voice was a high tremolo.

My mother smiled. "It was my idea."

"SKRIPNIK TOLD YOU ABOUT THE PAINTING?"

"No, no," Pearl said, looking alarmed. And she *did* feel my forehead. "Just one day we were talking. You know, how you do, about all the terrible problems these days, all the crime, and I happened to mention how I keep some money in the freezer, just in case," she finished in a whisper. Then, in her normal voice again, she added, "He liked the idea. 'Cold cash,' he called it. So I figured maybe—"

I felt ill, dizzy. "Well, you were right. That's it." I gently placed the watercolor study on the kitchen counter.

"But God, What now?"

I must have begun trembling, because my mother pulled me away from the box on the kitchen counter like you would a mourner from a coffin and did her best to wrap me in her arms, my greater height nonwithstanding. "Shhh, don't, baby doll, it's okay. Is that picture yours?"

"No, it's—it belongs . . ." I let myself be hugged for a moment, realizing I had no idea to whom this Chagall belonged. The Bender-Shlapentoks? But they had taken a check for it from Skripnik. Except the check was no good. But then Phyllis had given them another check. But that was for the big painting, which *wasn't* a Chagall.

"I don't *know* whose it is!" I wailed, finally overcome by the events of the past week.

Pearl began stroking my hair. "Don't worry, sweetie. Calm down, it'll be okay, honest. . . . Come on, enough tears; let's go get some dinner—" As Pearl talked she was pushing me toward the door, straightening my clothes, even putting on my jacket, which I had slung across the occasional table in the front hall. Those annoying kind of tears that won't stop even though you don't *want* to be crying were dribbling down my cheeks, no doubt melting my makeup and finishing off my last vestige of dignity. Shoulders heaving and breath coming in shaky sobs, I felt about five years old.

"Meezuz Ko-hen" we heard from behind us, and turned to see Shmuel-Slava descending, still gingerly, but triumphantly holding the dripping handkerchief aloft.

My prize, for a week well spent.

"Midge, honey," Pearl whispered behind me, putting on her gloves "are you sure this guy is right for you? Isn't he a little *old*? Tell you what, yesterday this caries case came in, a little chubby maybe, but he owns a hi-fi store on—"

"MOTHER!" I stopped dead in the doorway and turned around, ready to let her have it—and then I surprised myself.

By laughing.

I mean, what *could* you do? It had been the devil's own week, but whatever else you might say about it, it hadn't been dull. Assuming my tooth wasn't dead, then I had managed to get out of this with nothing that a hot shower and an ice pack on my lip couldn't put right. Oh, I was going to have to find something to do with Shmuel, I reflected as we went out and I closed the door on the devastation behind us, and I would have to put in some serious typewriter work tonight, to avoid having my editor throw Tammy, Tanesia, and me out on our ears tomorrow. And I had a strong hunch that I would do well to begin looking for a plumber, since I doubted that Sasha would give two hoots about *my* sink for a while. As for Russo, well, what's the point of growing old, if you don't have things to keep you awake at nights, wishing you'd done them differently?

But hey, I told myself, I'm alive, I'm on my own, and

I'm still calling my own shots, right? What more can a girl ask for, in these troubled times?

"Hey, Mid—*Margaret*!"

We all three looked down at the long, low red car that was just pulling into the space by the hydrant.

Russo got out of the car, waving at me. "Hey jeez, I'm such a dummy, I went off and forgot ya! Come on, let me make it up to ya, buy ya a drink!"

I looked at Pearl, who was looking back and forth between me and Russo like the net judge at a Ping-Pong match. I looked at Slava Skripnik, who even though he looked lost, tired, and hungry, still managed a twinkle whenever Pearl glanced at him.

"Make it dinner and I'll tell you where the missing picture is." I grinned, jumped the last two steps, and ran over to Russo's car; he answered with his sleepy-cat smile and went around to open the passenger door.

"Ma?" I said, turning back. "Mr. Skripnik needs a place to stay. Just for a few days, until Phyllis is feeling better. Be an angel, will you?" Then, to Russo. "Brooklyn or Bronx?"

He laughed. "Better make it Brooklyn. The places I go to in the Bronx, everybody would know I was taking you out before we finished the antipasto."

I froze, halfway down in the bucket seat. "You don't want to be seen with me?"

"Naw, naw," he said, and blushed. "It's just . . . my ma. She wants so bad to marry me off, if she finds out I'm out with a lady, before the coffee she'll be calling all the tux rental places to see who's giving the deals. The whole thing can get embarrassing sometimes, you know what I mean?"